AN ALE *of* TWO CITIES

Books by Sarah Fox

The Literary Pub Mystery Series

Wine and Punishment

An Ale of Two Cities

The Pancake House Mystery Series

The Crêpes of Wrath

For Whom the Bread Rolls

Of Spice and Men

Yeast of Eden

Crêpe Expectations

The Music Lover's Mystery Series

Dead Ringer

Death in A Major

Deadly Overtures

AN ALE *of* TWO CITIES

SARAH FOX

KENSINGTON BOOKS
www.kensingtonbooks.com

KENSINGTON BOOKS are published by

Kensington Publishing Corp.
119 West 40th Street
New York, NY 10018

All Kensington titles, imprints, and distributed lines are available at special quantity discounts for bulk purchases for sales promotion, premiums, fund-raising, educational, or institutional use. Special book excerpts or customized printings can also be created to fit specific needs. For details, write or phone the office of the Kensington Special Sales Manager: Attn. Special Sales Department. Kensington Publishing Corp, 119 West 40th Street, New York, NY 10018. Phone: 1-800-221-2647.

Library of Congress Card Catalogue Number: 2019945264

Kensington and the K logo Reg. U.S. Pat. & TM Off.

ISBN-13: 978-1-4967-1869-3
ISBN-10: 1-4967-1869-0
First Kensington Hardcover Edition: December 2019

ISBN-13: 978-1-4967-1872-3 (ebook)
ISBN-10: 1-4967-1872-0 (ebook)

10 9 8 7 6 5 4 3 2 1

Printed in the United States of America

AN ALE *of* TWO CITIES

Chapter 1

The town of Shady Creek was a winter wonderland. The first snowfall of the season had hit Vermont several weeks ago, not long after the last of the leaves had fallen, and others had followed close on its heels. Now, in early December, the snow lay in a thick layer on rooftops, tree boughs, and the surrounding countryside. I wasn't completely sold on the chilly temperatures, but even Ebenezer Scrooge would have had to admit that the snow-blanketed town was beautiful.

I paused outside the red door of the old stone gristmill that housed my cozy apartment and my literary-themed pub, the Inkwell. Maybe I was biased, but I thought the mill was the prettiest building in town, especially now that nature had decorated it with a layer of snow. The red-trimmed windows and red waterwheel made the place look cheery, even festive, and I'd seen several tourists snapping photos of the building in recent days. I'd taken a few photos myself, and had uploaded them to the Inkwell's Web site and social media accounts.

The cold air bit at my cheeks as I fastened the top button of my blue, puffy, down jacket and pulled my matching scarf up over the bottom half of my face. No snow had fallen overnight, to my relief. That meant I didn't have to worry about shoveling the walkway before the pub opened at noon. And no shoveling meant I was free to head for the village green—much whiter than green at the moment—to check out the opening day festivities of Shady Creek's annual Winter Carnival.

I crossed the footbridge over the creek that had given the town its name. The water in the middle of the creek remained unfrozen and babbled its way between the snowy banks, sounding cheerful as usual. As I made my way across Creekside Road to the village green, I saw that plenty of people had arrived before me.

A welcoming fire burned in a metal fire pit near the bandstand, and several people had gathered around the flames, chatting and sipping drinks from take-out cups, most likely from the Village Bean, the local coffee shop. The bandstand had been tastefully decorated for the season. Several swags made from evergreen boughs tied with bright red bows hung on the outside of the structure, and multicolored lights had also been strung around it. The lights weren't on at the moment, but every night since Thanksgiving, they'd lit up the bandstand with a festive glow.

Directly within my line of sight was a large white canopy, beneath which a few men and women with clipboards had gathered. Several huge blocks of clear ice sat here and there around the green, waiting to be transformed into anything from an angel to a polar bear. The village green was the site of the ice sculpture competition, the first event of the Winter Carnival. I'd never attended an ice sculpture competition before, so I was excited to watch this one unfold, especially since one of my employees, Mel Costas, was among the competitors. Even though I knew Mel was a talented artist, it had surprised me to learn she was taking part in the event, but she'd told me she'd been competing for years.

Apparently she'd won the last two competitions, as well as one several years ago. I had my fingers crossed that she'd win this time too. Every year there was a cash prize for the creator of the winning sculpture, but this year the stakes were higher. Not only would the winner receive a check for five thousand dollars, he or she would also be featured in *Collage*, a national arts magazine. If Mel won, the magazine coverage could give her and her art some valuable exposure. If more people knew about her work, she'd get more buyers, both online and when tourists visited Shady Creek, as many did, especially during leaf peeper season and special events like the Winter Carnival.

Although several people were milling about near the canopy, it wasn't hard for me to pick out Mel from the crowd. At nearly five foot ten, she was on the tall side, and her blond and electric blue hair drew my eye easily.

I wasn't sure how she could stand to have her head uncovered in this weather, but it did make her easier to spot.

"Morning," I said after I made my way around two men to reach Mel's side. "How are things going?"

"Hey, Sadie," Mel greeted. "So far so good. The competition will be getting underway in a few minutes."

"Are you nervous?" She didn't appear to be, but she didn't often show what she was feeling.

"Nah," she replied. "More pumped than anything. I love this event."

"I can't wait to see your sculpture." I glanced around. "Where's Zoe?"

Zoe Trimble was the twin sister of one of my new employees—Teagan, one of the Inkwell's chefs. When I'd bought the pub, it was without a cook. It took me a few months to find the right candidates to take over in the kitchen, but I was glad I'd held out until Teagan and Booker, the other chef I'd hired, had come along.

Like Mel, Zoe was an artist. She was interested in ice sculpting, so she planned to hang around and learn whatever she could from watching the competitors. Mel had promised to explain the various steps and techniques as she worked.

"She's gone to get coffees from the Village Bean," Mel replied. "She'll be back soon."

I tugged my knitted hat down over my ears and eyed Mel's uncovered head. "Don't you want a hat? It's freezing out here."

She laughed. "It's not so bad, and I'll warm up once I get to work. I'll probably need one tonight, though."

The competitors had thirty hours to create their sculptures from several blocks of ice. At least some of the entrants would work through the night to get finished in time. I shivered just thinking about it. It was cold enough for me at the moment, with the sun peeking through the gray clouds overhead. I'd probably turn into an ice statue myself if I stayed outdoors all night.

"There's Alma," I said, waving to a woman with long, graying hair.

She smiled and waved back before consulting a clipboard.

I'd first met Alma Potts at the Inkwell, where she'd become a regular customer. She loved reading, like I did, and when she'd found out I was planning to host book clubs at the pub, she'd been eager to get involved. The last time we'd spoken, she mentioned that she was the head organizer of the ice sculpture competition.

"May I have your attention, please?" Alma's voice rang out over the snow-covered green. A sound system had been set up for the event, with speakers and a microphone beneath the canopy. "All competitors please go to your assigned stations. We'll be starting shortly."

I walked with Mel toward her carving station near the bandstand. Even before the carnival preparations had begun on the green, the snow had been packed down by people walking here and there and by kids playing. That made it easy to get around, and the carnival's organizers had cleared pathways through any areas that had escaped the trampling of booted feet over the past few weeks.

As we reached Mel's blocks of ice, Zoe jogged up behind us, a take-out cup clutched in each gloved hand.

"Just in time," I remarked as she handed one of the two cups to Mel.

Zoe's breath puffed out in a cloud. "There was a long line. Everyone seems to want coffee this morning."

I could have used one myself. I'd had coffee with my breakfast less than an hour ago, but a hot drink would have hit the spot right then, especially since I could feel my toes going numb inside my boots.

Zoe was dressed more warmly than Mel, with a hat pulled down over her wavy, dark blond hair, but she still wasn't as bundled up as I was with my scarf, hat, mittens, and puffy, knee-length jacket. Apparently I was more susceptible to the cold than my Vermont-born counterparts. I'd spent a few years of my life in Boston and Minneapolis, but I was from Knoxville and I'd never really been able to get used to cold winters.

As Mel did a final check of all her tools, I studied her competition, the carvers spread out around the green. I recognized a few faces, but there were also some I'd never seen before. People traveled from other towns and even other states to compete, I'd been told, so that explained the unfamiliar faces. Not that I necessarily would have recognized everyone anyway. I'd only lived in Shady Creek for about six months. I'd met a lot of people at the Inkwell during that time, but there were still plenty of townsfolk I didn't know.

A commotion at the eastern end of the green drew my attention. A tall man with his dark hair slicked back strode past the canopy. Something about the way he held himself gave me the impression that he thought he owned the entire village green. Maybe it was the way he kept his nose in the air and ignored everyone around him, even though several people had formed a small crowd, scurrying to keep up with his long strides.

"Darn," Zoe said when she noticed the new arrival. "I was hoping he wouldn't show up."

Mel turned around to see whom she was talking about. "Ignore him," she advised.

"Who is he?" I asked.

The man had arrived at the last unoccupied carving station and now faced his followers, his chest puffing out as he radiated self-importance.

"Federico Mancini," Mel replied. "Better known around here as Freddy."

"He's a local?" I said with surprise, wondering why he was completely unfamiliar to me when he seemed to want everyone to notice him.

"He grew up here in Shady Creek," Mel said. "He moved away when he was about nineteen or so. I don't think he's been back since. Not until today. From what I've heard, he thinks this town is beneath him now."

Freddy appeared to be in his midthirties, a few years older than me, so he must have been gone for well over a decade.

"Why the sudden reappearance?" I asked.

Mel returned her attention to her tools. "Probably so he can rub his success in our faces."

"He's a chef in Boston now," Zoe explained. "And he owns a restaurant. A pretty fancy one, I think. I've never been there myself, but I've heard people talk about it from time to time."

I'd lived in Boston for over two years before coming to Shady Creek when my life in the big city fell to pieces, but I'd never heard of Freddy Mancini. That wasn't surprising, though. As much as I loved good food, I'd never been part of the foodie scene in Boston or anywhere else, and I'd never had the budget to eat out at expensive restaurants.

I continued to watch Freddy as he spoke to the small crowd around him, clearly enjoying the attention. A couple of people held out their smartphones to record what he was saying. I noticed Joey Fontana of the *Shady Creek Tribune* among those gathered around the chef. If the others were reporters as well, which at least some of them seemed to be, I didn't know which newspapers they worked for. Joey and his father owned the *Tribune*, the only local paper, and I knew both of their part-time coworkers by sight. I'd never seen the other reporters before.

"Are there journalists here from out of town to cover the event?" I asked.

"Looks like it," Zoe said before taking a sip of her coffee.

"Is that usual?"

"Not really," Mel replied. "It's typically just the local paper that covers the Winter Carnival, but other reporters have shown up once or twice when somebody high profile has come to compete. Not in recent years, though. At least, not that I recall. Freddy's won a handful of competitions around the country and even a couple around the world, so I guess he's attracted some additional interest."

"Hopefully that's good for the town," I said. If more people knew about Shady Creek, maybe more would come to visit.

"*He* sure isn't," a male voice muttered close by.

The owner of the voice was walking past us. More like stomping past, actually. Black hair stuck out from beneath his dark green wool hat and his stormy eyes were nearly black as well. With his hands stuffed into the pockets of his jeans, he positively glowered at the world around him as he headed across the green, away from Freddy and the gaggle of reporters.

"What's with him?" I asked once the man was out of earshot.

"That's Leo Mancini," Zoe said in a low voice.

"Freddy's half brother," Mel added.

"It doesn't sound like there's much brotherly love between them," I said.

Mel shrugged. "There never really was."

That was sad. I wondered what was behind their animosity,

but I didn't dwell on it for long. Any thoughts of Leo and Freddy fluttered out of my mind as Alma's voice rang out through the cold air again.

"Welcome, everyone, to the thirty-first annual Shady Creek Winter Carnival!"

I clapped my mitted hands along with everyone else. A few people in the crowd added whistles and cheers.

"Before the ice-sculpting competition gets started, I'd like to give a shout out to the people and businesses that made this event possible."

As Alma went on to thank the sponsors and all of the volunteers who'd organized the competition, a striking woman with long dark hair detached herself from the crowd still gathered around Freddy. She was texting on her smartphone, but she glanced up as she passed by. She did a double take, recognition and surprise registering on her face.

"Jade!" Freddy bellowed.

The woman nearly jumped and then quickly backtracked toward the chef.

I glanced Mel's way and caught a quick glimpse of surprise and recognition on her face as well before a neutral expression took over.

I was about to ask her who Jade was when Alma called out, "Let the sculpting begin!"

Mel set aside her coffee and picked up her tools.

The competition was underway.

Chapter 2

When Mel fired up a chain saw, I backed away and let her get down to work. I could barely feel my toes, and my fingers felt like icicles, so I claimed a spot by the fire pit, greedily soaking up any warmth I could from the crackling and popping flames. I had a decent view of all the competitors from where I stood, and it was clear that not everyone had the same approach. Some were tracing their patterns onto their ice blocks while others, like Mel, were going freehand.

"Not competing today?" someone said from behind me.

I glanced over my shoulder to see Joey Fontana coming to join me by the fire. He wore a wool hat over his dark hair and had a camera hanging around his neck. As usual, he had a smile on his face. I'd never known him to be in anything but a good mood, even back in the fall when hounding me for an interview I didn't want to give.

I couldn't help but smile back at him.

"Trust me, it's a good thing I'm not," I replied. "I don't think I could make a block of ice look like much of anything. And if I tried, I'd probably end up injuring myself."

"Sounds like we're two of a kind," Joey said, still grinning.

He snapped a photo of Mel in action before training his camera on Freddy.

I watched as the chef powered up a chain saw and cut through a block of ice like it was butter. "I guess it's a big story that Federico Mancini is here."

"It sure is," Joey agreed. "Made all the better by his connection to the town. This is where his story started, and it's a good story. It'll probably make the front page of the next issue of the *Tribune*."

"Don't forget that others are competing too."

Joey caught my drift right away. "Like Mel Costas. Don't worry. I already interviewed her and I'll be taking photos of everyone as they work. After all, it's not guaranteed that Freddy will be the winner."

"Of course it's not. Mel has a good track record."

Joey's grin widened. "You're not biased or anything."

"There's nothing wrong with believing in my friends," I said in my own defense.

"Just how much do you believe in Mel?" another man asked as he sidled up to the fire pit.

It was Bert Caldwell, I realized. The owner of a local cheese company, Bert was tall with a generous paunch. As had been the case on every other occasion I'd seen him, he wore a baseball cap with his company's logo on the front.

I had to silently question his sanity. A baseball cap wouldn't provide much warmth for his ears.

"What does that mean?" I asked him.

Bert glanced around as if to see if anyone else was within earshot. There were three women on the other side of the fire pit, but they were engrossed in their conversation, laughing and chatting.

"I'm taking bets," Bert said once he was satisfied we wouldn't be overheard. "A bit of friendly wagering."

"Is that legal?" I glanced from him to Joey.

The reporter gave an unconcerned shrug and used the camera slung around his neck to snap another photo of Freddy wielding his chain saw.

"Doesn't matter if the wrong people don't find out," Bert said.

"You're saying this in front of a reporter," I pointed out.

"Joey's not about to say anything. He's already placed his bet."

I narrowed my eyes at Joey. "Did you put your money on Mel?"

"Sorry, that's confidential information," he said, not the least bit abashed.

In other words, he'd bet on someone else. I decided to not let that bother me. Mel didn't need the support of every town resident. I had confidence in her and I knew the wagering wouldn't psych her out in the least if she found out about it.

"So, how about it?" Bert asked me. "Are you in?"

"I'm most definitely *out*," I said.

To emphasize my point, I headed off on a circuit of the green to check out what all the competitors were up to. I believed in Mel enough to stake some money on her, but I had an aversion to all types of gambling since my ex-boyfriend's addiction had destroyed our relationship. I also didn't want to end up getting into any trouble. I'd been through enough in the past year, what with breaking up with my boyfriend—who'd later been killed—and losing my job in Boston. On top of that, I was still finding my feet as a business owner. The last thing I needed was to get caught breaking the law.

I didn't spend much time at each competitor's station. Since the event was in its earliest stages, I couldn't yet see the artists' visions taking shape. Still, I was impressed by the way they wielded their power and hand tools with such ease and confidence, cutting, chipping, and scraping the ice without hesitation. I didn't doubt that if I'd attempted to sculpt a block of ice, it would have ended up cracked, shattered, or otherwise destroyed.

The last competitor I stopped to watch was Freddy Mancini. By then, all the reporters, including Joey, had disappeared. They'd probably gone off in search of someplace warmer, with plans to check in on the competition now and then. Bert Caldwell, however, was still hanging around. At the moment, he was next to the fire pit, in conversation with Jade, the woman who seemed to be somehow linked to Freddy. I was certain she and Mel had recognized each other earlier. That in itself wasn't so strange, but what had piqued my curiosity was the fact that there had been something more than surprise and recognition in their eyes when they saw each other. Something I couldn't quite put my finger on.

Whatever had passed between them wasn't any of my business, but that didn't dampen my curiosity. It never did. Some people—and one person in particular—had been known to call me nosey, and I had to admit to myself that it wasn't an unwarranted descriptor. I wasn't keen on admitting that to anyone else, though.

As Freddy set down his chain saw and grabbed a chisel, Jade left Bert by the fire pit and returned to the chef's side. He shot a suspicious glance Bert's way before focusing on Jade.

"What was all that about?" he asked, sounding grumpy.

"Just a local man asking questions about the competition," she replied. "Do you need anything at the moment? A coffee, maybe?"

"What I *need* is to be left alone so I can focus," Freddy groused.

He attacked one of his ice blocks with the chisel. Behind him, Jade rolled her eyes.

"I'll be over by the fire keeping warm, then," she said to him.

"Get me a coffee first!" he ordered, not taking his eyes off his work.

"Of course," Jade said. Her tone was smooth and polite, but I thought I detected a flicker of anger in her brown eyes.

I couldn't blame her. If he'd spoken to me like that, I probably would have been tempted to bury him under his blocks of ice. Actually, I was tempted to do that even though he hadn't been speaking to me. I hoped he didn't intend to stay in Shady Creek beyond the end of the competition. I especially hoped he wouldn't decide to show up at the Inkwell. No doubt he'd find fault with everything.

Jade strode away from Freddy, heading across the green in the direction of the Village Bean. My curiosity got the better of me and I hurried to catch up to her.

"Excuse me," I said as I reached her side. "Do you work for Freddy Mancini?"

Jade slowed her pace and smiled at me. She was a beautiful woman, probably in her early thirties, with long dark hair and thick eyelashes that made me immediately envious. My eyelashes were practically invisible without mascara.

"I'm his personal assistant, Jade Castellano," she said. "Are you a reporter?"

"No. Just a curious onlooker. And a friend of Mel Costas," I added. "Do you know her?"

Jade hesitated, both in her steps and in her speech. "I did once," she said after a moment.

"Maybe you'll have a chance to catch up with her after the competition."

She smiled again, but this time it seemed forced. "Maybe." She glanced down at the phone she held in one leather-gloved hand. "Excuse me, but I have some work to take care of."

"Of course," I said.

I drew to a stop and watched her walk away, my curiosity unsatisfied.

There was a story there. I was sure of it. But Jade clearly wasn't going to fill me in. Maybe Mel would, but I wouldn't count on that. Mel and I got along well, and I considered her a friend as well as an employee, but she wasn't one to easily share details about her personal life.

For all the good it would do, I reminded myself that it wasn't any of my business and decided to focus on what *was* my business—getting the Inkwell ready to open for the day.

The first thing I did when I returned to the Inkwell was put on a pot of coffee. I didn't even wait to shed my coat, scarf, and hat, only removing my mittens to make the job easier. While the coffee brewed, I passed through a door marked PRIVATE and trudged up the stairs to my apartment, where I finally removed my outer layers.

"Brrr," I said, rubbing my hands as I approached my white-haired, blue-eyed cat where he slept on the back of the couch. "You've got the right idea, Wimsey. It's a good day to stay indoors."

Wimsey closed his eyes, a content and somewhat self-satisfied expression on his furry face as I stroked his long, silky coat. I got a faint purr out of him at first, but then he shut off his motor and shook his head, as if to say, "Enough, human!"

He only liked cuddling on a limited basis.

I made a quick trip to the bathroom to check my appearance in the mirror. Removing my wool hat had left my red hair full of static. I ran a brush through it, but that only made matters worse, so I splashed a bit of water on my hands and smoothed them over my hair.

The result wasn't perfect but it would do. I didn't waste any more time; I could practically hear the brewing coffee calling my name from downstairs. Back down behind the bar, I savored each sip of my hot drink as I gazed around my beloved pub. I'd purchased the business and building back in the summer while I was in Shady Creek visiting my aunt Gilda and trying to pick up the pieces of my former life. I'd never intended to remain in Vermont, but I'd fallen in love with the charming town and the character-filled, renovated gristmill.

After sinking most of my life savings into the purchase, I'd transformed the run-of-the-mill pub into one that reflected my lifelong love of books and literature. My extensive book collection was on display on the wooden shelf that ran around the main room of the pub. The wide plank floors and wood beams gave the pub character, as did the old barrels that had been worked into the construction of the bar.

Recently, I'd added some seasonal decorations to create a festive atmosphere. Fairy lights and garlands were strung around the pub, and I'd placed some rustic-looking candle lanterns here and there, each one decorated with red bows and sprigs of holly. My favorite holiday addition was the beautiful eight-foot Christmas tree standing in one corner. Naturally, I'd given it a literary theme and had decked it out with some ornaments I'd collected over the years and others that I'd recently purchased on Etsy. There were silhouettes of characters from Jane Austen's novels, figurines of Winnie the Pooh and his friends, and colorful baubles featuring elegant Elvish writing. I'd also found several adorable miniature books to put on the tree with tiny covers from classics like *The Wind in the Willows*, *Anne of Green Gables*, and the first Nancy Drew adventure, *The Secret of the Old Clock*. Perched on the top of the tree was a deerstalker hat as an ode to Sherlock Holmes.

Outside the pub, Mel and Damien, one of my other employees, had helped me put up lights around the front door and all of the windows. The large red door also had a cheery wreath hanging on it, one I'd made myself during a workshop at the local public library a week earlier. I wasn't the most artistic person, so I was quite pleased with how well the wreath had turned out. I'd already received several compliments on it, and I was glad my patrons seemed to like all of my decorating efforts.

I was halfway through my cup of coffee when Booker James burst in through the pub's front door, bringing a blast of frosty air with him.

"It's sure cold out there," he said with a shiver.

"You're telling me."

Booker pulled off his hat and shook out his multitude of shoulder-length braids. "Aside from the cold, how are things going?"

"Great, especially now that I'm inside with a nice hot cup of coffee."

"A hot drink sounds good." Booker made his way behind the bar. "I'd better put the kettle on."

He preferred tea to coffee, and always drank it out of one of the teacups his grandmother had given him, never out of a mug. It had taken me a while to get used to seeing the six-foot-four former college football player drinking his tea out of a china cup patterned with flowers. Now I couldn't imagine him drinking it any other way.

Booker disappeared through the door that led to the pub's kitchen and employee cloakroom. When he reappeared several minutes later, he had his freshly brewed tea with him, in a cup decorated with red and purple sweet peas.

I'd counted myself lucky when Booker accepted the job I'd offered him several weeks earlier. He brought an upbeat energy to the Inkwell and was easy to get along with. He could also work magic in the kitchen. With Teagan's help, he'd put together a menu that had so far been a hit with the pub's customers.

Like me, Booker was new to Shady Creek. He'd moved here to be with his girlfriend, who'd decided to return to her hometown after finishing college. A string of injuries had put an end to Booker's football career aspirations, so he'd pursued his other passions—cooking and music. He typically worked the earlier shift at the Inkwell so he was free for evening gigs with his band.

"Teagan and I were chatting about the menu yesterday," Booker said as he leaned against the bar and sipped his tea. "What do you think of a cold soup for when the warm weather hits?"

"I think that's a fantastic idea," I said. "I'm guessing you have a recipe in mind."

"We were thinking something citrusy. Maybe grapefruit with avocado?"

"I've never tasted anything like that, but it sounds delicious."

"We'll make sure it is," he assured me.

Ever since I'd opened the pub, I'd wanted to have literary-themed food on the menu. But until I'd hired Booker and Teagan in late October, I hadn't had a chef to make that a reality. Before the chefs had joined my staff, I'd only been able to offer the Inkwell's patrons soup from the local deli and premade meat and veggie pies to go along with their cocktails, local craft beers, and other drinks.

Thanks to Booker's and Teagan's creativity in the kitchen, however, my vision for the pub was truly taking shape. The menu now offered appetizers, a soup of the day, salads, a few entrées, and a couple of scrumptious desserts. At first I'd only added a handful of food items to the menu to test the waters, so to speak. When the initial dishes went over well with the pub's customers, the two chefs had collaborated to come up with several more, and now patrons came to the Inkwell for the food almost as much as for the drinks.

"Don't forget—today we're debuting the Paradise Lox," Booker said before drinking down the last of his tea.

"I definitely haven't forgotten." I finished my coffee and took my empty mug into the kitchen, Booker following behind me.

The Paradise Lox was the latest appetizer to be added to the menu. Each crostino was topped with salmon cream cheese mixed with lemon and dill, and—of course—lox. I'd been very thorough about taste-testing the appetizer. The first bite had wowed my taste buds, so naturally I'd had to try plenty more to be absolutely sure the appetizer was right for the menu.

"Remember we have to save some for the customers," Booker teased as he headed for the large sink.

"I'll try to restrain myself," I said. "But I can't guarantee that I won't indulge a little bit."

I put my mug in the dishwasher and left the kitchen while Booker washed his hands. He would start preparing the food now so that when the Inkwell opened, we'd be ready to serve hungry townsfolk and tourists.

Thankfully, there were plenty of the latter in town for the Winter Carnival. After moving to Shady Creek, I'd quickly learned that it was a town that loved its events. The annual Autumn Festival was the biggest draw for tourists, taking place during prime leaf-peeping season. Visitors hadn't arrived in quite the same droves for the Winter Carnival, but there were still plenty of tourists bringing in extra trade for me and all my fellow business owners.

That helped me sleep well at night. This was the first time I'd owned a business, and I was anxious to make a success out of it. There were plenty of townsfolk who were regulars at the Inkwell, but without an influx of tourists now and then throughout the year, I would have been struggling to make ends meet.

I busied myself with preparing the Inkwell for opening. I dusted the shelves and decor, and made sure that all the napkin dispensers and salt and pepper shakers were full. By the time the hour hand on the Guinness wall clock reached the twelve, I detected some delicious smells wafting from the kitchen. I swept my gaze across the pub one last time, checking to make sure everything was in order. I couldn't help but smile as I did so. In the few months since I'd purchased the pub, I'd come to love it. It almost felt like it was an extension of me now. I was proud of the Inkwell, and I was gratified that the townsfolk had embraced it as well as me.

Life was good in Shady Creek. And, as I opened the pub for the day, I had no reason to believe that would change anytime soon.

Chapter 3

By midafternoon there was enough of a crowd in the pub to keep me and Booker busy. Normally Mel would have been working the afternoon shift, but since she was taking part in the ice sculpture competition, I had to make do behind the bar on my own. There were a few familiar faces among the patrons, but also several tourists seeking out a warm place to enjoy some food and a drink or two before heading back out to take in the carnival's festivities.

As I pulled pints, mixed cocktails, and delivered orders to tables, I caught snippets of conversations about the ice sculpture competition. Excitement was building, as it was now possible to see some components of the sculptures taking shape. I was hoping I'd have a chance to slip out for a few minutes later in the day so I could check out Mel's progress and that of her fellow competitors. Although Booker and I were the only Inkwell staff members working at the moment, Damien would arrive in the early evening for a shift and Teagan would take over in the kitchen. If we weren't too busy later on, I might be able to sneak a few minutes away while Damien held down the fort.

In the late afternoon, my aunt Gilda arrived at the pub, bringing a big smile to my face. She had her friend and coworker, Betty, with her. Aunt Gilda owned a salon at the eastern end of the village green and Betty rented a chair from her. They were often among the first to know what was going on in town, thanks to their regular chats with their clients. Once someone had spent half an hour in Aunt Gilda's chair, she usually knew their entire life story. She wasn't much different from a bartender in that regard. People often confided in her as she cut and styled their hair.

My aunt had her dyed auburn hair in an up-do, the way she usually wore it, and her ears were pink from the cold.

I greeted them both with hugs. "I don't know how you can go outside without wearing a hat," I said. "My ears are going numb just thinking about it."

Aunt Gilda patted my back before sitting down at the table she and Betty had claimed. "I know how you feel about the cold, honey, and I can't disagree. But it only takes two minutes to get here from the salon, so I figured I'd survive."

"I guess you'll be getting a break from the cold weather soon," I said, not without a pang of disappointment.

Aunt Gilda usually spent Christmas in Savannah, where her lifelong best friend and several of her cousins lived. Most years she went there for at least two weeks, to enjoy the company of friends and family as well as the Savannah weather. I didn't want to close down the Inkwell for more than a day or two over the holidays, so I'd be staying in Shady Creek for Christmas. My mom was spending the holiday with my older brother, Michael, and his wife in Knoxville, and my younger brother, Taylor, usually went traveling overseas at that time of year. In other words, I wouldn't have any family with me to celebrate the holiday.

I tried not to think about that as I took Gilda's and Betty's orders for Lord of the Fries, Paradise Lox, and two Evil Stepmother mocktails. Christmas was one of my favorite times of year, but I was already feeling stabs of loneliness whenever I thought about spending it alone. The likelihood that I wouldn't have any family with me made me miss my dad even more than usual. He had passed away a few years ago and I didn't think I'd ever truly get used to not having him around. He'd loved Christmas as much as I did, and he was the one who'd instilled a love of books and reading in me at a very early age. I knew he would have loved the Inkwell and he would have been proud of what I'd done with it. I just wished he could be there to see it and to enjoy the holiday with me.

When Damien arrived, Aunt Gilda and Betty were still finishing up their appetizers, so I took the opportunity to grab a chair from an unoccupied table and join them for a short chat.

"Are you coming to the chili supper tonight?" Betty asked me.

I glanced around the pub. "I guess that depends on whether I can get away."

"You should try to," Aunt Gilda said. "You need to eat, and the chili supper is a Winter Carnival tradition."

I snagged a fry from her plate. "I'm not one to pass up free food if I don't have to. What time will you two be there?"

"We're planning to eat around seven. Should we save you a seat?"

"Please do," I said. "I'll try my best to be there, but I'll text you if I can't get away."

Beneath the chatter of the pub's patrons, the sound of quiet crying drew my attention. At a nearby table, a thirty-something woman with chestnut brown hair wiped her eyes with a tissue while another woman put an arm around her shoulders and spoke to her quietly.

Gilda and Betty had also noticed the crying woman.

"Poor Penny," Betty whispered with a shake of her head.

"What's wrong with her?" I kept my voice low too.

Aunt Gilda leaned closer to me. "She got the brush-off from Freddy Mancini earlier."

I had several questions I wanted to ask, but I bit them back as Penny and her companion got up from their table. Penny had stopped crying, but her eyes were rimmed with red and she looked as though her tears could start up again at any moment. Talking quietly together, she and her friend bundled up in their coats and scarves and headed for the door.

Even once they were gone, I spoke barely above a whisper. "What's Penny's connection to Freddy?"

"They were high school sweethearts," Aunt Gilda said.

"I have a hard time imagining Freddy as anyone's sweetheart at any point in time," I said.

"Ah, so you've met him."

"Not exactly. But I saw him out on the green when the sculpting was getting underway. He walked around with his nose in the air and he wasn't exactly charming to his personal assistant."

"That fits with what Gretchen Dingle told me this morning when I was doing her hair." Betty took a sip of her drink. "It also fits with what happened between him and Penny once his star was on the rise."

Aunt Gilda nodded. "This was before I moved to Shady Creek, but I've heard the story. Penny followed Freddy to Boston so he could train as a chef. After he finished culinary school, he got a job at a hotel restaurant. About a year or so later, he got on one of those TV chef competitions and won. Right after, he dumped Penny."

"Told her she wasn't sophisticated enough for him," Betty added.

"What a jerk!" I felt sorry for Penny.

"He got too big for his britches," Aunt Gilda said. "Poor Penny was gracious enough to approach him and wish him luck in the competition today."

"He pretended he didn't recognize her and told her he didn't need luck," Betty finished.

I frowned. "It doesn't sound like he's worth crying over."

"Few men are," Betty said. "But definitely not Freddy Mancini. That doesn't stop it from hurting, though."

"No, it doesn't."

I'd done plenty of crying after breaking things off with my ex the previous summer, even though he'd lied to me repeatedly over the years and had stolen my credit card to use for online gambling. Hearts weren't always sensible.

I pushed that thought aside. My ex had been murdered in October. Even though our relationship had been over for several months by then, it still hadn't been easy to accept that he was dead, and it wasn't something I liked to dwell on.

Aunt Gilda pushed back her chair and reached for her scarf. "Betty and I promised to help with the setup for the chili supper, so we'd better be on our way."

"I'm glad we had a chance to chat," I said. "And hopefully I'll see you later."

Both women pulled out their wallets.

"Don't worry about that," I said quickly. "Your food and drinks are on the house."

Aunt Gilda pressed several bills into my hand. "Honey, you can't keep doing that."

"You give me free haircuts," I reminded her as I tried to return the money.

We'd had this argument before. It was one I usually lost, but that didn't stop me from trying to press the issue now and again.

"You only get a few haircuts a year. Betty and I are in here every week." She closed my fingers around the money.

Betty handed over some bills of her own. "Gilda's right. You've got to let us pay."

"At least let me give you a free drink now and then," I said.

"Now and then." Gilda pulled me into a brief hug and kissed my cheek. "But not today. We'll see you later."

I saw them to the door and then got back to serving customers. Not long after Aunt Gilda and Betty left, there was a lull in business. A few patrons remained at the tables scattered around the pub, but they all had food and drink before them and didn't need any attention just then. I took the opportunity to slip behind the bar and speak with Damien for a moment. Although he'd arrived at the Inkwell bundled up in outerwear, he was now in his usual outfit of jeans and a short sleeve T-shirt that showed off the tattoos on his arms.

"Did you stop by the green on the way here?" I asked him.

"I did. And I talked to Mel. She says things are going well so far."

"That's good," I said. "I really hope she wins."

"She's got some tough competition, but I reckon she's still got a good chance."

Originally from England, Damien had lived in Shady Creek for close to twenty years and was raising two teenage daughters on his own. His wife had passed away from cancer when their girls were little more than toddlers. I didn't know if he had a woman in his life at the moment. Like Mel, he wasn't one to talk much about his personal life.

Damien and Mel had both worked at the pub before I bought it, and I counted myself extremely lucky that they'd wanted to keep their jobs when the business changed hands. They'd both proved invaluable on many occasions as I navigated my way through the choppy waters of running a business for the first time. I didn't know what I would have done without them.

Out of the corner of my eye, I noticed someone settle on a stool at the far end of the bar. I turned that way, a smile on my face, ready to greet whoever it was. Before I could get any words out of my mouth, my stomach did a funny little hop and my tongue tied itself up.

"Evening," Grayson Blake said, a hint of amusement in his blue eyes. "Expecting someone else?"

I was glad he'd mistaken my reaction for simple surprise. I didn't need him to know the effect he had on me.

I pulled myself together quickly. "No. I'm just not used to seeing you here."

Grayson owned the Spirit Hill Brewery and was my eastern neighbor. Our relationship—not much more than an acquaintance, really—hadn't started off on the best foot when I'd arrived in Shady Creek, but we'd smoothed things out since then. Mostly, anyway.

He still had a tendency to push my buttons and get me riled up. I served his award-winning beers at the Inkwell, but several weeks had passed since I'd last seen him in the pub. He could have free beer whenever he wanted at his place, so maybe he didn't see the point in coming by the Inkwell very often. If I were completely honest with myself, though, I'd been disappointed by the infrequency of his visits over the last couple of months. Not that I'd tell *him* that.

I had to admit—only to myself and my best friend, Shontelle—that Grayson was easy on the eyes. His dark hair was stylishly tousled and his eyes were a gorgeous shade of blue. He had a day or two's worth of stubble on his jaw, which made him even more attractive than usual.

I took a deep breath to calm the renewed fluttering in my stomach.

"I thought I'd get into the carnival spirit," he said. "I had a walk around town but now I need to warm up."

"Can I help you with that?"

Fire burned in my cheeks when I realized how that sounded. Grayson apparently realized it as well, seeing as he was grinning.

"With a drink!" I said in a rush. "I *meant*, can I get you a drink?"

He looked like he was holding back a laugh, but to my relief he picked up the menu I slid across the bar to him. "I've been wanting to try out one of your literary cocktails," he said as he scanned the list of drinks.

"You have?" For some reason that pleased me. I hadn't expected him to be interested in the cocktails I'd created, each one inspired by a book, author, or fictional character.

"The Malt in Our Stars sounds good," he said, his gaze still on the menu. "But I'm thinking the Count Dracula might be just the thing for a cold winter's evening."

I beamed at him. "I think it's the perfect winter evening drink."

"Then I'll give it a try."

"Any food to go with it?" I asked as he handed the menu back to me.

"I hear the fries are good."

"They're excellent. I'll have some for you in a minute."

I relayed Grayson's order for the Lord of the Fries appetizer to Teagan before mixing his drink. The Count Dracula cocktail was made from blood-orange juice, cranberry juice, cinnamon syrup, and coconut rum. It was a drink I'd already enjoyed a couple of times in front of a toasty fire since the winter weather had descended on Shady Creek.

"Did you check out the ice sculptures yet?" I asked as I placed a coaster in front of Grayson and set his drink on top.

"Right before I came here. It's amazing what the competitors can do with blocks of ice."

"It really is. I can't wait to see the final products tomorrow." I glanced around the pub.

Two men had signaled for refills of their beers, but Damien was looking after them.

"Speaking of tomorrow," I continued, returning my attention to Grayson, "the Inkwell's hosting a literary trivia night as part of the carnival."

Grayson nodded. "I saw a poster for it the other day."

I held my breath as he tried his drink. Relief washed over me when he smiled.

"You're right. The perfect drink for warming up."

"I'm glad you like it," I said with a smile of my own.

I heard a *ding* from the kitchen signaling that Grayson's fries were ready.

I excused myself and fetched the plate from the kitchen, carrying it over to Grayson. I had to leave him alone for a few minutes while he ate. Two patrons had recently left the pub, so I cleared and cleaned their table. As I did that, a group of half a dozen tourists arrived and I spent several minutes taking orders and mixing cocktails.

By the time I was able to focus on Grayson again, he was almost finished with his fries and his drink.

"Will you be signing up?" I asked, picking up our conversation where we'd left it.

"For the trivia night?"

"Yes. Maybe you could make up a team with some of your employees from the brewery."

"Actually, I won't be able to make it, though I can't speak for my employees."

"Oh." I tried to stem my disappointment. Maybe literary trivia wasn't his thing. "Not much of a reader?" I guessed, the thought only adding to my disappointment.

He swallowed the last of his drink and grinned. "If you think that, you didn't snoop far enough, Parker."

I sputtered, but he didn't give me a chance to tell him off for using that nickname. He slapped some bills on the bar and got up off his stool. "I'll see you around."

He was heading for the door by the time I'd recovered enough to send an icy glare his way.

I was still irked by Grayson's last comment when I donned my winter jacket twenty minutes later. I never appreciated it when he called me Parker, because it was short for *nosey* Parker. Making reference to the time when he'd caught me peeking through the windows of his house didn't exactly help my mood either. Maybe I had been a bit nosey at the time, but in my defense I was trying to figure out who'd murdered my ex. I'd been on the police suspect list and Grayson had been on mine, so I'd been attempting to learn more about him. Getting caught in the act wasn't my proudest moment, though. It probably ranked up in the top ten of my most embarrassing ones.

I mulled over what he'd said to me, aside from calling me Parker. What did he mean I hadn't snooped far enough? Not knowing the answer to that question only vexed me further.

Grayson Blake might be handsome, and he might be a talented craft brewer, but he could be so aggravating at times.

With a harrumph of annoyance, I pulled my hat down over my ears and stuffed my feet into my boots before clomping down the stairs and heading out the mill's back door. I tried my best to put Grayson out of my mind, but it wasn't so easy, in part because I was still smarting from the nickname he'd used and in part because it wasn't all that easy to forget about his blue eyes, even if the amusement that had lit them up had been at my expense.

I followed the shoveled pathway around the old gristmill and across the footbridge. I stopped at the edge of Creekside Road to wait for a car to pass by, its headlights cutting through the darkness. A light wind had picked up since I was last outside, and the temperature had plummeted. Two minutes hadn't yet passed since I'd left the pub and already I was shivering beneath my layers of winter clothing. The thought of sitting down with a steaming bowl of chili in the warmth of the town hall kept me going through the cold.

Despite the fact that my cheeks were already going numb, I stuck with my plan to check out the ice sculptures before heading over to the town hall at the western end of the village green. It had quieted down since I was last there. Gone were the spectators and the reporters. Even some of the competitors were missing. Two people I guessed were part of the event's organizing committee were huddled beneath the canopy, which was lit up by a string of twinkle lights, chatting with each other as they stomped their feet and rubbed their arms in an effort to keep warm.

Several spotlights illuminated the work areas, allowing me to see that competitors were at work at the two stations closest to the canopy. Another was chipping away at a block of ice at the midway point between the canopy and the bandstand, but I couldn't see anyone else. Mel's station was blocked from my view by the bandstand, but Freddy's half-finished sculpture was within sight, its creator absent.

I paused by his station to check out his work. It appeared as though he was carving an eagle caught in mid-take-off from a log. He had the general shapes roughed out, the details yet to come. Even so, I could tell that his sculpture would be impressive. I crossed my fingers inside my mittens, hoping Mel's work of art would have an extra wow factor. I'd wanted her to win the competition as soon as I'd found out she was taking part, but now that I knew what Freddy was like, I *really* didn't want him to place ahead of her.

The snow crunched beneath my feet as I rounded the bandstand. I smiled when I saw Mel standing before her sculpture, but the expression slipped from my face when she ran her gloved hands over her hair in a motion fraught with frustration.

"Mel? What's wrong?"

She spun around at the sound of my voice.

I noticed that something was missing. Several somethings, actually.

"Where are your tools?" I asked.

"Gone," Mel said, a mixture of disbelief and anger in her voice. "Somebody stole them."

Chapter 4

"Who would steal your tools?" I asked, shocked.

"I don't know," Mel said. "One of my fellow competitors?"

It was clear from her face that she didn't like that thought.

I scurried after her as she marched around the bandstand. When all the other carving stations were in view, she stopped and slowly swept her gaze from one to the other. It didn't appear as though anyone had extra tools lying around, but it wasn't as if I was qualified to judge that. Mel didn't storm over to any particular station, though, so I figured she'd come to the same conclusion as I had.

"There aren't many people around," I observed.

"Most people are over at the chili supper, grabbing a bite to eat before getting back to carving. That's where I was, but only for half an hour. Apparently that was long enough for someone to steal my tools." She pulled a knitted hat from the pocket of her jacket and crammed it down over her short hair. "I'd better ask if anyone saw anything."

She struck off across the snow-covered green toward the canopy where the two organizers were still huddled. I jogged to keep up with Mel's long strides. When we reached the canopy, she told the man and woman about her missing tools. They were suitably shocked, and neither had seen anything suspicious, although they pointed out that Mel's carving station was the hardest to see from their vantage point.

The other carvers present on the green came over to see what was going on. Mel filled them in, but none of them had witnessed anything either.

"I bet it was Freddy Mancini," one of the competitors said. He appeared to be in his midforties. "He was asking questions earlier, wanting to know who'd won in years past. Your name came up of course, Mel. He seemed pretty sure he'd win this year—full of himself, if you ask me—but maybe he decided to make it a bit easier for himself."

"I wouldn't put it past him," another man said.

Mel frowned. "I can't accuse anyone without proof."

"Let's have a look around and see if we can spot your tools somewhere," the woman from the organizing committee suggested.

According to the name tags hanging around their necks, her name was Ruby and the man with her was Dan.

The other sculptors returned to their work while Ruby made a circuit around the green with me and Mel. We didn't spot any of Mel's tools.

"How could anyone get away with all your tools without someone noticing?" I asked. "I know it's pretty quiet right now, but all these lights are on, and that would have been a lot of tools for one person to move in one go."

"I haven't noticed any vehicles parked by the green," Ruby said.

No parking was permitted on the streets bordering the green, so there was a good chance that any idling or unoccupied vehicles would have drawn her attention.

"I wonder . . ." I said as a thought struck me. I turned in a slow circle until I noticed a pile of snow heaped up against one side of the bandstand.

"What are you thinking?" Mel asked.

I approached the pile of snow and dug through it with my mittened hands. A second later Mel joined in. As soon as we'd brushed away the top couple of inches of snow, a bit of metal appeared.

Mel dug deeper and pulled the object out. "My chain saw! You're a genius, Sadie."

"I don't know about that," I said as we continued digging with renewed vigor, exposing more power tools. "But I'm glad we found them. Are they all here?"

Mel set aside everything we'd uncovered. "The power tools are, but not my hand tools."

We cleared the snow right down to the grass without finding anything more. With Ruby's help, we worked our way around the bandstand, checking beneath the snow banked up against the structure. By the time we'd finished, my mittens were wet and caked with snow, but we still hadn't found Mel's hand tools.

"I guess the smaller tools were easier to carry away," I said with disappointment. I hated to think of Mel being at a disadvantage in the competition.

"Will you be able to continue with your sculpture?" Ruby asked, her forehead creased with worry lines.

"I'm definitely not giving up," Mel said. "I've got another set of hand tools at my studio. Maybe I can get Zoe to run over and get them for me while I keep working with the tools I've got."

"That sounds like a good plan," Ruby said with obvious relief.

"It was still a dirty trick." I glanced around, but nobody was lurking in the shadows, watching us guiltily.

"I'll tell the committee what happened," Ruby assured us.

Mel brushed snow off her gloves. "And I'll make sure I don't leave my tools unattended again."

"That's probably for the best," I said. "And if your tools don't show up, you should report the theft to the police."

"We'll see what happens."

Ruby told us she'd get in touch with the other committee members as soon as possible, and then she hurried off back toward the canopy.

Mel tugged off one glove and dug her phone out of her jacket pocket.

"Did Zoe go home?" I asked as she tapped out a text message.

"No, she's at the town hall getting something to eat."

I thought for a second. "Maybe we should get a team together to be here in shifts. That way if you ever need a break, someone will be here who can keep an eye on things. Whoever hid your tools might not stop at that nasty prank."

"You're thinking they might try to trash my sculpture," Mel said, picking up on my line of thought.

"As much as I'd like to believe no one would do that, it's possible."

Mel picked up a power tool with a disc-like attachment. "I don't want anyone standing out here freezing in the middle of the night on my account. If I leave for any reason between now and the end of the competition, I'll let Ruby or Dan know. I'm sure they'll keep an eye on things."

"You really think that'll be enough?" I asked. "I don't mind helping out once the pub's closed for the night. And I'm sure I could find others to volunteer too."

Mel shook her head. "Thank you, Sadie, but don't worry about it. Really. Everything will be fine."

"Okay," I said, hoping she was right. "But if you change your mind, text me."

As Mel got back to sculpting, I studied her work in progress for the first time. I'd been so distracted by the missing tools that I hadn't taken in the incredible sight before me.

"Mel, this is amazing!" I said when she shut off her power tool. "It's a dragon, right? Sitting on a nest of eggs?"

Mel smiled. "It is. There's lots of work still to be done, but I'm glad you can at least tell what it's supposed to be."

"It's really incredible."

"Thanks. Hopefully the judges will think so."

"I'm sure they will. I can't wait to see it when it's finished."

I hung around for a few minutes longer while Mel continued to cut, carve, and shape her ice. A couple of other competitors drifted across the green from the direction of the town hall and resumed work on their own sculptures.

My toes were frozen and my stomach was grumbling, so I said good-bye to Mel and crunched through the snow to the western end of the village green. Although I was troubled by the fact that someone had tried to sabotage Mel's chances in the competition, I couldn't help but be cheered up by the town's holiday decorations. Every one of the old-fashioned streetlamps had been decked out with a wreath, and every tree and building had been strung with lights.

It was a beautiful sight, but I didn't linger on the green any longer. After checking that the way was clear, I quickly crossed the street to the old brick building that housed the town hall.

As soon as I had the door shut behind me, I pulled off my mittens and dug my phone out of the deep pocket of my jacket. Damien hadn't texted me to say he needed me back at the pub, so I figured I still had time to get myself some dinner. Even from the anteroom I could detect the delicious smell of chili cooking in the kitchen at the back of the building.

My mouth watered. I stuffed my mittens, hat, and scarf into the pockets of my jacket and hung it up in the cloakroom off to the left of the entry. Rubbing my hands, I made my way into the large main room, appreciating the warm temperature, even though my fingers and toes would take some time to thaw out.

I paused just inside the room, searching for familiar faces. A dozen folding tables had been set up and covered with red-and-white checkered cloths. There were probably twenty or thirty people there at the moment, eating and chatting, creating a low rumble of conversation.

A girl's voice called my name at the same moment as I noticed someone waving excitedly at me from across the room. A big smile spread across my face. My best friend's eight-year-old daughter was kneeling on her chair, desperately trying to get my attention.

"Sadie! Over here! We saved you a seat!"

I hurried down the center aisle to reach the table where Kiandra sat with her mom and grandmother as well as Betty and Aunt Gilda. On my way past another table, I spotted Zoe sitting with some of her friends. I was about to head her way to tell her about Mel's tools when she checked her phone and got up from the table. She said something to her friends and then headed for the door.

"Hi, Sadie," she said as she rushed past me. "I'm off to help Mel."

I said a quick hello before she disappeared.

Zoe had studio space in the same building as Mel. Hopefully she wouldn't have any problem finding the extra set of tools and Mel would have everything she needed in short order.

"Hi, everyone," I said as I pulled out the empty chair next to Kiandra. "Is there any food left?"

"Lots," Kiandra said, sliding off her knees to sit in her seat.

"You didn't eat it all?" I asked.

She giggled. "They have *pots and pots* of chili in the kitchen. I can't eat all that."

"Maybe if it were cake and ice cream," Shontelle said.

Kiandra's already bright eyes lit up. "Ice cream. Yum! Can we get some from the store before we go home?"

"You don't need ice cream in the middle of winter," her grandma Yvette said.

"I *always* need ice cream," Kiandra countered.

We laughed and I spent a minute or so catching up with everyone.

"You'd better go get yourself some food," Aunt Gilda said.

My stomach rumbled in agreement with her. "Right." I scooted my chair back. "I'll do that now."

I had to pass another dining table before getting to the one at the back of the room that had been set up for serving food. Freddy Mancini was sitting there with Jade Castellano and a couple of other people I recognized as his fellow competitors. Leo Mancini was across the room, eating with a group of guys around his age. With the two half brothers in the same room together, I was surprised it was so peaceful.

As I stood in line behind two other people at the serving table, a tall man with graying hair approached Freddy's table, a smile on his face.

"Freddy, it's so good to see you back here in Shady Creek," the man said.

"I go by *Federico* now," the chef said, disdain clear on his face.

The older man's smile faltered, but he quickly recovered. "Going up in the world, huh?"

"Unlike some people," Freddy muttered loudly enough for everyone around him to hear.

He turned away from the older man and started talking to Jade, giving her orders about his schedule for the next two days while she hurriedly tapped away at her phone.

The older man's smile slipped away entirely this time and his shoulders drooped with disappointment. Lara Hawkes, a member of the Inkwell's mystery book club, hurried up to him and took his arm.

"Come on, Dad," she said, steering him away while sending a death glare at the back of Freddy's head. "Let's get you home."

As soon as Lara and her father were out the door, Leo Mancini jerked his chair back and got to his feet in one abrupt motion. I suspected the peace was about to be broken.

Leo marched across the aisle separating his table from Freddy's and shoved his half brother's shoulder.

"What the hell was that?" he demanded.

"Who do you think you are?" Freddy shot back, brushing his shoulder as if Leo's touch had left a dirty mark.

"Eli was your mentor. You're where you are now because of him. And that's the way you treat him?"

Freddy sneered at Leo. "I'm where I am today because of my hard work and talent. I got here on my own."

Leo let out a humorless bark of laughter. "What a load of—"

"Gentlemen, how about we keep things down?" Eldon Howes interrupted. Although apparently off duty at the moment, the tall, fair-haired man was an officer with the Shady Creek Police Department. "This is a family event."

"*Family*," Leo said with distaste. "I don't think he knows the meaning of the word." He shot a disgusted look at his half brother as he spoke.

Freddy was about to retort when Eldon spoke up again. "Leo, how about you go finish your supper?"

Leo looked as though he would much rather have punched Freddy in the face, but when Eldon put a hand on his arm, Leo shot one last glare at his half brother before returning to his table, his expression as dark as a thundercloud.

I tried to relax my shoulders, realizing the tension in the room had worked its way into my muscles. Hopefully that would be the end of the drama. Although, with Freddy still present, I wouldn't have bet on it.

It was my turn to be served, so I focused on the woman dishing out the chili and crusty bread. Once I had my food, I filled a mug with hot chocolate from one of the urns at the end of the serving table. Then, with everything balanced on a tray, I returned to my seat.

"Did you catch all that drama?" I whispered to Aunt Gilda once I was sitting between her and Kiandra.

"Poor Eli," she said by way of response. "He used to run a restaurant here in town. I heard he took Freddy under his wing years ago, and was even the one who taught him to cook. And he did it purely out of the kindness of his heart. Freddy should be ashamed of himself."

"I don't think shame is within his range of emotions," I said.

"I'm sorry to say you're probably right about that."

"Why don't he and Leo get along? Not that it seems like Freddy gets along well with anyone, from what I've seen so far."

"I'm not sure what happened between them."

I glanced over my shoulder at Leo. He and his friends had finished eating and were getting up from their table. I wondered if he'd be able to leave the town hall without firing a parting shot at his half brother, but it quickly became clear that he wouldn't. He paused in the aisle between the rows of tables, his stormy gaze focused on Freddy.

"Good luck with the competition," he said, sounding anything but sincere.

"I don't need luck," Freddy snapped. "Especially not from you."

"Really?" Leo smirked. "Because even your assistant bet on someone else. What does that tell you?"

Still smug, Leo swaggered out of the town hall with his friends.

Freddy's face turned an alarming shade of red. He swung around in his seat to challenge Jade. "Is that true?"

Jade shrank away from him, her eyes wide. "It was just for fun."

"*Fun*? That's what you call your disloyalty?"

Jade sat up straighter, anger replacing the shock in her eyes. "You're overreacting."

"Overreacting?" Freddy bellowed. "How's *this* for overreacting? You're fired!"

Jade gaped at him as he shoved his chair back and got to his feet. Everyone in the room was staring at him now. He swept his disgusted gaze over all of us as he stormed down the aisle and out the door.

With her lips set in a hard line, Jade got up to leave as well. She walked at a more dignified pace, her head held high.

When she was gone, stunned silence weighed heavily over the room for a few seconds. Then murmured conversations started up, and everyone slowly resumed eating.

"I'm not sure I would have shown up if I knew what the entertainment would be like," I said quietly.

"Same here," Shontelle said, casting a worried glance at her daughter.

Kiandra didn't seem concerned by what had happened, however. She was dipping her bread into the remains of her chili while she filled her grandma in on what had happened at school that day. I dug into my own chili, enjoying the warmth and heartiness of the meal.

I spent a few minutes focused only on eating while everyone chatted around me. When Shontelle and Kiandra got up to leave, I left my chili long enough to give them each a hug. Then I got back to savoring the remains of my meal. I didn't look up again until I heard Aunt Gilda speak to a woman passing by our table.

"Everything all right, Sybil?"

The woman's light brown hair had streaks of gray in it and she appeared to be in her sixties. At the moment, her forehead was creased with worry lines.

"Have you seen Eli?" she asked Aunt Gilda. "I can't seem to track him down."

"He was here earlier, but he left with Lara about half an hour ago. It sounded like she was taking him home."

"Okay, thank you. I'll try phoning him again." She gave Aunt Gilda a brief, shaky smile before heading out of the room.

I scooped up the last spoonful of my chili. "I should really be getting back to the Inkwell."

Aunt Gilda patted my hand. "I'm glad you were able to stop by."

"So am I."

I said my good-byes and retrieved my outerwear from the cloakroom, including my damp mittens. I grimaced as I pulled them on. Maybe I would have been better off without wearing them, but I ended up leaving them on. It wouldn't take me long to get back to the pub.

I tried to brace myself before opening the door and heading back out into the cold air, but that still didn't prepare me for the icy blast that hit me as soon as I left the warmth of the town hall. My cheeks prickled and the inside of my nose felt like it had been instantly freeze dried.

Anxious to get back to the pub and out of the cold, I hurried down the steps to the sidewalk. As I set off northward along Hemlock Street, a loud clatter startled me. It sounded like it had come from behind the town hall. I peered down the gap between the town hall and the neighboring building, but didn't see anything.

I was about to keep going when I stopped again. There *was* something there, just not anything moving. It looked like there was a big lump halfway down the gap between buildings. I stepped into the dark space, leaving the cheery glow of the nearest streetlamp behind.

"Hello?" I called out, apprehension shimmying up my spine.

There was no response. The only sound I could hear was that of my feet crunching on the snow.

I stopped after taking a few steps. My apprehension had now morphed into fear.

The lump looked like it could be a person lying on the ground.

I wanted to turn around and run, but I couldn't. What if

someone needed help? I swallowed my fear and moved deeper into the shadowy gap.

"Hello?" I said again. "Are you all right?"

As before, I was met only with silence.

After another step, I froze.

It was dark, but my eyes were adjusting, and the shadows didn't keep me from recognizing the lump on the ground as Freddy Mancini.

The darkness also didn't stop me from seeing the ice pick stuck into his chest.

Chapter 5

I let out a strangled cry and stepped back so fast that I nearly fell over. I tried to retrieve my phone from my pocket, but my hands were too clumsy in their mittens.

"Help!" I yelled as I tore off my mittens so I could grasp my phone.

I yelled again as I tried to wake up the device with cold, shaking fingers.

No one was close enough to hear me. I tore out of the gap between the buildings and onto the sidewalk. I called for help once more, this time directing my voice toward the village green.

I was about to run up the steps and into the town hall to find someone when I heard swift footsteps crunching through the snow. Mel was running across the green toward me.

"Mel!" I said with a rush of relief as she reached my side. "It's Freddy."

I pointed into the shadows, my hand trembling.

Mel cautiously approached Freddy, and I followed. She crouched down and pulled off one of her gloves, touching her fingers to Freddy's neck. When she turned back my way, her face was grim.

"Have you called nine-one-one?" she asked.

"I'm just about to." I tried waking up my phone again, without success. I slapped a hand to my forehead, realizing I'd meant to charge it that morning. "The battery died."

"I'll call." Mel unzipped her jacket and fished her phone out of an inside pocket.

I had to turn away then. Now that my eyes had become more adjusted to the darkness, I could see the stain where Freddy's blood had seeped into the snow.

Swallowing hard, I tried to keep my emotions under control. I hadn't liked what little I'd seen of the man, but who could have done such a thing?

With that question circling in my mind, I truly registered for the first time that we were at the scene of a crime. I didn't think there was any possible way that Freddy could have ended up on his back, an ice pick through his heart, as a result of an accident.

Mel had finished speaking with the 911 operator, so I asked if I could borrow her phone.

"Do you have a flashlight app on here?" I asked as she handed me the device.

She pointed out the app. "Why?"

The light came on and I directed it toward Freddy's body, even though I would have preferred to look anywhere else.

I shuddered at the sight of Freddy's pasty face and his blood-soaked jacket. The red snow around his body made my stomach churn. Still, I leaned forward, catching sight of something. A small tuft of orange wool was caught on a rough spot on the ice pick's wooden handle.

"Sadie, we should back off," Mel said. "This is a crime scene."

She was right, and I didn't really want to keep looking at

Freddy anyway. I returned her phone to her and shoved my useless one into my pocket as we moved to the front of the town hall. I pulled my damp mittens back on, shivering harder now, and only partly from the cold.

I had to stifle another shudder as we stood on the sidewalk, waiting for the police to arrive. It was eerie, knowing a murder had taken place so close to where we stood. And it must have happened recently. Freddy hadn't left the town hall all that long ago.

I jumped when a car door slammed somewhere in the distance. My heart pounded as I glanced left, and then right, worried Freddy's killer might leap out at us at any moment.

"Whoever killed him is probably long gone," Mel said as if she'd read my thoughts.

Ruby and Dan jogged across the green toward us. As they crossed the street, Mel and I stepped forward so they wouldn't go past the town hall steps.

"Is something wrong, Mel?" Ruby asked. "We saw you take off running like your house was on fire."

"I heard Sadie call for help," Mel said.

Everyone's eyes turned to me.

"It's Freddy," I said. "He's dead."

Ruby gasped, her eyes going wide.

Dan gaped at us for a second or two. "How? Where?" he managed to ask eventually.

I pointed at the space between the buildings. "Down there. And it looks like he was murdered."

"Murdered?" Ruby echoed the word faintly.

Despite the fact that her cheeks were pink from the cold, she looked like she was about to pass out. Mel and I each grabbed one of her arms.

"Maybe you should sit down," I suggested.

We helped her over to a bench next to the town hall steps and she sank down. I sat next to her, feeling a tad shaky myself.

"Has anyone called the police?" Dan asked.

Mel told him she had. He took a step toward the shadowy space next to the building, but Mel put out an arm to stop him.

"It's a crime scene. We should stay back. Besides, it's not a pretty sight."

Dan nodded. "Right." He glanced around helplessly, like he didn't know what to do next.

By then we'd drawn the attention of the other competitors and a few people who'd emerged from the town hall. They all migrated toward us, asking why we were gathered on the sidewalk. When they were all together in a group, Mel explained the situation and asked them to stay put. After a moment of shocked silence, they started pelting questions at her.

"I don't have any answers for you," she said, raising her voice to speak over them. "Let's wait for the police to arrive."

Judging by the sirens piercing through the night air, that wouldn't take long.

A group of people coming from the direction of the Inkwell headed our way.

"What's going on?" one of them asked.

"Freddy Mancini's been murdered," a woman called out.

After another chorus of gasps, the newcomers pressed closer. Despite Mel's instructions to the contrary, a few individuals tried to shuffle around to the side of the building to get a look at Freddy's body.

"Ms. Coleman? What's going on?" A tall, muscular man stood on the sidewalk, his form more imposing than usual with the extra bulk from his winter jacket.

"Jason!" I exhaled with relief. He was the head of security at Grayson's brewery. "There's been a murder. The body's between the buildings." I pointed. "And these people are getting too close to the crime scene."

That was all I needed to say. Jason immediately took charge.

"Everyone back up," he ordered, herding the crowd toward the town hall steps. "No one but the police can go in there."

The curious onlookers shot questions at him, but he ignored them and continued to direct them farther way. By then, two police cruisers had pulled up to the curb, their sirens shut off now but their lights still flashing.

Satisfied that everyone was well away from the crime scene, Jason turned to meet the approaching officers. He exchanged a few quiet words with them and then pointed in the direction of Freddy's body. After that, he returned to the base of the steps, standing like a statue, his arms crossed over his broad chest, his gaze on the police as they disappeared between the two buildings.

It didn't take long for the officers to return to the sidewalk. The female officer came our way, while her male counterpart spoke into his radio.

"Who was first on the scene?" Officer Rogers asked.

I knew her name from interactions we'd had back in the fall when my ex was killed and someone had vandalized the pub.

I raised my hand.

"Ms. Coleman," she said, obviously remembering me as well. "Did you make the call?"

"That was me," Mel spoke up.

"I'll speak to you each in turn," Rogers said. "Could you join me for a moment, Ms. Coleman?"

I nodded and got up from the bench, following Officer Rogers away from the curious crowd watching us. The male police officer, whose name I didn't know, was still speaking quietly into his radio.

Once we were out of earshot of the onlookers, Officer Rogers asked me how I'd come to find Freddy's body. I relayed the story to her and then answered her questions about what I'd seen and heard in the moments before and after I'd stumbled upon Freddy. I mentioned the clatter I'd heard, but I couldn't tell her what had caused it.

Was it Freddy's killer, knocking something over as he or she made an escape?

By the time I'd given her all the information I had, I was shivering uncontrollably. While Rogers motioned for Mel to join her, I headed across Creekside Road to the Inkwell. Rogers had told me I could leave the scene, and I couldn't get away fast enough. I needed to get warm and I didn't want the crowd of onlookers peppering me with questions.

I hurried across the footbridge and into the Inkwell. The warmth of the pub enveloped me like a hug as soon as I had the door shut behind me. Unfortunately, that wasn't enough to stop my shivering. The cold had seeped into my bones by then.

My teeth chattering, I forced a smile onto my face and greeted customers as I made my way across the room to the bar, where Damien was mixing cocktails.

"I'm sorry I was gone so long," I said. "And my phone died. Did I miss any texts from you?"

"No," he replied. "But I was going to check in with you if you didn't show up soon."

"I'm sorry," I said again. "I was delayed unexpectedly."

Damien set a Count Dracula cocktail on a tray along with two Huckleberry Gins and a pint of beer. "Did that have anything to do with the police presence on Hemlock Street?"

"You know about that?"

"A couple of customers came in and spread the news."

"So you know about Freddy?"

"As in Mancini?" Damien asked. "The chef who's competing in the ice sculpture competition?"

"That's him. Do you know him?"

"Not personally." He eyed me with apprehension. "What happened?"

I lowered my voice. "He's dead. Murdered."

"Freddy Mancini's been murdered?" a woman said from nearby.

Apparently, I hadn't lowered my voice far enough.

Vera Anderson, the owner of a local boutique, had just emerged from the short corridor that led to the washrooms. "Is that why the police are across the way? Who did it?" She snapped the questions at me as if she were an impatient teacher and me a disagreeable student.

"Yes and I don't know," I said.

She turned her back on me as she produced her phone from her designer handbag and headed briskly for the table where two of her friends were waiting for her.

Now that Vera knew about the murder, I didn't doubt that the whole town would know about it in short order. I felt a twinge of guilt for letting the cat out of the bag, but I figured it wouldn't have taken much longer for the news to spread anyway. News and rumors alike tended to travel at turbo speed in Shady Creek.

I rubbed my arms, still suffering from the effects of standing out in the cold for so long. Not to mention the effects of finding Freddy's body.

Damien picked up the tray of drinks. "You look half frozen. You'd better get a hot drink into you."

That sounded like a good idea. First, though, I hurried upstairs to my apartment to shed my winter gear. Wimsey was cozied up on the couch, nice and toasty warm. I allowed myself a few seconds to cuddle him, but then I returned to the pub, where I immediately made myself a cup of tea.

I tried to take a sip of the drink right away, only to end up burning my tongue, so I set the cup aside reluctantly. The pub was fairly busy, so I got to work, helping Damien with taking orders, mixing drinks, and serving customers, sneaking sips of my tea whenever I could spare a moment. The hot drink and the work helped to warm me up, and slowly the deep chill left my bones. I couldn't say the same for the eerie prickling sensation that kept running up and down my spine.

Almost everyone in the Inkwell was talking about the murder now; theories about who might have done the deed were thrown around. I heard one of Vera Anderson's friends suggest that the murderer could have been a woman scorned by the successful chef. Across the room, as I delivered pints to some Inkwell regulars, I heard a man say it was probably a mob hit, related to Freddy's business dealings in Boston.

I didn't put too much stock in what people were saying. The theories would probably continue to fly around until the killer was caught. Still, I couldn't help but wonder about the crime myself. In just one day, Freddy had managed to upset several people, any one of whom might have struck out at him in anger.

But which one?

I didn't have the answer to that question, but maybe the culprit wasn't anyone I knew. If Freddy could ruffle so many feathers here in Shady Creek in the space of a single day, surely he'd made plenty of enemies in Boston.

The problem was that his murder had happened here, not in the city where he lived and worked. And that was why I couldn't rid myself of the prickle running along my spine. With a killer lurking in Shady Creek, how could any of us townsfolk feel safe?

Chapter 6

I slept late the next morning. Or, as late as Wimsey would let me, anyway. When he meowed into my ear, I rolled onto my back with a groan. He climbed up onto my shoulder and I cracked open my eyes to find his blue ones staring back at me. I closed my eyes again, but he tapped my chin with his paw and meowed more insistently. I knew from experience that he wasn't about to give up. He wanted his breakfast, and he wasn't known for his patience where meals were concerned.

My vision still bleary from sleep, I stumbled into the kitchen and dutifully provided His Lordship with breakfast and fresh water. Then I attended to my own most pressing need by putting some coffee on to brew. A niggling feeling of dread and apprehension worked its way into my mind, but it wasn't until I was heading for the shower that the previous day's events came rushing back to me and I remembered Freddy's death.

His murder.

Not even a hot shower could wash away the memory of Freddy lying in the bloodstained snow with an ice pick in his chest. I wanted to hear news of the killer's arrest, to know the case had been wrapped up quickly, peace and order restored in Shady Creek. That wasn't to be, however. When I finally got myself out the door after a cup of coffee and two slices of toast, it didn't take me long to find out that the murderer was still on the loose.

As soon as I stepped out the front door, I saw that the police were busy over by the town hall. An officer was stationed on each side of the building to keep people away and I recognized Detective Marquez and Police Chief Walters on the green, speaking with some of Mel's competitors. Freddy's unfinished sculpture stood abandoned, a reminder of the life cut short.

Mel was hard at work on her dragon and I decided not to interrupt her. Eldon Howes was the officer stationed on this side of the town hall, so I crossed the corner of the green to approach him.

"Morning, Officer Howes," I greeted. "Has anyone been arrested yet?"

"Not yet," he said, "but the investigation is still in its early stages."

I couldn't help but feel disappointed, though I knew he was right. Freddy hadn't even been dead for twenty-four hours. No doubt the police still had plenty of work ahead of them, but I hoped they'd catch the culprit before too long.

I recalled the tuft of orange wool I'd seen snagged on the ice pick. I'd mentioned it to Officer Rogers, but she hadn't given me any indication as to whether it was of any interest to her. Was it significant or had it been there long before the killer had used the tool to kill Freddy?

As much as I wanted to know the answer to that question, I knew I might never find out.

I wished Officer Howes a good day and he tipped his hat at me. I crossed the green, thinking about the murder and not taking much time to admire the almost-finished sculptures. Was someone so desperate to win the money and magazine coverage that they had killed Freddy to improve their chances of becoming the victorious sculptor? If that was the case, was Mel in danger?

That thought stopped me in my tracks. I considered sharing my concern with Mel, but she was so intent on her work that I didn't want to disturb her. She was safe at the moment; she was out in the open with police officers close by. I'd have to warn her later on, though. If Freddy's killer had been motivated by a desire to win the competition, he or she might well lash out again, and it was no secret that Mel was one of the frontrunners.

Comforted by the fact that Detective Marquez and Chief Walters were still on the green, I continued on my way to Aunt Gilda's salon. Betty and my aunt were busy with clients, cutting and styling their hair, but Gilda put down her scissors as soon as she saw me.

"I just heard about you finding Freddy," she said as she pulled me into a hug. "That must have been terrible."

"It was."

She stepped back and held me at arm's length. "Are you all right? Do you need something to eat or drink? I baked some forgotten cookies yesterday."

"I'm okay," I assured her. "And I can't stay long, but I won't say no to a cookie."

"They're over with the coffee and tea." Aunt Gilda picked up her scissors again.

I helped myself to one of the meringue-and-chocolate-chip forgotten cookies, a traditional Christmas treat in my family. They got their name from the fact that, once baked, they stayed in the oven overnight.

Betty and the two women having their hair cut wanted to hear the story of how I'd found Freddy, so I stayed long enough to give them a brief outline of the events. On my way out of the salon, I snagged another forgotten cookie and munched on it as I made my way to Shontelle's shop, the Treasure Chest. If she didn't already know about my unfortunate discovery, I wanted her to hear about it from me.

Instead of going straight into the store, I peeked through the large front window. Shontelle had her hands full with at least three customers browsing and another three lined up at the cash counter. I decided not to bother her and instead sent her a text message once I'd returned home.

With that done, I decided to focus on something positive. The pub's trivia night was taking place that evening, and I was both excited and nervous. It was the first event of its kind that I'd hosted at the Inkwell and I wanted it to go off without a hitch. It was also my way of contributing to the carnival's festivities. I'd started planning the trivia night several weeks ago, and I knew I had everything organized and ready to go. Still, I went over all the details again in an attempt to settle my jitters. It helped a bit, but not much, and I was glad when Booker showed up, his company a welcome distraction from my nervousness.

"Remember the summer soup we talked about yesterday?" he asked once he'd shed all his winter gear and left it in the cloakroom.

"Of course. It sounds so good."

"Well, now you can see if it tastes good too. I worked on the recipe last night and brought you a sample."

"You've made my day," I said with a smile.

"You might want to hold off on saying that until you've tried it."

He removed the lid from a container and handed it to me along with a spoon.

The soup was green, but a pleasant shade, not a gross one.

I dipped the spoon into it. My eyes widened as soon as I got my first taste. The soup was refreshing and delicious.

"Booker, you've done it again!" I said as soon as I'd swallowed. "This is amazing!"

"Great," he said with a big smile. "I was hoping you'd think so. Now it needs a name."

I took a second to enjoy another spoonful of the soup before saying, "How about A Time to Chill?"

"That's perfect," Booker said, still smiling. His expression sobered a moment later. "I'm guessing you've heard about the murder."

"I'm the one who found Freddy's body."

Booker's eyes nearly popped out of his head. "No way! That's awful, Sadie. Are you okay?"

I assured him I was as well as I could be considering the circumstances. That was true. I had to suppress a shudder every time I remembered how Freddy had looked lying dead in the snow, but I was otherwise holding up well.

After we'd chatted for another minute or so, Booker headed into the kitchen to do some prep work while I finished off the sample of soup. I was looking forward to having it on the menu once warmer weather hit.

Soon it was time to open the Inkwell for the day. When I opened the front door to switch the wooden CLOSED sign to OPEN, Mel was on her way up the flagstone path.

"Sorry I'm late," she said as she hurried through the door.

I quickly pulled it closed against the cold outside air.

"Late?" I said. "You're scheduled to take the day off, remember?"

"That was so I could work on my sculpture, but I finished up a little while ago. Is it all right if I work my shift?"

"Of course it is. And I can't wait to see your sculpture now that it's done."

Mel disappeared into the cloakroom and, when she returned a moment later, the pub was still empty, our first customers of the day yet to arrive.

She massaged her neck and rolled her shoulders as she joined me behind the bar.

"What's wrong?" I asked. It wasn't like her to look so stressed. "Are you worried about the competition?"

"No, it's not that." She hesitated before continuing. "I had to go to the police station this morning."

"What for? I thought Officer Rogers talked to you last night."

"She did, but Detective Marquez wanted to see me today."

I took a second to absorb that information. Detective Marquez had investigated my ex's murder back in the fall. I'd ended up on her suspect list for a while, a position I most definitely hadn't enjoyed. As I searched Mel's face, apprehension settled heavily in the pit of my stomach.

"Why would Detective Marquez want to talk to you?" I asked.

Mel rubbed a fist across her forehead. "She heard there'd been an incident between me and Freddy."

"Incident?"

"It wasn't a big deal. Around midafternoon yesterday, the reporters came back to the green. They spent some time talking to me before going back to Freddy. I think it bugged him that they paid attention to someone other than him. I could hear him trash-talking me. I tried to ignore him, but then one of the reporters—one from out of town—came over to get my reaction. I said I didn't need to engage in trash talk. My work would speak for itself."

"Good for you," I said.

"Freddy wasn't so approving. He made sure all the reporters heard him when he said if my work spoke with the same hillbilly accent as I did, no one would be able to understand it."

My jaw dropped. "What a jerk! That's a horrible thing to say, never mind the fact that you don't have a hillbilly accent. And he's from Shady Creek just like you are!" I clenched my hands into fists. "I could punch him!"

"Someone beat you to it," Mel reminded me. "Just not with their fists."

I reigned in my emotions. "Hold on. Are you a suspect?"

Mel responded with a grim nod.

My indignation returned full force. "That's insane!"

"Actually, it was inevitable, even without the incident on the green."

"What do you mean?" I asked, my apprehension making a comeback.

"There's something I didn't tell you last night," she said. "The ice pick that was used to kill Freddy . . . it's mine."

Chapter 7

It took me several seconds to process what Mel had said.

"Are you sure?" I asked once her words had sunk in.

"Positive. I engraved my initials on the handles of all the tools in that set. I told Officer Rogers last night that I recognized the ice pick, and today Detective Marquez confirmed that it's mine."

My chest grew tight with worry. "Did you tell them that your tools were stolen?"

"Of course, and it turns out the police found my hand tools in a garbage can in the alley behind the town hall. But they probably think I could have faked the theft to deflect suspicion away from me."

"But that's insane! And it would mean you'd planned to kill Freddy ahead of time."

Mel shrugged. "I bet the police will think it's possible."

"What's *actually* possible is that you could be in danger."

"Because the killer might be trying to eliminate his or her competition?"

"Yes. You and Freddy were the frontrunners. Maybe someone wanted to improve their chances of winning."

"Seems a bit drastic to murder someone over an ice sculpture competition."

"But not impossible, so be careful, okay?"

"I will be." She gave me a bleak smile. "Maybe having the cops watching me isn't so bad after all. That's got to keep me safer, right?"

I frowned at the reminder that she was under suspicion. "You can't be the only suspect. Plenty of others had far more reason to want to harm him than you did." I snapped my fingers as memories surfaced. "There's his half brother for starters. And his personal assistant. He fired her in front of everyone at the chili supper last night."

Mel shifted a line of glasses on a shelf, even though they were already tidy.

I sensed she was avoiding my gaze, and that triggered another memory.

"How do you know Jade Castellano?" I asked.

Mel glanced my way, but only for a split second. "What makes you think I know her?"

"You recognized each other yesterday."

She finally stopped moving the glasses around and faced me. "We dated for a while a few years ago."

I let that information sink in, realizing it explained the depth of the look that had passed between them. "Here in Shady Creek?"

"No, in Boston. I spent a couple of years there. Jade is a city girl through and through. I never expected to see her here."

"Did you talk to her at all yesterday?"

"I did."

"Before or after Freddy fired her?" I asked when she didn't offer any more information.

"After. Not long before you found Freddy."

"Was she upset?"

Mel leveled her gaze at me. "Jade didn't kill Freddy."

The first customers of the day arrived at that moment, so I didn't argue with her, but I couldn't help but wonder if she was wrong.

As darkness fell, I became a bundle of nerves. I was anxious for Mel, but I was also nervous about the trivia contest. I desperately wanted it to go over well with my customers.

"Relax," Damien said when he caught me drumming my fingers against the bar. "Everything's going to be fine. You're as prepared for trivia night as you can be."

"I know," I said, stilling my fingers. "But I want it to be a success."

"There's no reason why it shouldn't be."

He left me then to deliver plates of Lord of the Fries and To Be or Nacho Be to hungry patrons. I would have loved a platter of the delicious nachos myself. My stomach was rumbling with hunger and the nachos were piled with all my favorite toppings—red peppers, black olives, and plenty of cheese—with sides of salsa, sour cream, and guacamole.

Despite my hunger, however, I didn't think I'd be able to eat even if I had time. My stomach might have been rumbling, but it was also tied up in knots. We had a good crowd already, more than an hour before the trivia contest would begin, and that was a promising sign. Still, I knew I wouldn't be able to relax or enjoy a meal until the event was over.

Shortly before six, Damien assured me that he could hold down the fort for a few minutes while I slipped across the road to find out the results of the ice sculpture competition. I bundled up in record time and hurried over to the green, which was once again lit up by several spotlights as well as all the decorative twinkle lights. I had a few minutes to spare before the results of the competition would be announced, so I made a circuit of the sculptures, each one leaving me in awe of the artists' talent.

My favorite sculpture was, of course, Mel's impressive dragon, posed as if about to take flight from its nest of eggs. All the works of art wowed me, but my other favorites included a grizzly bear with two frolicking cubs, a jolly Santa Claus with a sack full of presents, and a tall ship, its sails appearing to billow in an imaginary wind.

I was snapping a photo of the ship with my phone when Alma's voice rang out over the village green, calling for everyone's attention. I quickly joined the throngs of locals and tourists crowding around the canopy where Alma was stationed with the microphone. Judging by the number of people present, it appeared as though Freddy's murder hadn't driven away many tourists. The relief that knowledge brought me came with a twinge of guilt, but the reality was that I needed the tourists' business if I wanted to keep the Inkwell's doors open.

"In light of recent events," Alma was saying to the crowd, "we'd like to begin with a moment of silence in honor of one of our competitors, Federico Mancini, who tragically passed away last night."

The crowd fell quiet, the only sounds from a passing car and a wailing toddler, who was quickly whisked away by his parents.

"Thank you, everyone," Alma said several seconds later. "We're so glad all of you were able to join us here tonight. I hope you've enjoyed the beautiful ice sculptures that are on display."

The audience responded by applauding, the sound muted by gloves and mittens. When the clapping died off, Alma continued.

"I'll now announce the winners of the competition. Thank you so much to everyone who participated, and to our volunteers and sponsors, who made this event possible." She opened an envelope and removed a piece of paper. "In third place, we have Emilio Caraveos and his sculpture of a grizzly bear and her cubs."

I clapped along with everyone else, adding in a cheer along with a few others. I didn't recognize Emilio when he went up to receive his trophy, so I thought he might be from out of town.

"And in second place," Alma continued, "Douglas Baker and his sailing ship."

Again, I joined in with the cheering and applauding. At the same time, my stomach gave a nervous flip-flop. I caught sight of Mel standing near Alma. She didn't appear as nervous as I felt, but I knew she was invested in the competition and wanted to win. The magazine coverage could be huge for her.

"Finally, we have our winner," Alma said, before pausing for dramatic effect. "First place in this year's ice-sculpting competition goes to . . . Shady Creek's own Melanie Costas!"

The crowd went crazy, and I did too. I jumped up and down, cheering for Mel as she approached Alma, a big smile on her face.

Joey Fontana and the other reporters crowded around her, snapping photographs as she accepted her trophy and check. I was about to squeeze my way through the crowd to get closer to Mel when I spotted Jade Castellano on the outskirts of the mass of people. She was clapping and smiling brightly, until Detective Marquez approached her, discretely flashing her badge.

The smiled slipped from Jade's face as Marquez spoke to her. She cast an uncertain glance in Mel's direction, but then she nodded and followed the detective away from the festive crowd. As Jade disappeared from sight, I wondered once again if Mel was wrong about her.

Chapter 8

In the end, I contented myself with waving at Mel and giving her two thumbs up. She grinned in response before the crowd around her pulled her attention back to them. I knew I'd see her the next day, if not later that night, so I figured I'd head back to the Inkwell and speak to her another time. She was in high demand at the moment and it was almost time for the trivia contest to begin.

As I worked my way around the clusters of people still on the green, I caught sight of Grayson on the other side of Sycamore Street. I was in the midst of raising my hand to wave at him when he stopped in front of Lumière, Shady Creek's classiest restaurant, and opened the door. He disappeared inside without seeing me.

I dropped my hand and resumed walking along the edge of the green. He'd said he wouldn't be at the trivia night, but never said why. It wasn't any of my business, of course, but now that I'd seen him going into the restaurant, it crossed my mind that he might have a date. With whom, I had no idea, and I wasn't sure I wanted to know. As much as I tried to tell myself that it didn't matter if he was seeing someone, I couldn't ignore the twist of disappointment in my stomach.

Fortunately, I didn't dwell too long on the thought of Grayson on a dinner date. When I returned to the Inkwell and saw how the crowd had swelled in my absence, a rush of happiness overshadowed any disappointment. The pub was so full that I had to open one of the two side rooms for overflow. That room—which I'd named the Stewart Room after one of my favorite authors, Mary Stewart—was decorated for the holidays with a small Christmas tree, twinkle lights, lots of LED candles, and the collection of snow globes I'd amassed over the years. Some of the customers who weren't planning to participate in the trivia contest had shifted into the Stewart Room, leaving more space for the trivia teams in the main area.

"We've got a good crowd," Damien commented as he passed by me on his way to the kitchen.

"We do," I agreed before he disappeared through the door.

Clutching a sheaf of papers, I smiled at the packed room, pleased to see many familiar faces along with a few new ones.

"Could I have your attention, please?" I said to the room at large.

No one heard me, and all the conversations taking place at the various tables continued.

"Hello!" I tried again.

This time, the occupants of the two tables closest to me turned their attention my way, but everyone else continued to chatter and focus on their food and drinks.

Bobby Dormer, an Inkwell regular, was seated at the table in front of me. He stood up and addressed the crowd. "Listen up, everyone!" he said loudly, his voice easily carrying across the room.

The conversations died off and dozens of pairs of eyes turned my way.

"Thank you," I said to Bobby with a smile.

He lowered his six-foot-three frame back into his chair and saluted me with his pint glass before taking a drink of his beer.

"Thank you all for coming tonight," I said to everyone in the room. "It's great to see so many people here for the Inkwell's first ever literary trivia night! If you haven't already done so, please assemble your teams. I'll pass out the answer sheets, and then we'll get going."

I made a circuit of the room, providing each team with a sheet of paper with a spot for the team's name and numbered lines for the answers to the trivia questions. When each team was supplied with an answer sheet and at least one writing implement, I stationed myself on a stool at the end of the bar, facing out toward the tables.

I quickly outlined the rules and announced the prize—an Inkwell gift certificate for each member of the winning team.

"Any questions?" I asked, surveying the participants.

Nobody spoke up or raised their hand.

"All right then," I said with a flurry of fresh nerves and excitement. "Here's the first question: What is the title of the Charles Dickens novel that was unfinished at the time of his death?"

Around the pub, people leaned over their tables to confer with their teammates in lowered voices. A couple of teams wrote an answer on their sheet right away, while others continued to discuss the matter. I kept an eye on the stopwatch on my phone, making sure to leave a consistent amount of time between each question.

The Spirit Hill Brewery didn't have a team present, but I recognized Juliana, a young woman who did public relations for Grayson's company. Apparently she was also an avid runner because she was a member of the local running group's trivia team.

Seeing Juliana reminded me of Grayson and his possible date. I swiftly shoved all thoughts of him out of my mind and consulted my quizmaster sheet.

"Moving on," I said to everyone. "Question number two: This famous mystery author wrote general fiction under the pseudonym Mary Westmacott."

I wasn't surprised to see fellow redhead and mystery-lover Cordelia King brighten and quickly whisper something to the other members of her team. If I'd read her lips correctly, she had the right answer—Agatha Christie.

Over at the next table, Sybil Hawkes said something to her fellow members of the Knitters' Guild team. Her knitting needles flashed as she worked away at a pretty green scarf. Penny Blaine was on the same team and had a knitting project on the go as well. I wondered how she felt about Freddy's death. I couldn't tell from looking at her. She wasn't smiling, but she also didn't appear to be devastated. I couldn't tell what she was knitting—a sweater, maybe—but her yarn was a beautiful shade of blue. The other members of the Knitters' Guild had left their projects at home. Bakery owner Sofie Talbot, who was apparently the team's scribe for the evening, wrote something down on their answer sheet.

At a table to my left, Harriet Jones, the oldest and liveliest member of the Inkwell's romance book club, sat with members of her Zumba class, all of whom were at least ten years younger than her.

She sat back in her chair. "These questions are too tough for my old brain." She picked up her Evil Stepmother cocktail, as if to toast her teammates. "I'll do the drinking while you young folks do the thinking."

I smiled as she downed her drink and signaled to Damien that she wanted another.

It appeared as though every team had written down an answer to the last question, so I moved on to the next one.

I continued down my list while Damien took care of the food and drinks. Everyone participating in the quiz seemed to be into it, to my relief and delight. Over the next half hour, we worked through several more questions until only one item remained.

"This children's author and illustrator, born in 1866, was also a prize-winning sheep breeder," I read out, wondering how many people would know or guess that I was referring to Beatrix Potter.

I gave the teams a couple of minutes to come up with a response before I slid off my stool. "Okay, time's up, everyone. Please hand in your answers."

I made a circuit of the room, gathering up the answer sheets. When I had all of them in my hands, I returned to the bar. "The winning team will be announced shortly," I said to the crowd.

Leaving Damien in charge, I retreated to my cubbyhole of an office beneath the stairs that led up to my apartment. I sat at the battered wooden desk that had come with the pub and quickly marked the answer sheets. Only about a quarter of the teams had correctly answered the first question with *The Mystery of Edwin Drood*, but most had connected Agatha Christie to Mary Westmacott.

A team made up of all men who'd already been on their third round of beer by the time the quiz started had earned last place, with only two questions answered correctly. Most teams had fared far better. I was double-checking the results when a shadow appeared in the hallway outside the open office door.

"Mel!" I jumped up when she appeared in the doorway. "Congratulations!" I gave her a hug before stepping back, beaming at her. "Your sculpture is incredible. You definitely deserved to win."

"Thanks, Sadie," she said with a smile. "How's the trivia night going?"

"Great, I'm happy to say. We had a fantastic turnout and I'm about to announce the winning team." I pulled open a desk drawer to fetch the gift certificates for the winners.

"Have you seen Jade in here this evening?" Mel asked, an unusual note of worry beneath her words.

"No," I said slowly. "Should I have?"

"We were going to meet here."

"I saw her on the green earlier when you were getting your prize." I hesitated for a split second before continuing. "She left with Detective Marquez."

Mel's blue eyes seemed to darken. "Voluntarily?"

"I think so. She wasn't handcuffed or anything."

"I'd better go to the police station." She took a step back out of the office.

I opened my mouth to ask if that was a good idea, but I didn't get the chance. Mel was already disappearing out the mill's back door. There was probably no point in asking, anyway. Mel seemed determined to go, and maybe it wasn't a big deal. I had my doubts about Jade's innocence, but if Mel was right and she wasn't guilty, Jade would probably appreciate the sight of a familiar face.

If the police would let Mel anywhere near her.

I figured that depended on how much jeopardy Jade was in.

Pushing those thoughts aside, I gathered up the gift certificates and returned to the pub. It took me a moment to get everyone's attention again. When the quiz had ended, previous conversations had resumed and new ones had started up.

Bobby helped me out by hollering again, and the room fell quiet.

"Thanks so much to all of you for coming out for this event," I said, the gift certificates clutched in my hands. "I hope you've enjoyed yourselves, and be sure to check out all the other events going on during the Winter Carnival." I smiled at the room. "I'm pleased to say that the winner of the Inkwell's first-ever trivia night is . . . Knitters Gone Wilde!"

The Knitters' Guild team erupted into cheers while everyone else clapped. I handed out the gift certificates to Sybil, Penny, and their teammates. It made me happy to see how excited they were to receive their prizes.

With the trivia contest officially over, I got to work helping Damien with serving drinks. The kitchen had shut down for the night, but no one seemed in a hurry to leave the pub now that the event was over and, to my delight, everyone seemed to be thirsty.

I was in the midst of mixing two Evil Stepmother cocktails—made with white grape juice, ginger ale, sour mix, and vodka—when I noticed Leo Mancini sitting at the bar with Sibyl Hawkes's husband, Eli. Leo was halfway through a pint of beer. I didn't know if it was his first drink of the night, since Damien had served him.

"He deserved what he got," Leo grumbled into his drink.

Those words drew my attention. Was he talking about Freddy?

A moment later I knew for sure that he was.

"No one deserves to be murdered," Eli said, his voice gentle yet stern. "Freddy let his success go to his head, but underneath it all, I'm sure he was still a good guy."

Leo snorted. "If he ever made you think that, he was conning you. Freddy never cared about anyone but himself. Not you, not me, not anyone. And I'm telling you, it sure felt good when I—"

"Leo," Eli said sharply, cutting him off, "you're letting the booze talk for you. Come on, let me walk you home."

Leo protested at first, but gave in after more cajoling from Eli. He drained the last of his beer before getting up off his stool. Fortunately, he hadn't had enough to make him unsteady on his feet.

Eli put a hand to Leo's back, guiding him to the door.

I wanted to know what Leo had been about to say. What had felt good? Driving the ice pick into Freddy's chest?

I shuddered at the thought. Leo certainly had enough hate for his half brother to have struck out at him in anger. I was sure the police would have questioned Leo, as one of Freddy's family members, but how much did Detective Marquez and her colleagues know about him? Were they aware of the distinct lack of brotherly love between them? Had Leo or anyone else informed them about their unpleasant exchange at the chili supper?

In case no one had, I slipped into my office and left a short voice mail for Detective Marquez, telling her about the incident. I added that I hadn't thought to mention the confrontation when I'd spoken to Officer Rogers on the night of the murder. My mind had been spinning too much at the time to realize it could be important.

With that out of the way, I delivered the Evil Stepmother cocktails to waiting customers and took down an order for two pints of stout, a Happily Ever After cocktail, and a Milky Way Gargle Blaster. On my way back to the bar, I paused by Cordelia's table. She and her teammates were getting ready to leave, pushing back their chairs and gathering their jackets and other gear.

"Thanks for coming to the trivia night," I said to the group. "I hope you had a good time."

"It was so much fun," Cordelia enthused as she pulled a hat down over her crinkly red hair.

"I'm glad you enjoyed it," I said, smiling. "Have a good night."

I was passing the Knitters' Guild table when Penny picked up her tote bag. She grabbed it by a corner, causing it to tip some of its contents onto the floor.

I crouched down to help her retrieve a pen and a tube of lipstick. Something else rolled beneath the table, so I reached out and snatched it up. When my hand closed around the ball of soft, burnt-orange yarn, an icy chill spread through my body.

It was the same shade of orange as the wool I'd seen on the murder weapon.

Chapter 9

It didn't necessarily mean anything.

Ten minutes later, I was still repeating that in my head, still trying to convince myself. Somehow I'd managed to return the yarn to Penny with a smile on my face, despite how unnerved the sight of the ball of wool had left me. I really didn't know Penny, but she *seemed* harmless. Could she really have killed Freddy?

Yes, I decided. It was possible.

She certainly had a motive, after the way Freddy had snubbed her and reduced her to tears on the day of his death. And I knew from experience that even someone who seemed to be an unlikely suspect, or someone who wasn't a suspect at all, could be a killer. The murder of my ex, Eric, had taught me that.

The Inkwell's crowd eventually thinned out after the trivia contest ended, and with Damien on hand to help, the pub wasn't quite busy enough to keep my mind from going over the mystery of Freddy's murder again and again. Thinking about it didn't accomplish anything, unfortunately. I was still left with all the same questions and worries.

When I spotted Shontelle threading her way through the tables toward me, I welcomed the distraction.

She met up with me as I was coming out from behind the bar. "How are you holding up?" she asked as she pulled me into a hug.

"I'm okay."

She stepped back and searched my face. "Are you sure? It must have been awful to see the body. *Another* body."

"At least it wasn't someone I knew well this time." I realized what I'd said. "That sounds terrible."

"No. I know what you mean and it's totally understandable." She gave my arms a gentle squeeze before releasing me.

"Can I get you something to drink?" I offered.

"I can't stay. My mom's at my place with Kiandra, but I promised her I wouldn't be long. I just wanted to see for myself that you're okay."

"I am," I assured her.

"Evening, ladies." The familiar voice drew our attention.

Grayson shrugged out of his suit jacket. He claimed a stool at the bar, setting his jacket on the empty seat to his left.

"Evening," Shontelle returned, flashing him a smile while she gave me a subtle nudge with her elbow.

For some reason she thought Grayson and I would make a good couple. I'd pointed out to her on several occasions that we barely got along, but she always ignored me, a knowing smile on her face. I'd admitted to myself—though not to Shontelle or anyone else—that he'd given me butterflies once or twice, but that didn't change the fact that he had a habit of getting on my nerves. Besides, after all the lies I'd endured in my last relationship, I wasn't in any hurry to trust a man with even a small piece of my heart.

"I have to get going," Shontelle said.

"Already?" I suspected she was cutting her visit even shorter than planned because of Grayson's arrival.

"My mom will be wanting to get home." She gave me another quick hug. "We'll talk soon."

As Shontelle left, nervousness skittered through me. Knowing that she'd wanted me to be alone with Grayson made me all too aware of the fact that I was.

Except, we weren't really alone. There were other people in the pub. Not at the bar with us, but it wasn't like we were completely on our own. That thought helped to ease my nerves.

"I was thinking of trying the Malt in Our Stars tonight," Grayson said.

I gave myself a swift mental kick. He was a customer, and here I was forgetting to ask for his order.

"A good choice," I said. I set to work mixing the cocktail and soon placed it in front of him on the bar. I waited with anticipation as he took a sip.

"That's really good," he said once he'd swallowed. "The flavors are nicely balanced."

"Thank you." I smiled, and the last of my nervousness slipped away.

"How was the trivia contest?" he asked before taking another drink.

"I think it went really well. We had a great turnout and people seemed to enjoy themselves." I wrestled with my curiosity, but it was a battle I quickly lost. "How was your dinner?"

I thought I did a good job of making the question sound casual.

"Dinner?"

"I saw you going into Lumière earlier," I explained.

"Ah. I didn't end up eating there. I was supposed to meet someone, but she called to cancel after I'd been waiting half an hour."

She. So he *had* been on a date. Or had planned to be.

"First date?" I passed him a bowl of pretzels. "If so, it doesn't sound like things are off to a great start."

"Not a date," he said.

I tried to ignore the tiny spark of relief kindled by his words. I was glad it wasn't a date, but I shouldn't have cared. Since ending my relationship with Eric, I'd told myself time and time again that I wasn't ready to fall for anyone else. Unfortunately, it seemed my heart wasn't a good listener.

Grayson took a pretzel from the bowl. "It was supposed to be a business meeting with a producer from *Craft Nation*."

"Right!" I said. "I heard the show was going to feature your brewery in an episode. That's got to be exciting."

"It was. But the network got wind of Mancini's murder and now they're worried about filming an episode here while there's a killer on the loose."

"For safety reasons or for PR reasons?"

"Both, I gathered from the call I got this evening."

"So they pulled the plug?" I guessed.

"Temporarily, at least."

My heart sank for him. "I'm sorry to hear that."

I could tell he was disappointed. I would have been too, in his shoes. *Craft Nation* was a popular television show that featured craft breweries across the country. Getting coverage in one of its episodes would have given the Spirit Hill Brewery invaluable exposure. Heck, it would have been good for all businesses in Shady Creek if it had inspired more tourists to check out our town.

"Your drink's on the house tonight," I said, wanting to cheer him up, even if only a little bit.

"You don't have to do that," he protested.

"I want to. No arguments."

"Thank you. Will you join me?"

I glanced at the clock. "I wouldn't mind some tea."

A woman at a nearby table caught my eye.

"I'll just be a minute," I told Grayson.

The woman requested another Happily Ever After cocktail, so I returned to the bar and mixed the drink while my tea steeped.

"What's that one?" Grayson asked as I poured some coconut rum into the glass.

"Happily Ever After," I said. "It's one of the first drinks I put on the menu. The tropical flavors always make me think of romantic beach holidays, sun-warmed sand, ocean breezes. . . ."

I realized I had a dreamy expression on my face. I hoped Grayson hadn't noticed, but when I saw the amusement in his eyes, I knew I was out of luck there.

"Have you been on a lot of those?" Humor still danced in his eyes.

"No, actually," I said, sensing that my cheeks were turning red. "But a girl can dream."

I delivered the drink to the woman who'd ordered it and glanced around the pub. Damien had everything under control, so I fetched my tea and perched on the stool to Grayson's right. He'd shaved and donned a suit in preparation for his business meeting, but if he'd worn a tie, he'd shed it at some point. He'd also undone the top button of his shirt and had rolled his sleeves up to his elbows.

I tried not to get distracted by how close we were sitting or by his muscled forearms resting on the bar, but it wasn't an easy task, especially when our arms brushed.

I took a sip of my tea to give myself a second to focus.

"Is there anything you can do about the show?" I asked. "Any way you can change their minds?"

Grayson nudged the bowl of pretzels my way. "I don't think so. My only hope is for the murder to get solved quickly, which I'm sure everyone in Shady Creek would like."

"Definitely," I said before snacking on a salty pretzel.

"I heard you were the one to find Mancini. Are you all right?"

I had to avert my eyes when I saw the genuine concern in his. I didn't want my heart getting carried away.

"A little shaken up," I admitted. "But otherwise fine."

"That's two bodies you've found in less than three months."

"Technically, your dog found Eric's body in October," I reminded him. "It's not like I'm a cadaver magnet."

"I also heard that Mel was second on the scene."

It was more than just a casual statement and I wondered what he was getting at.

"She came running when I called for help."

"And with Mancini dead, she won the competition."

I spun on my stool to face him, my knees hitting his leg. "She would have won anyway! Did you see her sculpture?" I turned back to the bar and crunched down hard on a pretzel.

"Her ice pick was the murder weapon."

"How did you hear about that?" I didn't think it was widespread knowledge. I *hoped* it wasn't.

"I have my sources."

His vague reply sent my rising irritation up another notch. "Well, whatever your sources are saying, Mel's not a killer."

"How can you know for sure?"

"I just *know*."

It irked me that I hadn't come up with a better response than that. When I glanced his way, I could tell he wasn't convinced. Any butterflies that had been fluttering around in my stomach before had turned to stone.

I downed the last of my tea in one go and got up from the stool. My stomach grumbled loudly, annoyed that I still hadn't eaten anything, aside from a single pretzel.

Damien returned to the bar and grabbed three clean pint glasses.

"Is there anything I can do?" I asked as I picked up my empty mug.

"We need an Evil Stepmother and a Lovecraft," Damien said as he pulled a pint of India pale ale.

"I'm on it."

I made my way around the bar, relieved not to continue my conversation with Grayson. I had a feeling that discussing Mancini's murder with him would only vex me more.

After I'd mixed the drinks I ducked into the kitchen in search of something to eat. We were no longer taking food orders at that hour and Teagan was tidying up, but I hoped I'd find a snack of some sort.

"Hungry?" Teagan asked as soon as she saw me.

"Starving."

She smiled. "I left a plate of Paradise Lox in the fridge for you."

I almost ran across the kitchen. "Teagan, you're the best."

She took off her chef's coat. "I'll tell Booker you said that."

I couldn't protest because my mouth was full of bread, cheese, and lox.

Teagan laughed at the expression on my face—probably a strange mixture of bliss and alarm. "Just kidding. See you tomorrow."

I managed to wish her a good night between bites of my much-needed snack. As soon as I was done eating, I left the kitchen to get back to work.

"Is the brewery entering a team in the hockey tournament?" Damien was asking Grayson as he finished filling a pint glass.

"We signed up last week," Grayson replied. "How about you? Has the Inkwell got a team?"

"I'm up for it," Damien said, "but I don't know if we could get enough players together." To me, he added, "We need a Count Dracula and another Lovecraft."

"You want to play in the hockey tournament?" I asked him as I grabbed a bottle of Midori liqueur. I hadn't even known he played hockey.

"Sure, if I had a team."

I mixed together the ingredients for the Lovecraft. "Maybe we can put one together."

Damien considered that for a second. "Mel would probably play."

"I will too," I said.

"You play hockey?" Grayson said, his eyebrows raised.

"What's so surprising about that?"

He raised his hands in surrender. "Nothing. I just didn't realize you played."

I started on the Count Dracula and focused on the coconut rum I was adding to the cocktail shaker. "I've played a bit of hockey. Sort of." I chanced a quick glance at Grayson and suspected he was fighting a grin. "Maybe not in any sort of *organized* way, but it won't be high-level hockey, will it?"

"Some teams will be at a higher level than others, apparently." He was definitely fighting a grin.

I shook the cocktail shaker a little harder than necessary. "Sign us up, Damien, however that's done."

Damien set three pints of beer on a tray. His expression wasn't giving much away, but I thought I detected a hint of uncertainty in his eyes.

"We need seven players," he said. "We can ask Booker, and I think Teagan might have some hockey experience, but even then we'd be two players short."

"Do they all have to be connected to the pub?" I asked.

"Not necessarily."

I added the two cocktails to his tray. "Then I'm sure we can cobble together a team."

Grayson tried to cover up a laugh by taking a drink.

I ignored him. "I'll clean up table five," I said to Damien before heading over to a table recently vacated by a group of four women.

When I returned from depositing the dirty dishes in the kitchen, Joey Fontana had joined Grayson at the bar.

"Got any fresh coffee?" Joey asked me.

I glanced at the almost-empty pot. "I can put some on."

"Maybe I'll try that stout you've got on tap instead."

"Good choice," Grayson said. His glass was empty now and the pretzels were almost gone.

Joey helped himself to a few of the ones that remained. "Just half a pint, though. I can't stay long."

"Busy week at the paper?" I guessed.

The *Shady Creek Tribune* had only one issue per week, distributed on Wednesdays, but Joey wrote the majority of the content himself.

"That's for sure. Things were crazy enough with the carnival and the break-ins. Now all that's secondary to the murder."

"Have there been more break-ins?"

I'd heard of a couple over the past month. The burglars had targeted local businesses. So far, the police hadn't caught the culprits.

"There was one Wednesday night at Vera Anderson's boutique," Grayson spoke up.

Joey nodded. "Luckily she's got an alarm. It scared the burglars off before they had a chance to steal anything."

"That's good, at least. Knowing Vera, I'm sure she's been on the police department's case."

"You can say that again. And not just theirs. She showed up on my doorstep for an interview before I'd even asked for one."

That was easy to picture.

"Speaking of interviews," Joey continued. "I could use a couple of quotes from you."

I should have anticipated that. "Because I found Freddy's body?"

"And because you're my favorite interviewee."

"I bet you say that to everyone you interview."

Joey grinned. "But I only mean it with you."

Grayson stifled a laugh. Either that or he was choking. Since he cleared his throat and snatched the last pretzel from the bowl, I figured he'd live.

"I'm surprised you're only showing up now," I said to Joey. "It's been twenty-four hours since Freddy died."

"I've been running around town, tracking down those who knew him best. I just came from the police station. Apparently, the cops are questioning Freddy's personal assistant. *Ex*-personal assistant."

"Ex?" Grayson echoed.

"Freddy fired her shortly before he died," Joey explained.

I nodded. "At the chili supper."

Joey passed me some bills when I slid his beer across the bar to him. "Mel's at the station too."

"She's there to check on Jade." I didn't bother to mention that she'd been questioned earlier in the day. If Joey didn't know that already, I wasn't going to be the one to enlighten him.

"Why would Mel be checking on Freddy's assistant?" Joey asked, leaning forward with interest.

Oh, for the love of Miss Marple! Why hadn't I held my tongue? I didn't know if Mel would care if Joey found out about her past with Jade, but I didn't want the reporter connecting Mel to the murdered chef in any way. And now it was my fault that his reporter senses were tingling.

"Sorry, I'll be back in a moment." I hurried out from behind the bar, pretending someone had hailed me from across the pub.

I took the time to check on several patrons before making my way back to the bar, hoping Joey wouldn't question me about Mel again. He and Grayson were talking quietly. I thought that was good news for me, until I heard Mel's name right before they wrapped up their conversation.

Grayson stood and picked up his suit jacket. "Thanks for the drink, Sadie." He addressed Joey next. "Let me know what you find out."

Joey saluted him with his glass before draining the last of his beer.

I watched Grayson as he pulled on his suit jacket on his way to the door.

"Find out about what?" I asked Joey when Grayson had left the pub.

He grinned at me. "Sorry. Confidential. But how about those quotes?"

I knew he wouldn't give up until he got what he wanted, so I provided a brief statement about finding Freddy's body, leaving out any details, not that I had many. I didn't want to seem ghoulish, and I wasn't sure how much the police would want the public to know.

Fortunately, Joey didn't press me for details about Mel's connection to Jade. I didn't want her name appearing in the next issue of the paper for any reason other than her first-place finish in the ice sculpture competition. The damage might have been done already, though. Joey's quiet chat with Grayson had left me uneasy, especially since Grayson had Mel pegged as a suspect.

After Joey left the Inkwell, Damien joined me behind the bar, an unusual hint of concern in his eyes. It probably matched the look in my own eyes.

"Is it true Mel's a suspect in Freddy's murder?" he asked.

"Is that what people are saying?" I hated to think people were whispering about Mel behind her back.

"I've heard a few murmurs. Is there any truth to it?"

"Unfortunately, yes," I said.

And the police had questioned her a second time. That couldn't be a good sign.

In my head, I drew up my own list of suspects. There was no denying that Mel was in trouble, and I was determined to do whatever I could to help get her out of it.

Chapter 10

In the morning I tried to enjoy my usual routine of reading a book while lingering over my breakfast and a cup of coffee, but I soon found that I couldn't stay focused on the novel, despite the fact that it was full of suspense and intrigue. My mind kept drifting from the words on the page to the puzzle of Freddy's murder. I wanted Mel's name cleared, but I knew that could take time. If it happened at all.

That last thought drove me to put down my book.

The night before I'd identified three main suspects: Leo Mancini, Jade Castellano, and Penny Blaine. They all had motive to kill Freddy. Leo harbored a deep dislike, perhaps even hatred, for his half brother, and Freddy had treated Jade and Penny poorly, to say the least, in the hours before his death. What I needed to know was whether any of them had an opportunity to commit the crime. If one or more of them had an alibi, I could scratch them from my list. Maybe the killer wasn't even on my radar yet, but the more I narrowed down my list of suspects, the closer I'd get to identifying the culprit. And once the real killer was behind bars, Mel would be in the clear.

Before heading out to do some investigating, I spent time cleaning the Inkwell. I'd wiped down the tables and cleaned the floors in the main room after closing the night before, but I still had work to do. The mystery book club the pub hosted once a month would be meeting that evening in the Christie Room, so I wanted to make sure the space was in tip-top shape.

First, I made sure there was plenty of fuel for the wood-burning stove. With our current icy weather, a cozy fire was a must for evening meetings in the snug room. The tables were already clean, but I gave them each an extra wipe-down anyway. Then I swept the floor before getting out my feather duster and embarking on a campaign to make every surface shine.

The Christie Room was one of my favorite parts of the pub. Comfy chairs and side tables were clustered around the wood-burning stove, which always drew people close on a chilly evening. A few regular tables and chairs took up the rest of the floor space, but there was far more to the room than the furniture.

This part of the pub had the same plank floors, wood beams, and exposed stone walls as the main room, giving it plenty of charming character. Books from my personal collection lined the shelves along the walls, and the room's namesake—Dame Agatha Christie—observed the space from a portrait on one wall. I'd also decorated the room with an old typewriter and movie posters from Agatha Christie books that had been adapted for film.

Ever since I'd started hosting book clubs at the pub back in October, I'd received rave reviews of the cozy meeting space. The clubs had also been a hit, much to my relief and happiness. There was a romance book club in addition to the mystery one, and I was planning to launch a science fiction and fantasy club in the new year.

I was pleased with the great response from the community.

The current clubs were thriving and several people had already signed up to join the new group. I'd loved books for as long as I could remember and I was so glad I'd been able to work that passion into my business, and to use it to connect with people in my new home of Shady Creek.

As I dusted the bookshelves, my thoughts returned to my suspect list. I needed more information, and I figured a good place to start was with Mel. I paused in my cleaning to send her a quick text message, asking how things had gone for Jade at the police station. I didn't receive an immediate response, so I went back to dusting.

Since Mel had known Jade well in the past, she would know if Freddy's personal assistant had a temper. Judging by Mel's adamant declaration that Jade was innocent, I knew she might not appreciate me asking questions about her ex-girlfriend. But since Jade wasn't from Shady Creek, Mel was probably the only person who could tell me anything about her.

I was about to check my phone for text messages again when I stopped short with my hand to my pocket, staring at the shelf in front of me. Two of my most treasured books were missing. It wasn't glaringly obvious, since someone had shifted the other books on the shelf to minimize the gap, but as soon as I'd looked closely, I noticed that the volumes were gone.

I quickly scanned all the other shelves in the room, but the books hadn't been put back in a different spot. If someone had removed them from the shelf to look at them and had forgotten where they'd taken them from, the books should have been somewhere else in the room. But they weren't.

As I sank down into the nearest chair, a sense of loss and betrayal crashed over me like a powerful wave. Thoughts spun around in my head. Was it a tourist or a local who'd stolen the books?

Abandoning my duster on a table, I jumped up and hurried

from the room. I checked every corner of the pub, every table, every shelf. I even searched my apartment, in case I'd forgotten that I'd moved the books myself, even though I knew that wasn't the case.

I looked in every nook and cranny. The missing books were nowhere to be found. Returning to the Christie Room, I stared at the spot where the two mystery novels had been. Why would someone have stolen them? The copies of *Déjà Dead*, by Kathy Reichs, and *A Trick of the Light*, by Louise Penny, had no more monetary value than the prices stamped on the back covers. They weren't rare or difficult to find in any bookstore.

Maybe someone had simply decided that they wanted them and that had been enough to prompt them to steal the books. I hated to think the thief could have been someone I knew, someone who came to the Inkwell regularly. The books were there the last time I'd dusted the shelf, before the romance book club's meeting just over a week ago. I hadn't opened the room for overflow since then, so the most likely scenario was that someone from the club had stolen the books.

I didn't want to believe that, though. I knew each member of the club. Aunt Gilda and Shontelle were above suspicion, but I considered several of the other members to be friends of mine as well, the exception being Vera Anderson. I couldn't imagine Vera stealing books, or anything else for that matter, but that didn't mean it was impossible.

I sank down into a chair and stared glumly at the bookshelf and the gap that now seemed more conspicuous. I could easily purchase new copies of *Déjà Dead* and *A Trick of the Light*. The monetary aspect of it didn't bother me. The betrayal did to some extent, but mostly it was the fact that the books held significant sentimental value that had me feeling melancholy. Every year, starting when I was six years old, my dad had given me a book for Christmas. I'd kept every one of them. He always wrote an inscription inside and I treasured each volume, all the more so now, since my dad had passed away.

It had been five years since he'd died, but I still missed him all the time. The books he'd given me, the special messages he'd written inside, were like little pieces of him left behind to remind me of him and how much he'd loved me.

Whoever had taken the books most likely had no idea how much they meant to me, but it still hurt that someone had stolen them, and the loss was hitting me hard.

Tears prickled at my eyes. I blinked them away, not wanting to cry, but I had to fight to stop myself from breaking down. It wasn't just the missing books that had me so emotional, I realized. It was the upcoming Christmas season as well. My dad had loved Christmas, as did I, and we'd had so many traditions that we enjoyed together each year—decorating the house, picking out a Christmas tree, caroling, and making gingerbread houses. This year, I wouldn't only be without my dad, I'd be without any family.

"Maybe whoever took the books will return them," I said out loud, as if that could make the words more likely to come true. "Maybe they just wanted to borrow them and were afraid to ask."

The words rang hollow in the room around me. No matter how positive I tried to be, I knew I was unlikely to see the books again. It only made matters worse that I couldn't stop wondering who'd taken them. I didn't want to suspect anybody I knew, not even Vera Anderson, who was far from my favorite person.

Focus on something else, I told myself, not wanting to give my suspicions a chance to grow. *You need to clear Mel's name.*

That would distract me from all the sadness prompted by the discovery of the missing books, and a distraction was exactly what I needed.

I still hadn't received a response from Mel, so I put away my feather duster and donned my winter gear.

It was time to get sleuthing.

Mel lived in an apartment above the hardware store on Ashcroft Road, a couple of streets away from the village green. I followed the alleyway to the rear of the hardware store where a set of steps led up to a small balcony and the entrance to Mel's apartment. Her truck was parked next to the stairs, its windows covered in a thick layer of frost. The presence of her truck didn't necessarily mean she was home, since it was easy to walk most places in Shady Creek, but I hoped I'd find her there.

I held on to the railing with my gloved hand as I carefully made my way up the frosty steps. I'd almost reached the top of the stairway when I paused, listening. I could hear voices coming from Mel's apartment. One belonged to Mel. I wasn't positive about the other, but I thought it was Jade's voice.

"That's a false alibi," Mel said. Her voice was muffled by the door between us, but her words were still clear enough to make out. "And they'll know it's false, because it doesn't match up with what I told them."

I hesitated with one foot on the top step, wondering if I should retreat and return another time. I probably should have left, but the words "false alibi" had me frozen to the spot, waiting to hear more.

"I was trying to help," Jade said, sounding close to tears.

"I know you were, but it *hasn't* helped. It's made things worse for both of us. You should have told the truth."

Jade said something I couldn't hear.

"I think you should go back to the manor," Mel said, over what I thought was the sound of Jade crying.

That was my cue to leave or get caught eavesdropping.

As quietly as possible, I backed down the stairs. I'd only made it halfway down when the door to Mel's apartment opened. Jade stepped out onto the balcony, zipping up her form-hugging black jacket. She had tears on her cheeks, and when she glanced up and saw me, she quickly wiped them away with the back of her hand.

She pulled on a pair of gloves and then hurried down the stairs.

"Excuse me," she said quietly as she squeezed past me.

I watched her hurry off down the alley and then glanced up to see Mel standing in the open doorway, frowning.

"Is this a bad time?" I asked.

Mel's frown eased up, although she didn't quite smile. "No. Come on in."

I knocked the snow off my boots before stepping inside the door. Mel shut it behind me as I rubbed my gloved hands together, chilled from those few moments spent standing on the stairway.

"Come and sit down," Mel said as she headed toward the small kitchen to the left of the entryway.

"Are you sure?" I felt a bit awkward about overhearing part of her conversation with Jade. "I don't want to intrude."

"You're not intruding." Mel smiled before opening a cupboard. "I've got coffee."

That was enough to make up my mind. I wiggled my feet out of my boots and hung my coat and scarf on a hook by the door, stuffing my hat and gloves into one of my coat pockets. By the time I pulled out a chair at Mel's small kitchen table, she'd filled two mugs with steaming hot coffee.

I liked Mel's kitchen. It was small, and hadn't been updated in a long time, but the bright blue cupboards gave the room a cheery atmosphere.

"Is Jade okay?" I asked as Mel set cream and sugar on the table.

"I'm not really sure how to answer that." Mel took the seat across from me and poured a bit of cream into her mug. "She's shocked by Freddy's murder, but she wasn't close to him. I don't think anyone was. But the police . . ."

I stirred cream and sugar into my coffee. "They obviously didn't arrest her. That's a good thing, right?"

"They haven't arrested her *yet*," Mel amended.

"You think they will?"

She leaned back in her chair, one hand wrapped loosely around her mug. "Last night when the police questioned her, she told them she was with me between the time she left the town hall and a few minutes before you found Freddy."

"But she wasn't," I said. Even if I hadn't overheard anything, Mel's current demeanor would have told me I was right.

"No, not the whole time. But after she left the town hall she did come to see me."

"On the green?"

Mel nodded. "She was upset, crying. Freddy had fired her and she wanted to leave town, but she didn't have any transportation. Freddy hired a driver to bring them both to Shady Creek, and he wasn't scheduled to take them back to Boston until this morning. I convinced her to spend the night in town, but she didn't want to go back to Shady Creek Manor, where she had a room booked. She asked if she could crash at my place. I walked her over here, got her a pillow and some blankets to use on the couch, and then left. I stopped by my studio to get a tool Zoe couldn't find earlier when she picked up my spares. Then I went back to the green to work on my sculpture. A few minutes later, I heard you yelling for help."

"So right before Freddy was killed, you were both alone for . . . how long?"

Mel stared into her coffee. "It was probably fifteen minutes from the time I left my place to when I got back to the green."

"So neither of you has an alibi."

"No," Mel confirmed. "And the cops know Jade lied because I'd already told them the truth about leaving her at my place and going to my studio. I'm sure they think she was trying to cover up for me or herself."

"What's the real reason?" I asked.

"She had a motive for wanting Freddy dead and the cops think I did too. She wanted to keep us both off the suspect list."

Instead, she'd probably bumped their names right to the top.

Chapter 11

When I left Mel's place, I went straight to the salon. Aunt Gilda and Betty both had clients when I arrived, but it looked as though those appointments were in their final stages.

"Why don't you get yourself something hot to drink?" Aunt Gilda suggested over the sound of the hairdryer Betty was using. "You look like you could use it."

The walk from Mel's apartment had left me chilled to the bone—again—so despite the coffee I'd just had, I took Gilda up on her offer. There was a small table in the salon's waiting area with coffee, tea, and a selection of mismatched cups and saucers. I poured myself a cup of tea and checked out the snacks. Instead of forgotten cookies, today there was a plate of Aunt Gilda's gingerbread on the table. I helped myself to one of those as well, and then another. Gingerbread was my favorite holiday treat.

Aunt Gilda was straightening her client's hair with a flat iron, but she finished up shortly after I'd settled into a chair with my tea and cookies.

"What have you been up to this morning?" she asked once her client had paid and disappeared out the door into the cold.

"I visited Mel, but that's all I've done so far." I set my teacup on the coffee table beside a stack of magazines and joined my aunt across the room where she was sweeping up hair clippings. "She's a suspect in Freddy's murder," I said quietly.

Aunt Gilda halted midsweep. "What in the world?" She glanced at Betty's client, a woman in her fifties, who was in the midst of paying for her haircut. When the woman had left the salon seconds later, Gilda continued. "Why would Mel want to kill Freddy Mancini?"

"*Mel* killed him?" Betty sounded shocked as she came out from behind the counter.

"No, of course not," I said. "But she's a suspect. He trash-talked her to some of the reporters and he was her main competition. Plus, the ice pick used to kill Freddy belongs to her. Someone stole her tools earlier in the evening, but the cops might think she set that up because she planned to kill Freddy."

"If she'd planned to kill him, she wouldn't have used her own ice pick," Betty said. "Mel's smarter than that."

"She is," I agreed. "But the cops don't know that."

Aunt Gilda continued sweeping. "It doesn't sound good for her, but her supposed motive isn't that strong. Surely there are others who had far more reason to kill him."

"*I* think so," I said. "But it doesn't help that Freddy's assistant lied and said she and Mel were together when Freddy was killed. She told the police that after Mel had told them the truth—they were both on their own for a while around the time of the murder."

"Freddy's assistant?" Betty said. "Why would Mel have been with her?"

I explained about their history and how Jade had asked to crash at Mel's place after Freddy fired her.

"That's not good," Aunt Gilda said as she discarded the swept-up hair clippings. "What if the police believe she still has feelings for Jade? They might think she has an additional motive—revenge on behalf of Jade after Freddy fired her."

"I know," I said glumly. "That had occurred to me too."

"What about Jade?" Betty asked. "Do you think she might have killed Freddy?"

"Mel doesn't think so," I said. "But I'm not ready to rule her out."

Aunt Gilda tucked a lock of my red hair behind my ear. "Let the police take care of it, honey. I don't want you in any danger. I'm still shaken up from what happened to you back in October."

There were times when I still felt shaken up too, especially when I woke up from nightmares caused by my run-in with a murderer in the fall.

I gave my aunt a quick hug. "I'm not planning to do anything dangerous."

Aunt Gilda didn't look entirely convinced. She was about to say something when the bell above the salon's door jingled.

"Good morning, April," she called to the bundled-up woman who stepped inside.

"Do you know where I can find Penny Blaine?" I asked quickly, knowing I didn't have much time before April O'Hare took her spot in my aunt's chair.

"She works at Sibyl's yarn store across the green," Betty said before Aunt Gilda could answer.

"Sibyl as in Sibyl Hawkes?" I asked.

"That's her," Aunt Gilda confirmed. "Now, Sadie . . ."

"My hair's an absolute fright in this cold weather," April O'Hare said as she bustled over our way.

"Don't worry," I rushed to assure my aunt. "I just want to talk to her."

I didn't think I'd succeeded in reassuring her, but she got April settled at the hair-washing station and turned on the water. I drank down the last of my tea and took the cup into the small kitchenette in the back before getting all bundled up again.

I called out a cheery good-bye and waved as I ventured out into the cold, nibbling on another piece of gingerbread. I hesitated out front of the salon, half turning to go back inside. Part of me wanted to tell Aunt Gilda about the books that had gone missing from the Inkwell. She'd understand why I was so upset. But now she was busy chatting with April, and it wasn't something I wanted to talk about in front of anyone else.

Not wanting to let my spirits slump, I tried to push the missing books from my thoughts and crossed Sycamore Street to the village green. I took the opportunity to admire the ice sculptures in daylight while listening to a group of carolers singing the "Coventry Carol." They were dressed in Victorian outfits and I envied the women their cozy muffs.

As I snapped a few photos of the ice sculptures and carolers, I spotted a familiar figure across the green.

"Booker!" I called out, shoving my phone into my pocket.

Wearing a thick winter jacket and a hat pulled down over his shoulder-length braids, Booker was almost as bundled up as I was. All he was missing was a scarf.

"Morning, Sadie," he said as he came over my way. "Mel's sculpture is wicked good."

"It really is," I agreed.

"She definitely deserved to win."

I pulled my scarf up over my chin. "Has Damien talked to you about the hockey tournament yet?"

"No. What about it?"

"We decided the Inkwell should have a team. Do you play hockey?"

"Nope. I can't even skate. If we were talking football, soccer, or baseball, there'd be no problem, but skating . . . You might as well ask me to fly."

"Darn," I said with disappointment.

"Sorry. Is there anyone else you can ask?"

"Maybe." I was already sorting through the possibilities in my mind.

As I parted ways with Booker, I texted Cordelia, asking if she was interested in joining the team. By then, my fingers and toes were going numb, so I headed over to Purls of Wisdom on Hemlock Street. I hadn't been in the yarn store before. Although Aunt Gilda had taught me how to knit when I was ten, I'd never been very good at it. I could make a lumpy scarf if necessary, but I hadn't picked up a set of knitting needles in several years.

Even though knitting had never become a real hobby of mine, I couldn't help but admire the store as soon as I stepped inside. It was cozy and warm, as I'd hoped it would be, and the shelves were bursting with color. I wiped my feet on the mat inside the door and pulled off my gloves, unable to keep myself from fingering the soft balls of yarn on the nearest shelf.

"Good morning!" Sibyl Hawkes called out as she approached from the back of the store where several women were sitting around a table, working on knitting projects.

"Morning," I returned.

"It's Sadie, right?" She continued on before I could confirm that. "The trivia night at the pub was such a blast. Will you have more in the future?"

"I'm hoping to," I said. "I'm so glad you had a good time. And I was very impressed by your team's knowledge."

"Many of us knitters are avid readers," Sibyl said with a smile. "Now, is there anything I can help you with?"

"Actually, I was just going to have a look around, if that's all right."

I glanced at the women around the table. Penny was standing next to one of them, guiding her through a stitch.

"It's absolutely fine," Sybil assured me. "Don't worry about the class. We often have them going on while the store's open. Feel free to browse all you like."

A phone rang over on the checkout counter.

"Let me know if you need any help," Sibyl said before hurrying over to the phone.

I wandered slowly from shelf to shelf, fingering the balls of yarn and admiring the gorgeous colors. Every now and then I shot a sidelong glance toward the back of the store, wondering if I'd have a chance to talk to Penny. After ten minutes or so, I was about to give up and head back to the Inkwell when Penny's students pushed back their chairs and began packing up their projects.

I pretended to be interested in some unspun, braided fleece near the class table as the students slowly made their way out of the store, chatting with each other as they pulled on their winter gear. One woman stayed behind to speak with Penny for a few minutes, but eventually she too headed for the door.

Penny made a circuit of the table, pushing the chairs in, but I managed to catch her eye.

"Do you need any help?" she asked me.

"I'm just browsing, really," I said. "But I did want to offer my condolences to you."

"Condolences?" she echoed with confusion.

"I understand you were close to Freddy Mancini."

A dark shadow seemed to pass across her brown eyes. When she spoke again, there was an edge to her voice. "At one time, but not for many years." Her gaze sharpened. "You were the one who found his body."

"That's right."

Penny tucked the last chair under the table. "In that case, you're probably deserving of more sympathy than I am." When she saw the surprise on my face, she explained, "It might sound terrible, but I had no affection left for Freddy. Not even a drop. He didn't treat me well in the past or in the present." The shadow returned to darken her eyes again. Her hands tightened around the back of the chair she'd pushed under the table, her knuckles turning white. "Freddy was a self-absorbed, arrogant jerk."

The bitterness in her voice startled me. I'd known that Freddy had treated her badly on the day of his death, but after seeing her in tears at the Inkwell, I hadn't expected such anger from her. The other day she seemed much more hurt than wrathful. But maybe that hurt had since transformed.

Penny released her grip on the chair and forced a smile. "Sorry. It probably seems insensitive to talk about him like that now that he's dead, but he really wasn't a good man."

"That seems to be the general opinion of him," I said. "And I got to observe that myself at the chili supper."

"I heard he clashed with Leo there. That's what happened pretty much every time they crossed paths, especially since the Boston incident three years ago."

"Boston incident?" I asked with interest.

"Leo had lost his job here in town, so he went to Boston and asked Freddy to let him work at his restaurant. He was even willing to work as a dishwasher. But Freddy told him he wasn't sophisticated enough to set foot in his restaurant, let alone work there."

"Wow."

"Right? They didn't get along all that well before, but ever since there's been nothing but hatred between them."

All the more reason for Leo to be on my suspect list, I decided. I'd already known that he had no love for his half brother, but now I had to consider the possibility that Leo had wanted revenge. Maybe when Freddy showed up in Shady Creek, lording his success over everyone, it was all too much for Leo. Of course, Penny was one of my suspects too. How quickly had her hurt feelings morphed into anger? Had it happened before Freddy's death?

I couldn't forget the ball of burnt-orange yarn that had tumbled out of her bag at the pub.

There was a good chance I was talking to Freddy's killer right now.

Swallowing back a nervous lump that had suddenly lodged in my throat, I decided to steer the conversation in a slightly different direction. "You didn't make it to the chili supper yourself?" I asked casually.

"No." Penny straightened some balls of yarn on a shelf. "I had a headache, so I went to bed early that evening." She finished fiddling with the yarn. "This is your first Winter Carnival, right? Didn't you just move here a few months ago?"

"In the summer," I said.

"I know the murder has put a damper on things, but I hope you'll have a chance to enjoy the festivities. The carnival's always good fun."

The jingling of the bell above the shop's door announced the arrival of three women. One of them called out to Penny, and she waved back. As the group of women headed our way, I stepped back and smiled.

"It was nice talking to you."

"You too. And the trivia night was great, by the way. I'm looking forward to the next one."

"I'm glad to hear it."

The new arrivals began chattering to Penny, so I waved to Sibyl and left the shop.

I had plenty to think about. If Penny had gone to bed with a headache early on Thursday evening, she couldn't have killed Freddy. But could anyone confirm her alibi? I didn't know. Aunt Gilda would probably know if she lived alone or not, but finding out if her alibi would hold up would take some more digging. As for Leo, he definitely deserved more scrutiny. I didn't have any trouble picturing him lashing out at Freddy in a violent way, whether following some planning or in the heat of the moment.

Investigating that angle would have to wait for the time being, I realized as I checked my phone. Cordelia had replied to my text message, saying she was excited to join the Inkwell's hockey team. I'd texted Teagan the night before, asking if she would play in the tournament. I had a message from her as well, saying she definitely wanted to be on the team and that Zoe was willing to play too if we needed another person.

Over coffee that morning, Mel had assured me that she was willing to take part in the tournament. That meant we almost had enough players, but now our team needed jerseys. With the tournament set to start in two days, I didn't know if I'd have time to get custom-printed jerseys with the Inkwell logo on them, but I was hoping to at least get a set of matching hockey sweaters.

Shivering, I tucked my phone away and pulled my gloves back on. Damien and Mel were both experienced hockey players and would probably be the most skilled members of the Inkwell team. While Teagan had said in her message that she and her sister had some basic hockey skills, Cordelia had admitted that she'd never played the game. She could skate, though, she'd said, and she was enthusiastic. I figured that put her in pretty much the same category as me.

When I'd told Grayson that I'd never played hockey in any sort of organized way, what I meant was I'd only played a handful of street hockey games with my younger brother while growing up. But, like Cordelia, I could skate. Hopefully we wouldn't be a complete disaster during the tournament, because beating the brewery's team would be so sweet.

I turned a corner, heading for a store that did custom T-shirt and uniform printing. I stopped short a second later when a police car zoomed past me and pulled up to the curb. As two officers climbed out of the cruiser, a middle-aged woman burst out the front door of a small electronics store.

"They've robbed me!" the woman exclaimed to the officers. "They've robbed me blind!"

Chapter 12

As much as I wanted to know more about the robbery, I knew the police wouldn't want me following them into the electronics store. The officers had disappeared from sight now, the shop door drifting shut behind them, so I continued along my intended path to the business next door.

The picture-framing and custom printing store was small but cute, with a selection of different frames on one wall and T-shirts and uniforms on the opposite one. The counter was straight ahead of me as I stepped in the door. A woman in her fifties stood behind the counter, and a man of about the same age was in the process of making his way around it.

"I wonder what's going on," the man was saying, his gaze on the front window. He sent a distracted smile my way as he moved around me toward the door.

"Good morning," the woman greeted me. "It seems the police are next door. Any idea what happened?"

"All I know is that a woman was saying she was robbed," I said.

"Good heavens! That must have been Dolores. I hope she wasn't hurt. Robbed in broad daylight? How terrible!"

The man opened the store's door. "I'm going over there."

"Don't be getting in the way of the police, Ernie!" the woman called after him.

He gave no indication of whether he heard or not.

The woman gave me an apologetic smile. "Sorry about that. Things like this don't happen very often, so it causes quite a stir when it does."

"I understand," I assured her.

"I'm Geraldine." She took off her glasses and set them on the counter. "What can I do for you?"

I introduced myself and told her about my need for hockey jerseys.

"Ah, yes. We've been filling several orders like that for the tournament, but I'm afraid you've cut it too close if you're looking for custom printing. The tournament starts on Monday and we've already got so many orders that we can't rush one through."

"I was worried about that," I said, disappointed. "Unfortunately, we didn't decide to enter a team until last night."

"Don't despair." Geraldine came out from behind the counter. "There's nothing in the rules that says you have to have your team name or logo on the jerseys. If you're happy with your team members simply having the same blank jersey, I can still help you out."

"That would be all right." It wouldn't be as nice as having custom Inkwell sweaters, but it was definitely better than nothing.

If we weren't a disaster as a team and wanted to play again next year, I'd make sure to put our order in earlier.

"So you'll be needing seven, right?" Geraldine asked as she sorted through some jerseys on a display rack.

"That's right."

"Hmmm. We're almost sold out of most colors, and you won't want to have the same color as any other team anyway. But I think I have seven of one color in the back, a color no other team has ordered. Not from us, anyway. I won't be a minute."

She bustled behind the counter and disappeared through a doorway leading to the back of the building. As I waited, I wandered toward the front window and peered along the sidewalk to the electronics shop, but I couldn't see anybody.

"Here we are!"

At the sound of Geraldine's voice, I turned my back on the window. She hoisted an armful of jerseys onto the counter. "The most we have of any other color is five, but I've got a dozen of these ones in various sizes, so you can take your pick."

She sounded awfully cheery about that, probably because she was faced with an opportunity to sell jerseys that no one else would have wanted. Because who the Holly Golightly would buy mustard yellow hockey sweaters with maroon trim? Nobody who had more than two days to get uniforms together for their team, that was for sure.

I lifted one of the sweaters up off the counter, trying unsuccessfully to find a redeeming quality of some sort.

"You really don't have seven jerseys in another color?" I asked, trying my best not to sound horrified.

"I'm afraid not. I know they're not the prettiest, but they'll do the job."

The shop door opened and I turned away from the jerseys with relief. Ernie had returned, his round cheeks pink from the cold. As the door shut behind him, his glasses fogged up.

"Is Dolores all right?" Geraldine asked. "What happened over there?"

Ernie removed his glasses. "Dolores forgot to set her alarm last night. When she got to the store this morning, she realized someone had broken in and made off with thousands of dollars' worth of equipment."

"Oh dear. But she wasn't robbed in broad daylight?"

"Nope. No one was there when it happened. Except the thieves, of course."

"That's one small mercy."

"Does her store have security cameras?" I asked.

Ernie replaced his glasses on his nose, the lenses now clear. "She does. One out back, one out front, and one inside. She was showing the footage to the cops when I got there."

"So the thieves were caught on camera?" Geraldine said.

"They were, not that it does much good. There were two of them, wearing masks and hoods. Dressed all in black."

"It must be the same hooligans who committed the other recent break-ins," Geraldine said. "They hit the souvenir shop a couple of weeks ago, and Audrey Minton's store before that."

"And Vera Anderson's store the other day," I added.

Geraldine shook her head. "I can't believe this is happening in Shady Creek. And a murder too!"

"That's what happens when you get more tourists coming to town," Ernie said.

I somehow doubted tourists were responsible for a rash of burglaries spread out over several weeks, but I didn't say so.

"Now, how about these jerseys?" Geraldine asked, holding one up.

I forced myself not to cringe at the sight of it. "I'd better check what sizes I'm going to need." I sidled toward the door. "I'll be back later."

"Don't leave it too long or we might be out of these as well," Geraldine warned as I slipped out of the store.

I wasn't too concerned. All the other teams were probably far more organized than ours and already had jerseys—ones that weren't painful to look at.

Without being too obvious about it, I tried to peek through the front window of the electronics store as I passed by, but all I saw was the two uniformed officers speaking with Dolores. I hoped the police would find the thieves soon. It was unnerving to know they were sneaking around town at night, targeting businesses. I'd recently had motion-sensitive lights installed outside the pub, but maybe I should have purchased security cameras too.

I decided to put that thought aside for the time being so I could focus on my current mission: procuring jerseys for the hockey tournament. I knew the garish ones Geraldine had offered me might be my only real option, but I wanted to explore another possibility first. The maroon-trimmed, mustard-yellow sweaters would be a last resort.

Shivering as I walked down the street, I glanced up at the heavy gray clouds. They'd grown darker since I'd left the Inkwell and I figured there was a good chance we'd be getting fresh snow soon. I tugged my hat down farther over my ears and picked up my pace. A minute or so later I arrived at a secondhand sporting-goods shop.

I browsed around and spoke to the proprietor, but he couldn't help me. He didn't have seven matching jerseys in any size or color.

"Talk to Geraldine and Ernie over at the Fine Print," he advised.

"I was just there," I said. "They don't have enough of any color other than yellow."

"Nothing wrong with yellow."

That was easy for him to say when he hadn't seen the eyesores.

I thanked him and trudged back to the Fine Print. I decided to guess at the sizes my teammates would need and purchased seven of the ugly jerseys. Geraldine handed me the bag with a smile, and I couldn't help but wonder what expressions I'd see on my teammates' faces when I showed them their uniforms. Hopefully they wouldn't refuse to play in them.

With that task out of the way, I set off in the direction of the Inkwell. As I neared the village green, I spotted the first tiny snowflakes of the day, drifting their way down from the leaden sky. Despite how cold I was, I smiled. I might not love shoveling snow, but the flakes dancing down from the sky made the beautiful town even prettier.

Instead of cutting across the green, I headed for the Treasure

Chest, Shontelle's gift shop, located on Hillview Road. I knew her store would be cozy warm, and I liked to drop in for a chat now and then when there weren't too many customers keeping my friend busy.

A woman had just left the shop when I went inside, but I soon saw there were no other customers.

"Morning," I called out to Shontelle.

She was near the back of the shop, carefully removing some snow globes from a box and placing them on a shelf. I wandered over her way for a closer look at the display. I'd always loved snow globes and I'd amassed a good collection of them over the years.

"You've been out shopping, I see," she said, eyeing the bag in my hand. "Anything interesting?"

"Jerseys for the Inkwell's hockey team."

I made no move to show them to her. Instead, I picked up one of the snow globes to admire it. A cute polar bear and her adorable cub stood on an iceberg beneath the small glass dome.

"I didn't know you were entering the tournament," Shontelle said.

I tipped the globe upside down before returning it to the display, snow now falling on the bears. "We only decided last night. We're still short one player."

"Don't look at me." Shontelle placed the last snow globe on the shelf. "I can't even skate."

"Who's going skating?" a voice piped up. Kiandra came bouncing out of the back room. "Can I go too?" Her smile grew brighter when she saw me. "Hi, Sadie."

"Hi, sweetie. Are you helping your mom with the store today?"

"No, I was reading in the back."

"Nancy Drew?" I guessed. I'd been lending her books from the series one by one.

"Yep. I'm almost done."

"I'll have to bring you another one soon then."

"Yes, please!" She looked from her mom to me. "Are you going skating?"

"No one's going skating today, sweetheart," Shontelle said. "We were talking about the hockey tournament."

Kiandra's face fell. "Oh."

"You like ice-skating?" I asked her.

"Yes. I'm not very good, though. Last year was the first time I tried. I kept falling."

"Falling is part of learning," I said. "But I can help you, if you'd like."

Her face brightened. "Really?"

"Really."

"Did you hear that, Mom? Sadie's going to teach me to skate."

"She's much more qualified than I am," Shontelle said.

"Can we go today?" Kiandra asked, bouncing up on the balls of her feet.

"Honey, Sadie has to work today."

"Unfortunately, that's true," I said. "How about Monday after school?"

"Chelsea's birthday party is on Monday," Kiandra said with disappointment.

Shontelle ruffled her daughter's cloud of curly hair. "Don't sound so sad. You've been looking forward to that party."

"Yeah. But I really want to learn how to skate better."

"The outdoor rink is open all winter," I said. "And you'll be on holidays soon. We'll find a time that works."

"Okay." Her eyes brightened. "Sadie, did you know you can go on sleigh rides during the carnival?"

"I heard something about that."

"They're horse-drawn sleighs and the horses are so pretty. Have you ever been on a sleigh ride?"

"I have, but not for a long time," I said. Not since I'd lived in Minnesota, I realized. It really had been a long time.

Kiandra radiated excitement. "I'm going on a sleigh ride for Chelsea's birthday party."

"Then it sounds like you'll have lots of fun on Monday."

Shontelle glanced at her phone. "Kiandra, go upstairs and get changed into your dance clothes. Grandma will be here soon to walk you over to your class."

"Okay. Bye, Sadie!" She waved and disappeared into the back of the store where a stairway led up to their two-bedroom apartment.

"So," Shontelle said once we were alone, "how did things go with Grayson last night?"

"They didn't go anywhere." I pulled off my hat, finally warming up. "He was just there for a drink."

"If you say so."

I followed her as she headed into the back, carrying the box she'd emptied of snow globes. "What's that supposed to mean?"

She tucked the box inside a bigger one and slid them both onto a high shelf in the storeroom. "The man owns a brewery. It's not like he has to go to the pub to have a drink."

"Maybe he wanted to have a drink while socializing."

"It didn't look like he was meeting his buddies there." She headed back into the main part of the store.

I trailed in her wake. "You're reading far too much into things."

"Or you're not reading enough," she countered.

I decided a swift change of subject was in order. "The electronics store on Mulberry Street was broken into last night."

"Another break-in? I'm glad I've got an alarm, but it's still unnerving. Do the police have any suspects?"

"Not that I know of." I leaned against the counter while Shontelle checked something on the computer.

As I took a second to think, it crossed my mind that the disappearance of my books could be related to the recent burglaries, but I quickly dismissed that idea. The theft of two books was hardly on the same level as the other crimes.

"Speaking of suspects . . ." I said a moment later.

Shontelle's gaze snapped my way. "Do you know who killed Freddy Mancini?"

"No." *Not yet*, I added in my head. "But I've got a few people on my suspect list."

"Like Leo?" she guessed.

"And Penny Blaine."

"I heard he pretended not to recognize her, even though they dated for years. What a lowlife."

"Do you know if Penny lives alone?"

"I think she does. Why?"

"She told me she was in bed with a headache when Freddy was killed. I was wondering if anyone could confirm that."

Shontelle's eyebrows drew together. "But wasn't Freddy killed around eight o'clock?"

"Pretty close to it."

"Then *I* can confirm something," Shontelle said. "Penny was lying."

Chapter 13

On my way across the village green, I thought over what Shontelle had told me. When she and Kiandra had left the chili supper on the night of Freddy's death, they'd had to wait at the curb before crossing Hemlock Street because Penny had driven by in her old red Toyota. I'd asked Shontelle if she was absolutely certain it was Penny. She'd assured me that she'd recognized both the driver and the vehicle.

Penny had turned her car onto Creekside Road, heading east. Shontelle had also told me that Penny lived west of the green, so wherever she was headed that night, she wasn't going home. No matter which way I looked at it, Penny had told a blatant lie. And why lie if she didn't have anything to hide?

The fact that she'd driven north along Hemlock Street before turning onto Creekside Road put her in the vicinity of the scene of Freddy's death right around the time he was killed. The town hall was, after all, located near the corner of Hemlock and Creekside. And there was a window of only twenty minutes or so when Freddy could have been killed. The time when Shontelle and Kiandra left the chili supper was smack in the middle of that window.

Had Shontelle seen Penny fleeing the murder scene?

I didn't want to believe that Penny could be a murderer, but I knew from experience that a killer could turn out to be someone you least expected. And no matter my personal feelings, her lie had solidified her spot on my suspect list.

When I reached the northern edge of the village green, I paused at the edge of Creekside Road and smiled. After a car drove by, I pulled off one glove and fished my phone out of my bag so I could take a picture. One of the horse-drawn sleighs Kiandra had talked about was parked across the road, near the driveway that led to Grayson's brewery. The horses were gorgeous, with braided manes and caramel-colored coats.

I snapped a photo of the scene, just before a group of half a dozen tourists bustled across the road to the horses. By the time I was crossing the footbridge toward the pub, the tourists had all bundled into the sleigh. With a word from the driver, the horses set off to the east, the bells on their harnesses jingling merrily. I'd heard that a couple of landowners were allowing the sleigh rides to take place on their property, providing plenty of room for roaming over the snowy landscape. Hopefully I'd have a chance to go on a sleigh ride myself before the Winter Carnival drew to a close at the end of the following weekend.

In the meantime, I'd upload my photos of the sleigh and the ice sculptures to the Inkwell's social media accounts. I liked to showcase the town as well as the pub online, and the Inkwell's followers, only some of whom were locals, seemed to like it too.

Reaching the front door of the pub, I welcomed the warmth that wrapped around me as soon as I stepped inside. As I was defrosting, I checked the Guinness wall clock. I didn't have time to go snowshoeing before I opened the pub, but hopefully I'd have a chance the next day. Ever since the first snowfall of the season, snowshoeing had become my main form of exercise. I was trying to regain some of the fitness and athleticism of my youth. Over the last several years, I hadn't been as diligent about staying active, and I'd felt the effects of that when I'd tried going out on bike rides in the fall.

With the Winter Carnival underway, I had some extra motivation for exercising regularly. I was going to need every bit of the stamina I'd regained when I took part in the hockey tournament and the snowshoe race scheduled for Friday. I doubted I had a chance to be victorious in either contest, but I was still going to give the hockey games and the race my best effort.

I ate a quick lunch up in my apartment and then spent a moment replacing a bauble on the small Christmas tree in my living room. Apparently, Wimsey had decided it was fun to knock decorations off the lower branches. Not that he'd admitted responsibility on this occasion or any previous ones, but since he and I were the only ones with the opportunity to commit the offense, it wasn't difficult to figure out who the culprit was.

If only Freddy's murder was so easy to solve.

Once I'd rehung the bauble on a higher branch—the lower ones were starting to look quite bare—I returned downstairs.

Booker had arrived while I was in my apartment. I could hear him singing in the kitchen below, as he often did before the Inkwell opened for the day. At the moment he was in the winter spirit, singing an enthusiastic rendition of "Let It Snow," an appropriate choice, considering the weather.

I didn't mind his before-hours singing one bit. He had a pleasant tenor voice and I considered it free entertainment. As he wrapped up the song, I unlocked the front door and flipped the sign. The snow was falling thickly now, and I wondered if that would keep people away on a Saturday afternoon. It turned out that I needn't have worried. Many of the tourists in town for the carnival showed up, seeking refuge from the snow and a place to thaw out their fingers and toes. Several locals came in as well, including Jocy in the early evening.

He left his coat on one of the coatracks by the door and claimed a stool at the bar, as was his custom lately. Damien poured him a pint of beer while I took his order for To Be or Nacho Be to the kitchen. As I carried the platter of heavenly smelling nachos out to him a few minutes later, a lightbulb flashed on in my head.

"I don't suppose you play hockey, do you?" I asked Joey as I set the platter on the bar in front of him.

"Sure. I was on the local team when I was in school. Why?"

"The Inkwell's hockey team is short one player."

"You signed up for the tournament?"

"We did," Damien answered as he mixed a Count Dracula cocktail. "But we might live to regret the decision."

"No, we won't," I said, with far more confidence than I felt.

"Have you seen the schedule?" Damien asked. "It was posted on the carnival's Web site this morning."

"No," I said. "When is our first game?"

"Monday morning. We're playing the Spirit Hill Brewery."

Of course we were.

"Who else is on your team?" Joey asked.

"Aside from me and Damien, there's Mel, Teagan, Zoe, and Cordelia."

"Cordelia King?"

"Yes."

"Can she even skate?" Joey sounded doubtful. "I don't think I've ever seen her at the rink."

"She told me she can skate." I decided not to mention that she'd also told me she'd never played a game of hockey in her life. "And it's not like it's the Stanley Cup play-offs. It's all in good fun." Although, defeating Grayson's team would make it all the more enjoyable.

"I'm all about fun." Joey chomped down on a cheese-laden nacho. He swallowed before saying, "Count me in."

I smiled at him. "Perfect! We're all set then."

"You got us jerseys?" Damien asked as he returned to the bar from delivering two cocktails to a table.

"I did. I got them this morning." I didn't offer to show them off. "I guess I'm going to need some equipment, though. I've got skates, but nothing else. I should have thought about that while I was at the secondhand store. Cordelia needs gear too."

"The two of you can borrow what you need from my girls," Damien said. "They both play hockey."

"Perfect. Thank you. Too bad your daughters aren't old enough to play in the tournament."

"They're looking forward to the day they will be. I have to say I'm impressed you found us enough players. Oh, and I booked the rink for a practice session tomorrow morning," Damien added. "Ten o'clock. Can you both make it?"

Joey and I assured him that we could.

"I'll bring the girls' equipment for you in the morning then."

The oldest of Damien's teenage daughters was about my height, the youngest close to Cordelia's size. It was a relief not to have to go out and buy a full set of equipment for one tournament and I didn't doubt it would be welcome news for Cordelia too. She didn't even have skates of her own. I thought she was a good sport for agreeing to play for the Inkwell's team on such short notice.

Joey was too, and I told him so.

"Anything to help out my favorite pub owner," he said with a grin.

I left him to finish his nachos and got a fire going in the wood stove in the Christie Room. When the flames were dancing and crackling merrily, I straightened up and my gaze settled on the shelf with the missing books. I tried to ignore the ache in my chest that returned whenever I thought about the books or spending Christmas alone.

Fortunately, work provided me with a good distraction. We had a decent crowd in the pub and, not long after I got the fire going, the first arrivals for the mystery book club meeting showed up. Cordelia popped her head through the door and smiled when she saw me.

"Evening, Sadie."

"Evening. Thanks so much for joining the hockey team."

"Thank *you* for asking me," she said as she unbuttoned her coat. "I can't wait! I've never been on a sports team before."

I filled her in on the fact that we could borrow gear from Damien's daughters.

"That's a relief," she said. "I wouldn't even know what gear to buy."

"I'd be a little lost too," I admitted.

Lara Hawkes, Eli and Sybil's thirty-something daughter, was the next to arrive. We all exchanged greetings as they unbundled themselves.

"It's always so cozy in here," Cordelia said as she unwound a long scarf from around her neck. "So perfect for a night like tonight."

I noted their damp hats and coats. "I'm guessing it's still coming down out there."

"I'll say." Lara unbuttoned her coat. "We're supposed to get at least six inches overnight."

Cordelia pulled her knitted hat off her head, letting her long, crinkly orange hair spring free. The static from her wool hat had left her hair even puffier than usual. She tried to smooth it down, but without much success.

As Lara hung her coat over the back of a chair, my gaze latched on to her cable knit sweater. The earthy tones went well with her light brown hair, but what I really noticed was the burnt-orange yarn woven in with the shades of cream, brown, dark green, and deep red.

"That's a beautiful sweater," I managed to say, masking my surprise before Lara noticed me gaping at her.

She glanced down at the garment. "Thanks. It's one of my mom's creations."

"I was at her shop this morning," I said. "It was my first time going in there. It's a great place."

Lara smiled. "My mom loves it, and I do too."

"Do you knit?" I asked, figuring she probably did with Sybil for her mother.

"I do, but not like my mom does."

"I wish I could knit," Cordelia said forlornly. "My gran tried to teach me once, but I'm all thumbs."

"You probably just need practice," Lara said. "You could try one of the classes at my mom's store."

Cordelia pulled an armchair closer to the wood stove and sank into it. "That sounds like fun. I might do that."

Nettie Jo Kim, owner of the Village Bean coffee shop, arrived next. I took the women's drink orders while they waited for their fellow club members to show up, and I spent the next few minutes mixing cocktails. Cordelia had opted for the Poirot—made with cassis—while Lara had requested white wine and Nettie Jo ordered a Milky Way Gargle Blaster. That was one of my favorite drinks on the menu. Made with root beer, cream, and vanilla vodka, it tasted like a root beer float with an extra kick.

While I was mixing cocktails, Cordelia came out to the bar and requested three platters of nachos for the group to share. I relayed that order to Teagan and then set the three drinks on a tray. When I returned to the Christie Room, I noticed that another member of the book club had arrived.

Adam Hammerstein had already shed his outerwear to reveal one of his many sweater vests, worn—as usual—over a white shirt with the sleeves rolled up. He was a couple of years younger than me. He taught physics and math at the local high school and was an avid reader and keen amateur baker.

Adam nudged his black-framed glasses up higher on his nose and handed me a small box. "Happy holidays, Sadie. I wanted to share some of my baking."

Cordelia, Lara, and Nettie Jo already held similar boxes. We all peeked inside. Each one contained a variety of cookies and other delicious-looking goodies.

"Wow! Thank you, Adam," I said. "They smell amazing and I bet they taste even better."

"They do," Cordelia said. She'd already bitten a piece off one of the cookies from her box. "Thank you."

Nettie Jo and Lara chimed in with their thanks too.

"You're welcome," Adam said, clearly pleased by our response to his gifts. He waved his copy of the club's latest book of choice—*Death by Chocolate Lab,* by Bethany Blake. "This book was a lot of fun."

"Wasn't it?" Cordelia said before finishing off her cookie.

Nettie Jo settled deeper into her chair, her drink in one hand. "I loved Socrates, the basset hound."

"My favorite is the one-eared chihuahua," Adam said.

Cordelia selected another cookie from her box. "All the four-legged characters are great. I also love the two-legged ones. Especially the handsome police detective."

"Maybe we shouldn't get too far ahead of ourselves." Adam pulled a comfy chair closer to the wood stove. "The rest of the group's not here yet."

"Can I get you anything to drink while you wait for the others?" I asked Adam.

"Definitely, but I'll have to take a look at the menu."

I handed him one that was sitting on a nearby table.

My gaze settled on Lara's sweater again and I couldn't stop myself from fishing for some information. "Lara, you must know Penny Blaine well, since she works at your mom's store."

"Sure, Penny's a friend of mine." Lara frowned. "I feel so bad for her. This whole thing with Freddy Mancini hasn't been easy on her. Though to be honest, I have no idea what she ever saw in him."

"Did you all go to school together?" I asked.

"No, I'm a few years younger than them. Penny and I only became friends in the last five years or so when she started teaching classes at Purls of Wisdom. I remember Freddy from back then, but I didn't know much about him."

"I heard he didn't used to be so pompous." Cordelia slapped a hand over her mouth. "I shouldn't say things like that, should I?" Her words came out muffled.

"Why not?" Adam asked.

"Speaking ill of the dead," Nettie Jo said, and Cordelia nodded.

"But he *is* pompous." Lara stopped and realized what she'd said. "Was. Why should we make him out to be an angel just because he's dead?"

Nettie Jo set her drink on a side table and leaned forward in her chair, holding her hands out to soak in the warmth from the wood stove. "Did Penny think he was an angel? Even after the way he treated her the other day?"

"No," Lara said. "She knew he'd changed. She knew that all the way back when he dumped her. But it still hurt her when he snubbed her."

"Leo sure didn't think he was an angel," Adam commented.

"Is it true they couldn't stand each other?" Cordelia asked.

"That's what it seemed like to me," I said.

"I don't blame Leo." Lara's voice had taken on a blunt edge. "It's not like Freddy's worth mourning. The only reason he came back here was to thumb his nose at the town, at everyone who helped him along the road to success. If you ask me, Shady Creek is better off without him."

Her last words were laced with venom. Everyone in the room fell quiet, all eyes on Lara. Her face reddened and she stood up abruptly.

"Washroom," she said. "Excuse me."

She left the room with her back straight, her shoulders tense.

When she was gone, Adam requested a Count Dracula and I headed for the bar. Cordelia joined me on my way out of the room.

"Do you think she's okay?" she whispered.

"Lara? I hope so. She sure seemed angry, though. Probably because of the way Freddy acted toward her father at the chili supper."

Cordelia nodded, her eyes wide. "I heard about that. Poor Eli. He treated Freddy like a son, spent hours and hours with him teaching him how to cook when he was a kid. And then Freddy was so rude to him!"

"It was pretty bad," I said, remembering the exchange at the town hall.

"I'm not surprised Lara's taking it hard. She's really close with her dad, and she's been protective of him ever since he had a stroke four years ago." Cordelia drifted away from me as I reached the bar. "I'll go check on her."

As I mixed Adam's drink, I thought over what Cordelia had told me. It was understandable that Lara was angry at Freddy on her father's behalf, but just how angry was she? Angry enough to kill him?

It was a possibility, especially since the orange in her sweater was the same shade as the tuft I'd seen on the murder weapon.

Cordelia and Lara emerged from the washroom and returned to the Christie Room. I followed behind them with Adam's drink, thinking as I went that Lara was deserving of a spot on my suspect list.

Chapter 14

The next morning, Wimsey made sure I woke up in plenty of time to get ready for hockey practice. I snoozed my alarm when it went off, but that never did much good. As soon as I'd snuggled back down under the blankets, Wimsey climbed onto my pillow and meowed in my ear. When I tried to ignore him, he batted and clawed at the covers, trying to get them off me.

When my cat wanted his breakfast, he wasn't about to let anything get in his way, especially not five more minutes of heavenly slumber for his human servant.

Once I'd had a cup of coffee and a light breakfast of toast, I dressed warmly with leggings under a pair of sweatpants and a long-sleeved shirt beneath a sweater. I braided my hair, pulled on my boots and outer layers, and then braced myself before stepping outdoors.

The snow had stopped falling during the night, but the accumulation predictions had been accurate. Roughly six inches of fluffy new snow covered the footpath outside the pub's front door. I grabbed the shovel I'd left leaning against the side of the building and pushed it along ahead of me, clearing a narrow path as I went. I planned to do a better job of shoveling the walkway before the pub opened, but that would have to wait until after hockey practice.

When I reached Creekside Road, I backtracked a few paces and left the shovel leaning against the railing of the footbridge. Hoisting the bag holding my skates and the team jerseys over my shoulder, I picked my way through the fresh bank of snow the plow had left behind and made it out onto the street. Since there was no sidewalk on Creekside Road, I walked along the edge of the snowbank on the street, heading east toward the park where the outdoor rink had been set up for the winter.

I'd made it as far as the driveway leading up the hill to the Spirit Hill Brewery when I heard someone call my name. I paused, seeing Grayson coming down the driveway with his white German shepherd, Bowie, trotting at his side. Bowie broke into a loping run, bounding the rest of the way down the hill to see me. I set my bag on the ground and crouched down to ruffle the dog's gorgeous coat and to receive a warm, sloppy kiss on my cheek in return.

"How are you doing, bud? Do you like the snow?"

"He loves it," Grayson said as he reached us. He grinned as I straightened up and tried to retreat further into the depths of my coat. "More than you, I'm guessing."

"I have mixed feelings," I admitted. "It's beautiful, even kind of magical, but I'm not so keen on the shoveling or the cold."

"I hope you've got lots of layers on then. I hear your team's got the rink booked for practice this morning."

"That's where I'm headed." I picked up my bag, quickly checking to make sure it was zipped up tight. I didn't want Grayson to see the jerseys I'd bought for my teammates. He'd see them eventually, of course, but I could picture the amusement that would show on his face, and I wanted to delay that moment for as long as possible.

"When's your team practicing?" I asked, thinking maybe I

could gather some intel by watching the brewery's team before our game.

"We've been practicing twice a week for the past month. The next time we get on the ice is for tomorrow's game."

My stomach sank. "You've been practicing for a *month*?"

It was only when Grayson laughed that I realized I'd said that out loud. "Don't worry. We won't trounce you too badly."

My eyes narrowed. "Trounce us? What makes you think we'll be so easy to beat?"

"Maybe the fact that you just got your team together. And the fact that at least one of your teammates hasn't played hockey before in her life."

He knew about Cordelia?

"How did you hear about that?" I asked.

Humor lit up his blue eyes. "I have my sources," he said for the second time that week. He stepped out into the road. "Come on, Bowie." To me he added, "Have a good practice."

"I will," I said.

I let out a huff when I caught a glimpse of his infuriating grin before he turned away. I stormed along the road toward the park, hoping desperately that the Inkwell's hockey team wouldn't be as much of a disaster as I suspected it would be.

Despite heading for the rink with time to spare, I wasn't the first to arrive. Mel and Damien were already there and had helped Bobby Dormer, the rink's caretaker, clear the fresh snow off the ice. I was relieved to see that the park was otherwise empty. We didn't need an audience if our practice got off to a rough start.

The rest of the team arrived over the next few minutes, with Joey showing up last. Teagan and Zoe helped me brush the snow off the benches at the edge of the rink so we'd have somewhere to sit and get ready. I had to take more than a cursory look at the twins to figure out who was who. They were identical and I probably wouldn't have been able to tell them apart if not for the fact that Teagan had a broad streak of red through her dark blond hair and several more piercings in her ears than her sister did. Fortunately, her red streak wasn't completely hidden by her hat.

It took some time for me and Cordelia to get into all our gear, unused to it all as we were. Eventually, however, we had our shoulder pads, elbow pads, shin guards, hockey pants, socks, and skates on. The two of us were still seated on the bench when Damien skated over our way.

"Figure skates?" he said skeptically when he looked at my feet. He was already on the ice.

"There's no rule against wearing figure skates." I realized I didn't actually know if that was the case. "Is there?"

Damien shrugged and looked to Mel as she joined him on the ice.

"I don't think so," she said.

"I thought you said you'd played some recreational hockey." Damien sounded like he was regretting the whole idea of entering the tournament.

"A few games of *street* hockey over the years," I confessed.

Damien rolled his eyes heavenward.

"Don't worry," Mel told him. "She can skate."

His expression implied that he wasn't quite sure if he should believe that. "How about the jerseys?" he asked.

"Right," I said with reluctance. "The jerseys." I tried not to cringe as I pulled the first one out of my bag.

Everyone stared at the mustard yellow, maroon-trimmed sweater when I held it up. I didn't think it was overly dramatic to describe the silence that fell around us as horrified.

Joey was the first to speak. "You're kidding, right?"

"Unfortunately, no." I pulled another one out of the bag and checked the size. I tossed it at Joey. "Last-minute team means last-minute uniforms."

He made no move to put it on. "I don't think you could've found uglier ones if you'd tried."

"They aren't *that* bad," Cordelia said, sounding as if she was trying desperately to convince herself of the truth of her words.

Mel coughed into her hand. I strongly suspected she was covering up a laugh.

The twins weren't so successful. They were practically shaking with silent laughter.

"The colors don't matter," Damien said. "It's how we play as a team."

"Exactly," I agreed.

"We'll be the laughingstock of the whole tournament," Joey said.

I tossed two more sweaters at the still-laughing twins.

"Not if we win, we won't."

If I'd truly held some small spark of hope that we could win the hockey tournament, it got doused with icy cold water in the first few minutes of our practice.

Damien, Mel, and Joey zoomed around the ice with confidence, handling their sticks and the puck with ease. The twins could skate reasonably well—forward at least—but I knew anyone with any formal skating or hockey training would be able to outpace them easily. As for Cordelia . . .

She hadn't lied when she'd said she could skate, because she could. Just . . . not very well. And we soon found out that she didn't know how to stop.

"What do I do? What do I do?" she yelled frantically as she sailed toward a snowbank at the edge of the rink.

I opened my mouth to call out instructions to her, but it was too late. She plowed face-first into the snowbank.

I wasn't used to skating with protective gear on me, but that didn't slow me down. I was at her side in seconds. I grabbed one of her elbows while Damien took the other and we hauled her back to her feet.

"Are you okay?" I brushed snow off the cage protecting her face.

"I'm fine!" she said, as chipper as ever. "Sorry about that."

When she was steady on her feet, we released our hold on her, but Damien shot me a look over her helmeted head. It clearly said, "What have you got us into?"

"Maybe you'd be more comfortable in goal," I suggested to Cordelia.

"You mean have pucks shot at me?" She sounded terrified by the prospect.

She wobbled and her feet shot out from under her. She would have fallen if Damien and I hadn't caught her.

"I don't think that's such a good idea," Damien said, once we'd set her on her feet again. "A goalie needs to be able to move from side to side and up and down easily."

Cordelia nodded vigorously. "I'd be a terrible goalie."

The whole team had gathered around and she looked at all of us, her face falling. "I'm sorry, guys. I know I'm not a great skater, but I really wanted to play on the team. Maybe you should find somebody else."

"No way," I said firmly, hating the dejection on her face. "We'll manage. I don't have any real hockey experience either."

"But you skate like you've been doing it all your life," she pointed out.

"That's because I have."

"She was a competitive figure skater," Mel said.

"That's so cool," the twins piped up in unison.

Zoe removed her helmet. "Can you show us some—"

"Jumps and spins?" Teagan finished.

I glanced down. "Maybe not in this gear."

"We're here to play hockey, not put on an Ice Capades show," Joey said.

I punched him lightly in the arm. "We'll play hockey."

"Then let's get to it," Damien said. Before getting on the ice, we'd appointed him team captain. "Who wants to be in goal?"

Teagan's hand shot up. "Can I give it a try? I was always the goalie when we played shinny growing up."

Damien nodded. "We'll see how you do. Sadie, you're on defense."

"Oh." I'd hoped my few turns around the rink before Cordelia's fall would have shown him that I wasn't going to be entirely useless.

"It's because you're the best skater out of all of us," he explained. "A good D-man—"

"Or woman," Mel cut in.

Damien didn't let that trip him up. "Needs to be able to skate well backward. Plus, if the other team tries for a breakaway, you'll be able to beat most players down to our end."

I perked up, glad he appreciated my abilities.

"Joey, you're on D with Sadie. Zoe and Mel, you're forwards." When his gaze fell on Cordelia next, he hesitated.

"How about you only put me on when someone else is really, really tired?" she suggested.

Damien nodded, rather grimly I thought. "I'll play whatever position is needed."

I spent some time with Cordelia, teaching her how to stop, while everyone got warmed up. Then Damien ran us through some drills.

Things went well for the next few minutes. Cordelia stayed on her feet and I started to get more comfortable in my hockey gear. A short while later, however, I was dodging around orange pylons, trying to keep control of the puck on my stick, when Cordelia came barreling in my direction, her arms windmilling as her stick clattered to the ice.

"Sadie! I'm sorry!"

I hopped out of the way, just in time, and she went zooming past me.

Zoe wasn't so lucky.

Cordelia crashed into her and they fell to the ice in a heap.

"I'm so sorry, Zoe!" Cordelia said as I helped her up. "I panicked and forgot everything Sadie taught me."

With Cordelia back on her feet, I offered a hand down to Zoe. She grimaced and reached for her ankle instead.

"What's wrong? Are you hurt?" I asked as everyone gathered around.

"My ankle," Zoe said.

"I broke your ankle?" Cordelia practically wailed.

"No, no," Zoe rushed to assure her. "I'm pretty sure it's just twisted."

Damien and Joey lifted her up off the ice. She stood on her right foot and tried to put weight on her left. She winced, but bravely tried to skate.

Teagan had to grab her arm to stop her from falling. "Sorry, twin. You're sidelined."

"Maybe it'll be better by tomorrow," Zoe said, the hope behind her words sounding incredibly fragile.

Her sister raised an eyebrow at her.

Zoe's shoulders sagged. "I'm sorry, guys. You'll be short a player now."

"It's all my fault," Cordelia said. "I'm so sorry I hurt you, Zoe!"

"Don't worry about it," Zoe told her kindly. "There's always some risk to playing sports."

Cordelia still had guilt written all across her face, but she didn't say anything more.

Teagan and Mel helped Zoe off the ice and got her settled on one of the benches.

"Maybe we should take you to a doctor," Mel said.

Zoe waved off her concern. "I'll be fine. It's nothing serious. You guys keep practicing."

"Is there any point?" Joey asked quietly as I joined the guys in the middle of the rink. "With Zoe out and Cordelia being . . . well, *Cordelia*, we don't have enough players."

Damien's gaze zeroed in on something at one end of the rink. I followed his line of sight and saw Bobby standing behind one of the benches, his back to us as he talked on his cell phone.

"Does Bobby play?" I asked.

"He's not a great skater," Damien said, "but he's been in goal for a few recreational games."

"Is he on anyone else's team?" Joey asked.

"Not that I know of," Damien replied.

I skated down to the end of the rink. Bobby was still on the phone, so I waited patiently. I wasn't trying to eavesdrop, but my ears perked up when I heard what he was saying.

"I did as you asked, and I'm pretty sure the cops believed me when I told them I was with you. . . . Yes, I said you were home with a headache and I was keeping you company."

He paused, listening to the person on the other end, while I barely breathed.

"I was home alone all evening," he said after a moment, "so nobody can say I wasn't with you. Everything will be okay, Pen. I promise." He lowered his voice to say something I couldn't hear. Then he ended the call.

"Bobby."

He nearly jumped out of his skin at the sound of my voice. "Oh, hey, Sadie," he said when he'd turned around. He shoved his phone into his coat pocket.

Damien skated up behind me. "We've got a situation," he said to Bobby.

He explained what had happened to Zoe. Fortunately, Bobby agreed right away to join our team. It didn't take long to decide that he would take Teagan's place in goal. His size alone would be an asset when it came to keeping pucks out of the net.

I didn't have a jersey big enough to fit him, but we decided it wouldn't matter that much since he'd be in goal. I sensed that everyone was a bit envious of him for not having to wear mustard yellow. Heck, I was a tad envious myself. I figured we'd all survive, though.

Another team had arrived at the rink, ready for their practice, so we got off the ice to make way for them. Mel gave Zoe and Teagan a ride home in her truck and the rest of us left on foot. I walked with Joey, my skate bag over my shoulder.

"We'll be out of the tournament after the first game," he said as we crossed the park.

"Don't talk like that," I admonished, even though I suspected he might be right. "We need to stay positive."

"I might be more positive if I remember to have a stiff drink before tomorrow's game."

"No way," I said. "We need you completely sober."

"Then I'll have the stiff drink *after* the game, when I need to forget."

I might end up tempted to join him, but I didn't say so. I was trying to stick with a positive attitude.

"So," I said, changing the subject, "do you know anything new about the murder investigation?"

"Not really." He adjusted the strap of his hockey bag on his shoulder. "The police are being tight-lipped, which isn't surprising."

"Did you get the information Grayson wanted?"

"Grayson?" Joey echoed, confused.

"He wanted you to find out about something. The two of you were talking about it at the Inkwell the other night."

Understanding showed on Joey's face. "He wanted to know Mel's connection to Freddy's assistant."

Of course he did, because he seemed to think Mel was guilty. That stirred up a storm of emotions inside me.

"And, yep, I know they used to date," Joey continued. "I'm guessing you already knew that."

"I did, but Mel's my friend. I wasn't going to blab about her past."

"Unfortunately for me."

"You still figured it out," I reminded him.

He grinned. "I always do."

We parted ways at the corner of Creekside Road and Sycamore Street.

Once I was on my own, I couldn't think of anything other than Bobby's phone call.

I was certain he'd been talking to Penny Blaine. I was also sure that Penny had asked Bobby to lie for her, to bolster her alibi.

Her *false* alibi.

Did that mean she was guilty or just scared the police would think she was?

I was determined to find out one way or another.

Chapter 15

The Inkwell was more crowded than usual for a Sunday afternoon, thanks to all the tourists in town for the Winter Carnival. I was so busy serving customers and chatting about the pub and the inspiration behind the themed cocktails that I didn't have a chance to think about my suspect list or how I would eliminate any names from it. In the midafternoon, however, that problem rushed out from the shadows at the back of my mind and into a bright spotlight.

I was on my way back to the bar after serving a couple near one of the south-facing windows when I spotted Mel out by Creekside Road. She was on her break, and I'd assumed she was in the back room, but clearly that wasn't the case. And she wasn't alone. Daylight was seeping out of the gray sky, but I could still see well enough to recognize the woman she was speaking with.

Jade Castellano.

I glanced around to make sure no one was watching me. All of the customers seemed absorbed in their conversations or focused on their food and drinks, so I stepped closer to the window. Mel said something to Jade, and the other woman shook her head. A white car was parked illegally by the curb. Jade circled around the vehicle and opened the driver's door. She paused then and said a few words to Mel over the roof of the car before climbing inside and shutting the door.

As Jade drove away, Mel struck off through the snow toward the footbridge. I quickly tore myself away from the window and returned to the bar. I figured it would probably be best to pretend I hadn't seen anything. Mel most likely wouldn't want to know I'd been snooping, and whatever had passed between her and Jade was none of my business.

Knowing that didn't stifle my curiosity, though. Not even a little bit.

After Mel returned from her break, I kept catching myself on the verge of asking about her conversation with Jade. Each time, I bit my lip and forced myself to focus on mixing a cocktail or delivering a meal to a waiting customer. The fourth time I ended up in a wrestling match with my curiosity, I accidentally let a pint glass overflow as I was filling it with India pale ale.

"Oh, good Gandalf! Look what I've done!" I shook droplets of beer off my fingers and hurried over to the sink to wash my hands.

"Just ask," Mel said as she passed behind me.

I dried my hands with a towel. "Ask what?"

She slid a glass of whiskey across the bar to a man who handed her some bills in exchange. "You keep shooting glances my way," she said to me as she opened the cash register. "And you look like you're about to burst if you don't say something." She tucked the bills inside the register and closed it. "I'm guessing you saw me outside with Jade."

"I didn't want to pry," I said. "I'm sorry. I guess Grayson's right. I really am a nosey Parker." I couldn't help glancing around to make sure Grayson hadn't suddenly materialized to overhear me admitting that.

"Don't worry about it, Sadie," Mel said. "I don't have any secrets. Go ahead and ask whatever you want to ask."

I grabbed a clean pint glass and filled it more carefully than the last one. "It looked like Jade was leaving town," I said quietly, so no one else would overhear.

Mel took the freshly poured beer from me and set it on a tray along with three other pints. "She is."

We had to pause our conversation momentarily to attend to our customers. While Mel delivered the beers to a table occupied by four young men, I popped into the kitchen to pick up burgers and nachos. I delivered the food to a table in the corner and then collected some dirty dishes from another table on my way back to the bar.

"Do the police know she's leaving?" I asked once I'd deposited the dishes in the kitchen.

Mel was in the midst of mixing up two Evil Stepmother cocktails. "They know, and they don't care. She's no longer a suspect."

"What? Really? Why not?" The questions tumbled out of me in a rush.

Mel smiled for a split second as she added ginger ale to the two glasses. "She was on FaceTime with a friend in Boston when Freddy was killed. It took a while for the cops to check that out and confirm it, but now that they have, they know she didn't kill Freddy."

"But then why do they think she lied about you being with her? To help you out?"

Mel gave a grim nod. "They think she still has feelings for me and was trying to keep me out of trouble."

"Does she still have feelings for you?" I gave myself a mental kick. "That *really* isn't any of my business."

Mel's smile almost returned. "I think she might, but it doesn't matter. We're not getting back together."

"It sounds like it matters to the police."

She finished mixing the drinks before saying, "I guess it does."

I tried not to show my impatience as I waited for her to deliver the cocktails to two women sitting at the far end of the bar.

"So Jade's in the clear and you're still in trouble?" I said when she returned.

"That's about right." She appeared far calmer than I felt.

"But you haven't been arrested." I latched on to that fact. "That's a good sign."

"No one's been arrested yet," Mel pointed out. "I think they're waiting on some forensic evidence."

"Which won't point to you, since you're not the killer."

"My fingerprints will be on the murder weapon."

"Of course they will, but that doesn't prove anything. You never tried to hide the fact that it was your ice pick. Maybe someone else's prints will be on it too."

"It was cold out that night," Mel reminded me. "There's a good chance the killer was wearing gloves."

Defeat settled its heavy weight across my shoulders. I did my best to shake it off, but Mel's next statement thwarted my efforts.

"If the forensic evidence doesn't point at anyone else, I won't be surprised if I get questioned again."

"You should get in touch with a lawyer." I hated saying that. "Just in case."

"I already have."

"I was hoping I could clear your name." I couldn't keep the disappointment out of my voice. I really thought I could do more for her.

"I appreciate that you want to, Sadie, but it's not your job."

Maybe not. But if I didn't do it, who would?

The first thing I was aware of the next morning was the fact that I was nervous. It took a few seconds for me to remember why.

It was the day of the Inkwell's first hockey game.

And most likely our last.

No, no. Think positive, I told myself as I forced myself out of bed.

But when I met my gaze in the bathroom mirror, my hair messy and my eyes bleary with sleepiness, there was no escaping the truth: I knew we had very little chance of winning.

Although he hadn't come right out and said it, Damien believed that too.

"Cordelia's a menace on the ice," he'd said when he turned up for his shift the night before.

I'd cringed, not liking that he described my friend that way, but also unable to deny it.

"We'll just have to hope she's more of a menace to the other team than to us," I'd responded.

"We're playing for the fun of it, and for community involvement," I told my reflection, trying my best to sound convincing.

Maybe I could have believed that if we weren't playing the brewery's team. I'd always had a competitive streak, and it had served me well when I was a figure skater, but for some reason, Grayson Blake brought out that streak more than anyone or anything else. He thought it would be easy to beat the Inkwell's team. Remembering that got me fired up.

"If we're going down, we're going down fighting."

Heartened by the determination I saw in my eyes, I got ready to take on the day, no matter what hockey humiliations it might hold.

After getting dressed, I sent a text message to Teagan, asking how Zoe was doing. She responded a few minutes later. Zoe's ankle had swollen up, so Teagan had taken her to the medical clinic after our hockey practice. She'd been diagnosed with a sprain, but she was in good spirits and taking it easy for a few days. I asked Teagan to convey my well wishes to her sister and then set my phone aside so I could braid my hair.

I didn't feel like partaking of any of my usual breakfast foods and I had time to spare, so I decided to treat myself to something from the Village Bean. When I arrived at the coffee shop, it was nearly full of customers chatting over hot drinks and muffins or Danishes. The Winter Carnival was likely responsible for the booming business. That and the fact that it was Monday morning, a time when many people were desperate for caffeine. I had to wait in line behind two other customers, but it didn't take long for Nettie Jo and her assistant, Ruthie, to fill their orders.

"We had another great meeting the other night," Nettie Jo said to me when I reached the counter. "I'm so glad I joined the book club."

"I'm glad you did too," I said with a smile. "It's great to hear you're enjoying the meetings."

"We all are," she assured me.

I put in my order for a mocha latte and a white-chocolate cranberry scone.

"Did you hear about the dirt someone dished on Freddy Mancini?" Nettie Jo asked as she dug out my change from the cash register.

My curiosity perked up. "No. What dirt?"

She handed me some coins. "Some reporter from Boston wrote an article about Freddy, basically saying he was an arrogant jerk who was willing to step on anyone to be successful."

"So the reporter wrote the truth?"

A smile flickered on Nettie Jo's face as she snagged a scone with a set of tongs and put it on a plate. "Well, sure, but the article also made some accusations."

"What sort of accusations?"

With a smile Ruthie set my mocha latte on the counter and then disappeared into the back.

Nettie Jo continued once she was gone. "Whomever the reporter got his information from said Freddy treated his employees like servants, even harassed some of them. And the article suggests that Freddy got the money to set up his restaurant from the mob."

I took the plate Nettie Jo handed me. "The mob? Really?"

She shrugged. "That's what the article implies. Who knows if it's all true?"

"At least some of it is," I said. "I didn't have to spend much time around him to know that he wasn't a nice guy."

"I never went near him," Nettie Jo said. "And I'm kind of glad I didn't."

Two women came into the coffee shop and headed for the counter, so I picked up my order and thanked Nettie Jo. I left her serving the new customers and made my way toward the back of the coffee shop. I set my scone and drink on a small table and pulled out one of the two chairs. I'd just settled into it when I glanced at the lone woman at the neighboring table. She had her back to me, but I was pretty sure I recognized her. I leaned to the side to get a glimpse of her profile.

Grabbing my scone and latte, I got up and approached Penny's table. She had a half-finished latte in front of her, but her attention was focused on her phone as she scrolled through a Web site.

"Hi, Penny. Mind if I join you?"

Her gaze jerked up and she froze for a split second before smiling. "Oh, hi, Sadie. Sure."

She shoved her phone into her handbag as I pulled out the chair across from her. I slipped out of my jacket and lay it over the back of an empty chair before sitting down. When I got a closer look at Penny, I noticed that her eyes were rimmed with red. Her cheeks were a bit splotchy too. She didn't have tears in her eyes at the moment, but I was sure she'd been crying recently.

I pretended not to notice. "How are you doing today?"

"I'm all right, thanks." She wrapped her hands around her cup. "I hear your hockey team has a game today."

"In a couple of hours. Do you play?"

"Oh, no. I'm not athletic at all. But I might come and watch."

I tore a piece off my scone. "I guess you know Bobby is playing on the Inkwell's team. You're friends with him, right?"

Her cheeks went a bit pink. "Yes, we're friends. He told me he was filling in for someone last minute."

"Zoe Trimble. She hurt her ankle at practice."

"That's too bad, but I know Bobby's looking forward to playing."

I took a moment to savor a bite of my scone and a sip of my latte. "Have you and Bobby known each other your whole lives? You both grew up here in Shady Creek, right?"

"Yes. We weren't in the same grade at school, but we've known each other for a long time. He lived down the street from me when we were kids."

She took a long drink of her latte, nearly finishing it. She set down her cup and was about to say something when two women at a nearby table broke out into loud laughter. We glanced their way.

"An arrogant jerk who didn't even know how to do his own laundry," one of the women chortled.

I realized they were both looking at a tablet set on the table. They laughed again and then lowered their voices. I had a pretty good idea of what they were reading.

I took another bite of scone and turned my attention back to Penny. When I saw a tear trailing down her cheek, I quickly chewed and washed the bite down with a swig of my latte.

"Penny, what's wrong?" I asked.

She shook her head and wiped away the tear with the back of her hand. She picked up her cup, but her hand trembled, so she set it back down.

"It's nothing." She rummaged through her handbag until she came up with a crumpled tissue.

"It doesn't look like nothing," I said quietly. "Is it upsetting for you to hear the things people say about Freddy?"

She shook her head, adamant. "No, it's all true, after all. Well, maybe not the part about the mob. I think the reporter made that up. But the rest of it's true."

She scrunched her eyes shut as another tear escaped.

"Then what's wrong?" I asked gently.

She dabbed at the tear with the tissue and glanced around, as if worried she might be overheard.

Then she leaned closer and confessed in a distraught whisper, "I've done something terrible."

Chapter 16

I pushed the remains of my scone aside, my appetite slinking away.

"You killed Freddy?" I asked, my voice barely audible.

Although I'd already suspected she might have been the one to stab Freddy with Mel's ice pick, my voice betrayed how horrified I was to find myself sitting across from someone confessing to murder.

Penny's eyes widened to a startling size. "No!"

She said it so loudly that a few glances skittered our way.

Her cheeks turned bright pink and she stared at the tabletop. When all the gazes we'd drawn had focused elsewhere, she wrapped her hands tightly around her cup and lowered her voice. "Of course I didn't kill him. I could never do such a thing."

"But you said you did something terrible," I reminded her.

"And I did. Just . . . not *that*."

I waited for her to elaborate, but instead she closed her eyes and began crying silently.

I reached across the table and squeezed her arm. "What is it, Penny? If you didn't kill him, then surely whatever you've done can't be too bad."

"It's still pretty awful." She wiped her face with her tissue and drew in a deep, shuddery breath. The tears in her eyes subsided and she seemed to gather control of herself. "I spoke to a reporter about Freddy."

I turned those words over in my mind, connecting some dots. "The reporter who wrote the article everyone's talking about today?"

Penny nodded, staring into her cup. "It was a terrible thing to do. I wish I'd kept quiet, but now it's too late to change things."

"How did you end up talking to the reporter?"

"There were a few of them here from out of town to cover the ice-sculpting competition. Really, to cover Freddy's participation in the competition. He was well known in Boston's foodie circles and he'd won several ice sculpture competitions across the country."

"I remember seeing the reporters on the green," I said. "They did seem to be focused on Freddy, and he looked like he enjoyed the attention."

"He always did like to be in the spotlight." Penny turned her cup in a slow circle. "I went over to say hi to him. We didn't part on the best of terms years ago when we broke up—when he dumped me—but I wanted to know what he'd say when he saw me face to face. I should have let it be, but I couldn't, you know?"

I nodded, staying quiet, not wanting to interrupt her narrative.

"Freddy pretended he didn't know me. I could see in his eyes that he did, of course. But he wanted me to feel like I wasn't even worth remembering. We were together for *seven years* and he wanted me to believe he didn't recognize me." She gulped down the last of her latte and set the cup down hard, her grip on the handle so tight that her knuckles turned white. "I was so stunned at the time that I just turned and walked away. But one of the reporters had overheard. He approached me, saying he wanted to write an article about Freddy. The *real* Freddy. He'd seen the way Freddy had brushed me off and guessed that there was some history between us. By then I was angry, so I agreed to meet the reporter that night, out at the diner by the highway."

"So you weren't at home with a headache that night," I said, even though I'd already known that.

Penny glanced up briefly, sheepish. "I lied about that. By the time I was driving home from the diner, I already regretted telling the reporter all those things about Freddy. Everything I said was true, but I still shouldn't have talked to the man. And then the next morning I found out Freddy had been killed. I felt terrible. What I'd done seemed even worse with him dead. And when the police wanted to question me, I got so scared. So I lied. I thought if the police knew how angry I'd been at Freddy, they'd think I killed him."

"But the police know you lied," I said. "You were seen driving past the green right around the time Freddy was killed."

Penny's shoulders drooped. "I figured that was what happened. I should have known better than to lie. And now I've made it worse."

"How so?"

"The police questioned me again. Mostly about my alibi. They were trying to trip me up, to get me to change my story. I should have come clean, but I stuck with the lie. When they let me go . . ."

She closed her eyes as she fought off a fresh wave of tears.

"You asked Bobby to tell the police that he was with you that evening, to confirm that you were at home."

Penny's eyes flew open and she stared at me with surprise. "How do you know that?"

"I overheard Bobby when he was talking to you on his phone yesterday."

Penny dropped her face into her hands. "I never should have pulled poor Bobby into this mess. He's always so good to me and now I've gone and put him in hot water right along with me."

"It's not too late to set things right," I said.

"I'm pretty sure it is."

"It'll look better if you go to the police rather than having them come to you about your alibi again."

"I know, but . . ." She trailed off and shook her head. Avoiding my gaze, she grabbed her handbag and pushed back her chair. "Thanks for listening, Sadie."

"What are you going to do?" I asked as she rushed to pull on her jacket.

"I'm really not sure."

I didn't have a chance to say good-bye. She hurried out of the coffee shop, still zipping up her jacket, and disappeared from sight.

Penny and Jade had both made things worse for themselves by lying to the police. Jade, at least, was off the official suspect list. Penny was off mine now—I believed she'd told me the truth about everything—but I doubted the police had discounted her as the possible culprit.

I hoped she would talk to Detective Marquez and get everything sorted out, but there had been a lot of fear and uncertainty in her eyes when she'd left the Village Bean. Maybe it would be best if I approached the detective and told her everything Penny had shared with me.

That was probably a good idea, but it would have to wait. I needed to pick up a few groceries and then it would be time to head for the rink.

I hesitated, not sure if I should really wait until later in the day. I decided on a compromise.

As soon as I'd finished my scone and latte, I bundled up and stepped out into the cold. I quickly called Detective Marquez on my cell phone, hoping to arrange a meeting in the late afternoon. She didn't pick up, so I left a brief message and made my way down the street to the grocery store.

The clouds were parting overhead, exposing patches of blue sky. It was good that it wasn't likely to snow during the hockey game, but the icy wind whistling through town seemed to cut through my clothes and seep right down to my bones. Hopefully I'd stay plenty warm during the game, but at the moment every step along the sidewalk was unpleasant.

When I reached the store, I rushed inside as if I'd been waiting my whole life to get groceries. I snagged a basket from the stack by the door and set off down the produce aisle. I didn't have much time, but I wanted to make sure I had some food to eat after the game.

I put a few items in my basket on my way down the aisle to the back of the store, where I perused the selection of dairy products. I was in the midst of deciding between strawberry or blueberry yogurt when I picked up the sound of a familiar voice.

"I hear you didn't have much of a reunion with Freddy," Grayson was saying to someone.

Following the sound of his voice, I tiptoed toward the next aisle and peered down it. Grayson, grocery basket in hand, was talking to Eli Hawkes as he plunked a box of cereal into his cart.

I ducked out of sight before Grayson spotted me, but I hovered at the end of the aisle, listening.

"His success went to his head," Eli said without an ounce of rancor. "But I believe the boy I once knew was still in there somewhere. He would have seen the error of his ways eventually. If he'd had time." His voice almost broke with sadness.

"Not everyone was so understanding," Grayson said.

"Not everyone was as close to Freddy as I was. He was like the son I never had, a brother to my daughter."

"Was Lara close to Freddy?"

"They got along when they were younger. Lara's angry at him now, but that will fade in time. She didn't like the way Freddy talked to me at the chili supper, but underneath her anger she's grieving."

I wasn't so sure about that. I wanted to chance another peek around the corner, but I didn't dare. The last thing I wanted was for Grayson to catch me spying on him.

"Any idea who killed him?" Grayson asked outright.

"None. I hope the police will find whoever did it. And soon. Freddy might have let his success go to his head, but he didn't deserve to die." Again, Eli's voice sounded ready to break under the weight of his sadness.

"I'm sure the police are doing all they can," Grayson said kindly. "Take care of yourself, Mr. Hawkes."

Footsteps headed my way.

I darted into the next aisle and feigned interest in the products on the shelf, hoping I'd been quick enough.

The footsteps halted at the end of the aisle.

"Sadie?"

The hint of suspicion in his voice nudged my heart rate up, but I smiled brightly and hoped I appeared innocent. "Oh, hi, Grayson. Getting some groceries?"

His blue eyes watched me steadily. "Were you eavesdropping?"

"Eavesdropping? I don't know what you mean." I grabbed the closest product off the shelf. "I'm just getting some . . ." I glanced at the bottle in my hand.

Grayson took it from me and read the label. "Baby food?"

He was almost successful at fighting his grin, but not quite, and there was no mistaking the laughter in his eyes.

How did I always get myself into these situations?

I grabbed the bottle away from him and shoved it back on the shelf.

"Are you expecting?" he asked, his eyes still bright with amusement.

Heat rushed to my cheeks as I glared at him. "Do I *look* like I'm expecting?"

A flash of apprehension crossed his face, as if he realized he'd said the wrong thing. But he recovered so quickly I almost thought I'd imagined it.

"Definitely not. It's just that people usually buy baby food for . . . well, babies."

"For your information, I have a friend who . . ." I trailed off.

I had no idea where I was going with that. From the grin on Grayson's face, he knew it too.

"Oh, all right. Yes, I was eavesdropping. And you"—I poked him in the chest—"were investigating."

"I have a vested interest in the case getting solved quickly."

"So the *Craft Nation* execs will change their minds again?" I guessed.

"It's in my brewery's best interests."

"I hope you've got a better suspect than Mel, because she's innocent."

"So you say."

I put my hands on my hips, my grocery basket hitting my leg. "So I *know*." I decided I'd be better off finding out what information he had rather than arguing with him. "Aside from Mr. Hawkes, who else is on your suspect list?"

He didn't respond right away, waiting as a woman with two kids in tow passed by with her heavily loaded grocery cart.

"Penny Blaine, for starters," he said.

"She's innocent too."

"Really?" he said vaguely.

I wasn't sure if he'd actually heard me. He was too busy fishing his phone out of his coat pocket.

He checked the screen and then tucked the device away again. "As much as I'd like to keep chatting, I've got a hockey game to get to. I'll let you finish your shopping." He shot a glance at the shelf of baby food before grinning at me. "See you at the rink."

I wanted so badly to aim a sharp parting remark at his back, but I came up empty. Frustrated, I returned to the dairy products and grabbed a container of strawberry yogurt before heading for the checkout counter. By the time I got there, Grayson was already gone. I paid for my purchases and braved the cold once more.

I'd almost reached the village green when I noticed Penny standing on the sidewalk, speaking with Detective Marquez. A uniformed officer was also there, a marked cruiser parked by the curb.

Penny shook her head and wiped at her cheeks. I was too far away to see any tears on her face, but I knew she was crying.

As I hurried forward, Penny put her hands behind her back and Detective Marquez snapped a pair of handcuffs around her wrists. The detective's colleague led Penny toward the cruiser and opened the back door. Penny hesitated but then climbed inside. The uniformed officer got into the driver's seat and started the engine.

"Detective Marquez!" I called out.

She'd been about to step off the curb in front of her unmarked vehicle, but she stopped and waited for me to approach.

"Have you arrested Penny?" I asked when I reached her, my breath puffing out in a succession of little white clouds.

The cruiser had pulled away from the curb and was heading down the street.

"Yes. We believe she killed Freddy Mancini."

"It's because she lied about her alibi, isn't it?" I didn't wait for confirmation. "I know that looks bad, but she didn't kill Freddy. It's true she wasn't at home like she said she was, but she was on her way to meet a reporter."

"How do you know all this?" Marquez asked.

"I talked to her a little while ago. She told me everything."

"If you had information about the case, you should have contacted me."

I tried not to let the rebuke irritate me. "I left you a voice mail. I've got to get to a hockey game, but I was going to go to the station later today."

Marquez stepped off the curb, her expression unreadable. "Is there anything else you have to tell me?"

"Just that Penny got Bobby Dormer to lie for her, but I'm guessing you already figured that out. Despite her lies, I truly believe Penny's innocent."

Marquez opened the driver's door of her car and regarded me over the roof. "I'm afraid I need evidence, not opinions." Her expression softened slightly, as if she wanted to lessen the sting of that statement. "If Ms. Blaine is innocent, that will come out in the end." She climbed into the vehicle and shut the door.

Hoping she was right, I stood and watched as the detective drove away.

Chapter 17

Despite the chill of the wind biting at my face, I loved the familiar feel of zooming around the rink. I didn't have the same freedom as when I skated without all the hockey gear, but I still enjoyed being on the ice. I missed skating. I hadn't done enough of it since I'd given up competing in my late teens.

As I skated around, warming up, I scanned the small audience huddled on the benches that had been brushed free of snow. I spotted Shontelle sitting bundled up in her winter coat and scarf, a takeout cup from the Village Bean in hand. I waved at her, my excitement growing.

After my most recent encounter with Grayson, I was more determined than ever to play hard and give the brewery's team a run for their money. I was always embarrassing myself in front of him. It was time to turn things around.

My teammates and I had all donned our ugly jerseys. While I'd noticed a few raised eyebrows, no one had made any comments about our uniforms. Not that I'd heard, anyway. To their credit, my teammates hadn't raised any more complaints about the jerseys. Not even Joey.

Cordelia had yet to step on the ice. I figured she might need some encouragement after her collision with Zoe the day before, so I skated toward the bench at the side of the rink where she was sitting.

Before I could get there, Joey breezed up beside me.

"Hey, Sadie, have you ever been snowmobiling?"

The question took me by surprise. "No, I haven't. Why?"

"I bought a snowmobile a couple weeks ago. I could take you out on it sometime."

I stopped at the edge of the rink. I hadn't expected the invitation and I wasn't quite sure what to say.

Damien skated over to join us. "Ready to get down to business?"

"Definitely," I said.

He held out a hand to Cordelia. "Let's get you on the ice so you can warm up."

Cordelia didn't look too certain, but she took Damien's offered hand.

As they skated off together, I noticed Grayson standing a few feet away with his teammates, shooting glances my way. Or was it Joey he was looking at?

I wasn't sure and his expression wasn't giving me any clues.

I shrugged it off as the referee blew his whistle to get our attention. I hadn't answered Joey's question yet, but he no longer seemed to be expecting a response.

Donning my helmet, I fastened its strap.

It was time for the game to begin.

The first period didn't go as well as I would have liked.

I had high hopes in the beginning. Within the first few minutes of play, I got a breakaway and powered my way down the sheet of ice. I managed to keep control of the puck, but my shot was weak and easily deflected by Dennis, the goalie for the brewery's team. I had another chance to shoot at the net when

Mel sent a nice pass my way, but again my shot didn't have much oomph behind it and Dennis barely had to work to stop it with his goalie pads.

Down at the other end of the rink, Bobby managed to stop several shots from Grayson and his teammates, but the puck got by him twice, leaving the Inkwell's team down two-nothing by the time the first five-minute intermission rolled around. I shook off my frustration. We still had plenty of time to make a comeback.

"I wish I could do more," Cordelia said morosely as I sat down on the bench beside her.

"You did just fine," I told her before gulping down some water.

She'd only played two short shifts, but she'd managed not to crash into anyone.

She eyed the other team as they huddled around the bench next to ours. "I'm really glad there's no body-checking in this tournament."

"You and me both," I said.

One hit from Jason and my skeleton probably wouldn't stop rattling for a week.

I took another big drink of water before refastening my helmet. Damien tried to give me a few pointers on how to improve my shot, but the whistle blew, cutting his teaching session short.

When the second period got underway, things seemed more promising, for a short time, anyway. Damien, Mel, and Joey took the first shift and ended up with a great scoring chance. Unfortunately, they were defeated by Dennis.

After that, the brewery's team took control of the play and scored a third goal. It felt like the game was slipping away from us, but I wasn't about to give up and admit defeat.

I went out on the ice for my first shift of the second period with a renewed determination to score a goal. Teagan passed me the puck and I charged out of our zone. Grayson was defending his end, skating backward as I barreled toward him. When I darted to the right to get around him, he slipped and took half a second to regain his balance. By then I was past him. But once more, my shot wasn't good enough to get the best of the brewery's goalie.

I let out a growl of frustration as the whistle blew and Dennis tossed the puck to the referee. It wasn't my failure to score that had me aggravated, though.

I skated up to Grayson before he could get off the ice.

"What was that?" I demanded.

"It looked like a good scoring chance to me," he said.

"I'm talking about what you did *before* I had a chance to shoot."

"What did I do?" he asked.

I wasn't buying his innocent act. "You let me get right past you."

"You outskated me," he said. "That's all there was to it."

I poked him in the chest with the bulky fingers of my hockey glove. "You didn't really lose your balance."

"Guys!" Mel called from the face-off dot where everyone was waiting for us. "Come on."

I glared at Grayson, waiting.

He relented beneath my fierce gaze. "Your team's down three-nothing. I thought I'd be nice and give you a chance to score."

I was tempted to pull his jersey up over his head. "I don't want you to be nice!" I fumed. "If I get a goal, or even a chance to get one, I want to get it fair and square. Not because you let me."

He raised his hands in surrender. "Fair enough. From now on I won't pull any punches."

"Good," I said before skating back down the rink to get ready for the face-off.

A couple of shifts later, things started looking up for the

Inkwell team. Damien scored a beautiful goal and Mel scored another one barely two minutes later. For the first time in the game, our entire team was smiling.

"We're only down by one now," Cordelia said, far cheerier than she'd been earlier. "You can do this, guys!"

I nudged her in the arm as I sat next to her on the bench. "*We* can. We're all part of the team."

The next time I got on the ice, I didn't get any shots on goal, but I managed to prevent the brewery's team from testing our goalie a couple of times. As the second period was drawing to a close, I skated backward into the Inkwell's zone, Grayson charging toward me with the puck on his stick. I thought he was going to shoot at the net, but at the last second he passed the puck back to Jason, who circled around behind the goal.

By then, Mel had joined me down in our zone. I stood in front of the net, trying to block the shooting lane without getting in Bobby's way. Max—the other brewery player on the ice—joined his teammates and they passed the puck around, waiting for a good chance to shoot it at the goal.

When Grayson sent the puck Jason's way, I reached out with my stick and managed to intercept it. I grinned with triumph, ready to power down to the other end.

Before I'd gone two strides, I heard Cordelia yelp and then a semi smashed into me.

At least, that's what I thought had happened as I lay on my back, dazed and unable to draw air into my lungs.

I gasped, on the verge of panicking.

I closed my eyes, aware of nothing but pain and my inability to breathe.

"Take some deep breaths, Sadie."

I opened my eyes to find Grayson on his knees beside me.

"Relax. You'll be fine. Deep breaths."

I tried to do as he instructed. After what felt like forever, my lungs started working properly again. I drew in some much needed oxygen and then exhaled, focusing on nothing other than repeating that sequence over and over.

Damien was now kneeling on my other side, and I could see Mel and the rest of the players gathered around.

"You had the wind knocked out of you," Grayson said. "Does anything hurt?"

The pain in my back and chest had subsided, so I tried to sit up. Both Grayson and Damien put a hand on my shoulder to keep me down.

"I'm okay," I said. "Nothing hurts . . . too much."

"Maybe we should call the medical guys over here," Grayson said.

"Please don't," I said quickly, not wanting any fuss. "I'm okay. Really."

This time when I tried to sit up, they helped me. With Grayson holding one arm and Damien the other, I got to my feet. They skated with me over to the bench, still keeping hold of my arms. I probably could have made it on my own, but I wasn't feeling quite myself, so I appreciated having them there just in case.

Once I was safely seated on the bench, I took off my helmet.

Cordelia shifted down the bench toward me. "Are you okay, Sadie? I'm so sorry!"

"Why? What happened?" Now that I was upright, I could see that there definitely weren't any semis on the ice.

"I couldn't stop. I crashed into Jason and he crashed into you."

Jason. No wonder I felt like I'd been flattened by a Mack truck.

I patted Cordelia's arm, but then halted the movement as I winced with pain. "Don't worry about it. I'm fine."

Grayson was still hovering nearby, along with my teammates.

"You should probably call it a day," he said.

"No way," I protested. "There's still a third of the game to go."

"And you just got over a concussion a few weeks ago."

"I didn't hit my head this time." At least, I didn't think I had. It felt fine. It was my back and ribs that were unhappy.

"He's right, Sadie," Mel spoke up. "You took a hard hit. Better safe than sorry."

I wanted to argue further, but my aches and pains kept me quiet. I probably wouldn't have been of much use out there anyway.

Jason made his way through the small crowd gathered around me. "I'm really sorry about that, Sadie. If I could have avoided hitting you, I would have."

"I know. Don't worry. Either of you," I said, looking between Cordelia and Jason. "I'm okay."

Next to hurry over to check on me was Shontelle. I told her I was okay as well. She offered to drive me home, but I wanted to stay and watch the rest of the game. Finally, everyone seemed reassured that I wasn't seriously hurt and the game got back underway.

As I watched the start of the third and final period, I became aware of people chatting on a bench a few feet behind me. My attention shifted from the game to the spectators' conversation.

"I thought Penny was coming to watch," a woman said.

"She was planning to." I recognized Sibyl Hawkes's voice. "Something must have come up."

Clearly they hadn't heard about Penny's arrest.

"I brought her the merino-alpaca blend she wanted to buy off me."

"Oh, that's gorgeous," Sibyl said. I tried to glance over my shoulder, but my back muscles shouted at me to stop. "What's she planning to make with it?"

"Some gloves for Bobby."

"I thought she already made gloves for Bobby."

"She did, but that man is always losing things."

"You spun that yarn yourself, right?" Sibyl asked.

"I did."

"Do you have more? I'd love to make Eli some gloves out of that."

"Sure. I'll bring a couple of skeins by the shop later this week."

"Speaking of Eli," Sybil said, "I need to get home. He's been feeling down since Freddy got killed, so I'm making him his favorite dinner tonight—shepherd's pie with rice pudding for dessert. It might not be much, but I'm hoping it'll cheer him up a little bit."

"I really envy you and Eli. You'd do anything for each other, wouldn't you?"

"We would." I could hear the smile in Sibyl's voice.

"The only thing my one-time husband did for me was give me my beautiful daughter," Sibyl's companion went on. "Then he took off for Tallahassee with some floozy."

I stopped listening to the women and refocused on the game as Jason shot the puck at the Inkwell's net. Fortunately, Bobby blocked it.

That was the only highlight for our team during the last part of the game.

Cordelia didn't want to get back on the ice—she was convinced she'd end up killing someone—and with me sidelined that meant that Damien, Mel, Teagan, and Joey were the only players left, aside from Bobby in goal. They hardly got any chance to rest during the third period, and the brewery's team easily outplayed them, scoring another two goals to win the game five-two.

With my back stiffening up, it wasn't easy to get all my gear off. Mel helped me with my skates and I managed the rest, slowly. Jason came over to apologize again, and I assured him he didn't need to feel bad.

Damien was taking all the borrowed gear back home, so all I had to carry was my skate bag. Still, I accepted gladly when Mel offered me a ride home in her truck. Shontelle had already left to get back to her store.

Once I was in my cozy apartment with Wimsey, I went straight to the bathroom, never before so grateful for the deep clawfoot tub. A nice long soak in hot water was what my back needed. If I was lucky, maybe it would relax my mind as well as my muscles and bring some clarity to the mystery of who had killed Freddy Mancini.

Chapter 18

I took it easy for the rest of the day. I really didn't feel bad, thanks to my long, hot bath and a couple of ibuprofen, and I figured I'd be fully recovered by the time of the snowshoe race later in the week. Nevertheless, I wasn't about to pass up an excuse to spend an entire afternoon reading. That was something I rarely had the chance to do anymore, since the Inkwell kept me busy most days of the week. I'd recently started a book by an author I loved, Louise Penny, and I was looking forward to getting back to the story. I lounged on the couch with Wimsey, immersed in the fictional town of Three Pines, while a toasty fire crackled in the wood stove to keep me warm.

By early evening, however, I'd finished the book. I couldn't start another one right away, not when I had a book hangover from the one I'd just read, so when I received a text message from Shontelle, asking if I planned to go to the bonfire that night, I decided I would.

The bonfire was part of the Winter Carnival. There was one every night for the duration of the festivities, at the same park where the outdoor rink was located. I hadn't attended one yet, but I'd been hoping to do so. I made sure to bundle up in several layers, knowing it would be even colder out now that the sun had set.

When I stepped outside, I almost changed my mind and went back indoors. The wind had died down since I was last out, but the temperature had plummeted. I hesitated on the footpath, but then pressed onward. There would be hot chocolate and apple cider at the bonfire, and that knowledge gave me the motivation I needed to keep going.

Plenty of people had arrived at the park ahead of me. I estimated that there were two dozen adults milling about with several children running around, chasing each other and playing in the snow. I traced a circle around the fire, searching for Shontelle. The leaping orange flames highlighted people's faces, but my friend's wasn't among them.

I found myself a spot to stand close enough to the fire to feel its warmth, and checked my phone. Shontelle had sent me a second message, apologizing and saying she wasn't coming after all. Kiandra had fallen fast asleep on the couch and Shontelle didn't want to wake her.

I sent her a quick note in reply, and then checked my other messages.

My younger brother, Taylor, had sent me a video of a lion at a zoo, casually walking along and accidentally falling into a pool of water, startling himself and his companion.

It's a reenactment of the time you fell into the river at Volunteer Landing! his accompanying message read.

Very funny, I wrote in reply, following it up with an emoji with its tongue sticking out.

Where are you off to this year? I asked in another message.

Costa Rica, he wrote back. **Surfing holiday!**

Awesome! was my response, even though a heavy weight had settled in my chest.

It was a reminder that I'd be alone for the holidays.

My sinking spirits brought to mind my missing books. They hadn't reappeared, not that I'd really expected them to.

I stuffed my phone deep into my pocket and sat on one of the rough-hewn benches set around the fire. I stared into the flames, watching them dance and flicker. They mesmerized me, and slowly the rest of the world seemed to fade away. I'd almost forgotten where I was when someone sat down next to me, breaking the spell.

"Hot chocolate?" Grayson offered me one of the two cups he held.

I accepted it without hesitation. "Thank you." I felt the warmth of the cup through my gloves and it helped to chase away some of the chill of the night air.

"Are you disappointed about the game?" he asked.

"The game? No. Why would you think that?"

"You look a bit . . . melancholy. Or is it your injuries?"

The dancing flames were reflected in his eyes. I had to avert my gaze from his before I became entranced.

"I'm not really injured," I said. "Just a few sore muscles." I took a sip of hot chocolate, savoring the flavor and the warmth. "The game was fun. Up to a point, anyway." I softened my last words with a hint of a smile.

"Having been body-checked by Jason several times in my life, I know it's like getting hit by a truck."

"That's what I thought had happened at first." I shook my head. "Poor Cordelia. I don't think we'll ever get her back out on the ice."

"That might be for the best," Grayson said with a grin.

I elbowed him in the ribs, almost causing him to spill his hot chocolate. "She didn't *mean* any harm."

"I know," he said, recovering quickly. "But if she does get back on the ice, maybe she should have a few skating lessons before trying to play another hockey game."

"That would be a good idea," I agreed.

I stared into the fire again, wrestling with my low spirits, trying to raise them, but without success.

"So if it's not the game or injuries that have you feeling down, what is it?"

I glanced his way, about to deny that I was anything but happy. The genuine concern in his eyes threw me off. I hesitated, but then I answered truthfully.

"Christmas. And stolen books."

"You don't like Christmas?"

"I love it. But this year I don't have anyone to spend it with. Aunt Gilda goes to Savannah for the holidays each year, my mom's going to celebrate with my older brother and his wife in Knoxville, and my younger brother will be in Costa Rica. I could visit my older brother along with my mom, but I don't want to close the Inkwell for more than a day."

"What about Shontelle? The two of you are close, aren't you?"

"Yes. And I know she'd invite me over if I told her I'd be on my own, but she's got her mom and Kiandra, and one of her aunts is coming to visit. I don't want to intrude." I forced a smile. "I'll be okay, though. I'll just have a quiet holiday. Maybe I'll make some headway through my teetering to-be-read pile."

Grayson was the one staring into the fire now.

I realized I didn't know anything about his family. "What about you? What do you do for the holidays?"

"Some years I spend a couple of days in Syracuse with Jason and his folks, but this year I thought I'd stay in Shady Creek. It'll be a quiet holiday for me too."

"You don't have any family to celebrate with?"

"I don't have any family left, aside from a few cousins I hardly know. I was raised by my mom and grandmother, but they've both been gone for years now."

My heart ached with a pang of sympathy. "And here I am complaining. I'm sorry."

"Don't be. Of course you're sad you'll be on your own."

We both fell silent, the conversations going on around us blurring together in the background. I wondered if I should suggest that we spend the holidays together, but I couldn't get the words out. I didn't know him well enough for that, did I? I didn't want to be lonely, and I didn't want him to be either, but what if asking made things awkward between us? He probably wouldn't want to spend Christmas with me, anyway. Would he?

I took a sip of hot chocolate, confusion and indecision making me restless.

"What about the stolen books?" Grayson asked.

With my thoughts about Christmas going in circles in my head, it took me a second to process his question.

"Two books disappeared off one of the shelves in the Inkwell. And not just any books." I explained about the gifts from my dad, the inscriptions he'd written inside each one.

"Maybe someone borrowed them and will bring them back eventually."

"Maybe." I wasn't holding out much hope.

Silence overtook us again. I'd finished my hot chocolate by the time Grayson next spoke.

"So you're going snowmobiling?" he asked.

"You mean with Joey?"

Grayson nodded before downing the last of his hot chocolate.

"I haven't said yes yet."

"Are you going to?"

I studied his face, trying to gauge why he was asking. He kept his eyes on the snapping and crackling flames.

"I don't know. When I go out in nature I like to enjoy the peace and quiet. I'm not sure zooming around on a noisy machine is for me. Don't tell him I said that, though. It was nice of him to ask."

Grayson finally turned his gaze on me. "You know why he asked, right?"

"Yes." I reached for his cup. "Are you done?"

He handed me the cup and I got up and tossed it into the bin set out for that purpose, adding my own along with it.

I'd made a quick getaway, and I doubted that had escaped Grayson's notice. I did know why Joey had invited me snowmobiling. I'd suspected for a few weeks now that he had some feelings for me, but I didn't want to talk about it, especially not with Grayson.

I returned to the bench but didn't sit down. My back muscles were aching again and my toes were numb, despite the warmth from the bonfire.

"I think I might head home now," I said.

Grayson stood up. "I'll walk with you, if that's all right."

"I'd like that."

We skirted around the crowd enjoying the bonfire and left the chatter and laughter behind us. The noise died away until all I could hear was the sound of us crunching through the snow. An icy crust had formed over it and the tiny crystals sparkled in the moonlight.

As we passed by a group of three large evergreens, I noticed a flicker of movement between the trunks. Almost at the same moment, I heard a hushed voice speaking in an urgent tone.

I stopped in my tracks and Grayson halted next to me. Before he had a chance to ask why I'd stopped, I grabbed his arm and pointed toward a shadowy figure.

Leo Mancini had stepped into the light from a nearby streetlamp, his face illuminated briefly before he paced back into the shadows. I wouldn't have paid much attention if I hadn't heard what he was saying into his cell phone as the shadows swallowed him up.

"But if the cops search my place, I'm done for."

I glanced at Grayson and could tell he'd heard Leo's words too. He was listening as intently as I was now.

"We need to . . . tonight . . ." The sound of snow crunching beneath Leo's boots drowned out some of what he was saying.

"Fine," he said after a pause, not sounding the least bit happy. "Tomorrow night. You'd better be there. I've had the cops breathing down my neck lately. Even dead, Freddy hasn't stopped messing up my life."

We didn't hear anything further. Leo stomped off toward the bonfire without ever noticing us. We remained motionless until he was well out of earshot.

I realized I was still holding on to Grayson's arm and quickly released it.

"You know what this means, right?" I said.

"Leo's got something to hide."

"Yes, but not just that."

Even in the dim light from the streetlamp I could see suspicion growing in Grayson's eyes.

"What else?" he asked.

I thought it was obvious. "We don't have much time to find out what it is."

Chapter 19

Grayson easily kept pace at my side as I hurried along the street.

"Why do *we* need to find out what it is?" he asked.

"Who else is going to look into it?"

"The police. It's their job to investigate crime."

"You're not the police. That hasn't stopped you from digging for clues." I waited for a car to pass by before crossing the road. "Besides, the cops arrested Penny for Freddy's murder. They're not looking for his killer anymore."

"So why would Leo be worried about the cops finding evidence at his place that would tie him to the murder? It seems to me he should be relaxed now."

I stopped in my tracks. "Good point." I started walking again, just as Grayson had stopped beside me. "But maybe he thinks the case against Penny will fall apart because he knows she's not guilty. Maybe he thinks her arrest has simply bought him a bit more time."

"Okay, let's say for argument's sake that Leo killed Freddy. What kind of evidence would he be hiding? The murder weapon was found at the scene."

We shared a glance.

"Bloodstained clothes," I said, knowing Grayson was thinking the same thing. I picked up my pace. "But why wouldn't he have washed or burned any bloody clothes by now?"

"He's not the sharpest tool in the shed. But why would he have to wait for someone to help him? It doesn't add up."

"Maybe not," I conceded, "but he's definitely hiding *something*."

We'd reached the corner of Sycamore Street and Creekside Road. I stopped beneath one of the old-fashioned streetlamps and pulled out my phone, wincing as I tugged off one glove so I could use the touch screen.

Grayson peered over my shoulder "What are you doing?"

"Trying to find out where Leo lives."

"I think he's out on Hartley Road somewhere."

I found his name in an online directory. "Got it. You're right. It won't take long to get there."

I struck off along the edge of Creekside Road.

Grayson jogged to catch up with me and took my arm, pulling me to a halt. "Hold on. You're not planning to go out there now, are you?"

"Would you rather I wait until he's home?" I tugged my arm free and got moving again.

Grayson matched my strides easily. "He could show up there anytime. You don't know how long he'll stay at the park. Maybe he's already on his way home."

I hesitated.

Grayson stepped in front of me, blocking my path. "Leo works at the Lockwood Creamery. I think he has an early shift."

I considered that. "So first thing in the morning would be safer."

"Going to the police would be safer."

"What can they do? We overheard a snippet of one side of a

conversation. Is that really enough to get a warrant to search his place?"

"Unlikely."

I slipped past him and continued on down the road.

"Sadie."

I spun around, getting tired of his attempts to dissuade me from investigating.

"I'll pick you up at four-thirty."

"I thought you weren't interested in being my sidekick," I said, remembering a conversation we'd had back in the fall.

A muscle in his jaw twitched. "How about we do this as equal partners?"

I considered the idea. "I can live with that."

"Four-thirty then."

I crossed the road and made my way over the footbridge. When I glanced back at the street before unlocking the Inkwell's front door, I saw Grayson still standing by the snowbank, watching me.

I waved to him and then hurried through the door, locking up behind me.

As much as I wanted to find out right away what Leo was hiding, I knew Grayson's plan was the smart one.

Hopefully by daybreak we'd know Leo's secret.

When my alarm went off at the unearthly hour of four o'clock the next morning, I couldn't help but question my sanity. I wasn't a morning person, but I could handle waking up early on occasion. Maybe not without a lot of yawning and some good strong coffee, but I could do it.

This, however, was pushing it. Even Wimsey was still sound asleep, thoughts of breakfast not yet entering his mind. He cracked open one eye as I threw back the covers and swung my feet over the side of the bed. Then he went right back to snoozing.

I desperately wanted to do the same, especially when my bare feet hit the cold floorboards. With great longing, my gaze drifted back toward my pillow. I almost gave in to the temptation to snuggle back under the covers. The only thing that got me moving off the bed and into the bathroom was my curiosity.

I really, *really* wanted to know what Leo didn't want the police to find.

When I apprehensively ventured out the Inkwell's front door into the darkness and frigid cold, I was relieved to see Grayson's vehicle already by the curb, the engine running. I scurried across the footbridge and climbed into his black sports car as quickly as I could, eager to shut the door on the frosty air.

"Morning," I managed to say before I clapped a hand over my mouth to cover up a big yawn.

Grayson eyed the backpack I was stashing by my feet. "I thought we were going down the road to Leo Mancini's place, not on a vacation to the Caribbean."

I tucked a thermos of coffee into one of the cup holders in the center console. "I figured we'd need snacks and binoculars. I also brought a flashlight and a camera with a much better zoom than my phone. If we're going on a stakeout, we need to do it right." I secured my seat belt with a snap. "Besides, I couldn't go on a Caribbean vacation with one tiny backpack." I nudged the bag with my foot. "There's no way I could fit all my swimsuits, sundresses, flip-flops, and reading material in this little thing."

Grayson put the car into gear and set off along the dark road.

"Not that I'm an overpacker," I said quickly. "Just a . . . sufficient packer."

He flicked his gaze my way but said nothing.

Why had I felt the need to tell him that? It wasn't like we were ever going on vacation together.

I sank deeper into my seat and kept quiet as we drove along. Outside the center of town, there were no streetlights, so the road was shrouded in thick darkness. I couldn't see anything other than what showed up in the beams of the car's headlights. I spotted a mailbox at the side of a driveway, but otherwise it seemed like there were only trees on either side of the road.

The car's headlights illuminated a sharp turn up ahead. I gripped the edge of my seat, only relaxing my fingers once we were safely around the bend.

"You've got winter tires on this thing, right?"

"Of course." He shot a brief glance my way. "You can relax. I'm a good driver."

"I wasn't worried," I said.

I thought I saw his eyebrows go up a fraction of an inch, but it was hard to tell for sure in the darkness.

I fell silent again, staying that way for nearly five minutes.

When the headlights illuminated a driveway with metal numbers attached to a wooden post, I sat up straighter.

"You missed Leo's driveway," I said as we continued along the curving, unlit road.

Grayson slowed down. At first I thought he was going to turn around, but instead he took a left onto an unpaved road that disappeared between a mixture of bare-limbed trees and evergreens.

"This road curves around the back of Leo's property," he said, just as I was about to ask him what he was doing. "He'd likely notice us if we drove right up to his front door. This way we can check things out more covertly."

"Good plan," I said.

Grayson drove slowly, the car bumping and jostling as he navigated the uneven surface. The road curved around to the left and he pulled to a stop when a gap through the trees gave us a view of a snow-covered acreage.

Grayson cut the headlights, but not the engine. I was glad of that. The inside of the car was only just getting comfortably warm.

Once he'd engaged the parking brake, Grayson leaned my way and reached one arm into the backseat. His face came within inches of mine. My heart flip-flopped, but then he was back on his side of the car, hopefully unaware of the effect he'd had on me.

I peered at the shadowy object he was holding. "You brought binoculars too?"

He put them to his eyes, training them on the dark shapes of buildings in the distance. "I'm betting these will be more useful than yours."

"What makes you say that?" I asked, feeling oddly defensive of the ones I'd brought.

"I'm guessing yours aren't night-vision binoculars."

"You have night-vision binoculars?" I couldn't keep a note of awe out of my voice.

Grayson handed them over to me. I lifted them to my eyes and scanned Leo's property. It was cool to be able to see so much despite the darkness. In the distance was a small two-story house, all of its windows currently dark. Near the house were a small shed and what I guessed was a detached garage. Closer to us was a larger outbuilding, no visible clues as to its use. At the moment, nothing stirred on the property.

"These are amazing," I said as I handed the binoculars back to Grayson. Suspicion overtook my enthusiasm. "Why do you have them?"

"One of the tools of the trade."

I watched him skeptically through the darkness. "Why does a craft brewer need night-vision binoculars?"

"Tools of my *previous* trade," he clarified.

"Which was?" Before he had a chance to respond, I asked another question. "A less-than-honest trade?"

I'd heard rumors that he had a criminal past, but when I'd asked him about it back in the fall, he'd laughed and walked away without explanation. My curiosity had remained unsatisfied ever since.

One of the second-story windows of Leo's house lit up.

"Looks like he's awake," Grayson said.

"You've never given me a straight answer," I said, my attention split between him and the house. "Are you a criminal?"

"If you even suspect that's a possibility, you shouldn't be sitting in a car with me on a dark and lonely road."

"A reformed criminal, I should have said. I don't believe you're one now."

"That makes a change."

I knew he was referring to the time when I'd suspected him of murder and arson.

"You still haven't answered my question," I pointed out.

He kept his eyes on Leo's house while I studied his shadowed profile.

"I'm not a criminal," he said at last.

I couldn't leave it at that. "Have you ever been?"

He faltered—just slightly—before responding, "No."

"You hesitated."

"I've never been arrested." He raised the binoculars to his eyes.

"But you've broken the law," I said, interpreting what he'd left out.

"Haven't you?"

"Of course not." I reconsidered my answer. "Well . . ."

He lowered the binoculars and focused his gaze on me. The corners of his mouth twitched. "Confession time."

I heard a definite note of humor in his voice.

"Technically, I suppose I stole a gobstopper from a candy store. But it's not like they could have sold it anyway," I hurried to add, "because I found it on the floor."

"You ate a gobstopper you found on the floor of a store?" he asked with a strange mixture of amazement and disgust.

"I was six!" I defended myself. "Of course I wouldn't do that *now*."

"Really?"

I punched him lightly in the arm. "You're trying to distract me, but it's not working. It's your turn to confess."

"All right." The amusement had disappeared from his voice. "But this stays between you and me."

Despite the rumors I'd heard about him, I wasn't expecting what he said next.

"I was involved in the drug trade."

Chapter 20

I gaped at Grayson in the darkness. "Dealing drugs? Smuggling?" I had trouble believing either could be possible. A few months ago, maybe, but not now.

"Nothing so nefarious," he said, to my relief. "The Chicago neighborhood I grew up in wasn't the worst, but it also wasn't anywhere close to the best. When I was twelve, I got recruited by some older kids. Sometimes I delivered packages, other times I acted as a lookout."

"Did you know what you were doing? What *they* were doing?"

"Sure. I wasn't completely naive at that age. What I didn't understand back then was the devastating effect of drugs on people's lives, on the community. To me it was an easy way to earn some money and get attention from the older kids."

"But you never got caught?"

"Not by the cops. My mom got wind of what I was doing through the neighborhood grapevine and whisked us both off to Syracuse to live with my grandmother." He trained the binoculars on Leo's house. "Best thing she could have done for me."

"Was she a single mother?"

Grayson lowered the binoculars and nodded. "So was my grandmother. The two strongest women I've ever known."

He shut off the car's engine. It was toasty warm inside, so we'd probably be okay for a while without the heater on.

I picked up the thermos of coffee and unscrewed the lid. "So that's why there's a rumor that you have a criminal past?"

"It can't be. No one in this town but me and Jason knew about that until now."

I felt a flicker of warmth in my chest from the knowledge that he'd confided in me. "So how did the rumor start then?"

"I could make a guess."

I poured coffee into the mug that was nestled into the lid of the thermos. "Want some?"

He accepted the steaming drink. "Thanks." He took a sip before saying anything further. "I was taken home by a police officer once when I was fourteen. I was friends with Jason by then and he's never let me live it down. Someone probably overheard him teasing me about it one day. He likes to make it sound worse than it was."

"You've known Jason a long time then."

"Twenty years."

I tried to picture the two men as gangly teenagers, but somehow couldn't quite manage it.

"So why did the police officer take you home?" I asked, determined to get the whole story out of him.

One side of Grayson's mouth angled up in a grin. "I was playing street hockey with Jason and some other friends when I accidentally shot a puck right through Old Man McGregor's front window."

"I'm guessing he was no Mr. Rogers."

"Not even close. He made your standard grumpy old man seem like a happy-go-lucky angel. And I made the shot just as a police car was cruising down the street."

"Uh oh."

"Old Man McGregor would have liked to tar and feather me right there on his front lawn, so I was actually lucky the officer was there to step in. My mom paid for the damage to the window and I spent the rest of the summer mowing lawns to earn enough money to pay her back."

"And that's the extent of your criminal history?"

"That's it. Nothing quite as gross as eating a gobstopper stolen off a sticky, dirty floor where hundreds of feet had tramped."

"I was six!"

He laughed and I busied myself with pouring another cup of coffee, trying to ignore the way the sound of his laughter set off a flutter of butterfly wings in my stomach.

I checked the time on my phone as I sipped at my coffee. It was well after five now. The second-story light in Leo's house had switched off a few minutes earlier. A downstairs window had lit up seconds later, but no one had emerged from the house. We couldn't see the front door from our vantage point, but the detached garage was within view. Leo wouldn't be able to get to his vehicle without us seeing him, and the Lockwood Creamery was too far away for him to go to work on foot.

"Shouldn't he have left by now?" I asked.

Grayson glanced at his phone. "I thought he'd be gone by five."

"Don't tell me he's taking the day off." I didn't like to think that I might have robbed myself of several hours of sleep for nothing.

"Maybe he'll leave soon," Grayson said.

"Hopefully." I took a sip of coffee as I sifted back through everything we'd talked about. "What trade?"

Grayson was about to take a drink of his own coffee but stopped. "Sorry?"

"You said the night-vision binoculars were a tool of your former trade," I reminded him.

He swallowed a sip of coffee and set the cup down on the

center console. "I was a private investigator before I took up brewing beer."

"Really?"

That intrigued me to no end, but before I could ask him anything more about his previous profession, my phone rang.

"It's my mom," I said apologetically, once I'd checked the device.

My mother was of the view that any minute spent sleeping after five o'clock was a minute wasted. She often called me early with the intention of leaving a voice mail, knowing I'd still be asleep. She hated texting and refused to have any part of it, so she always called when she wanted to talk to me.

I hesitated, wondering if I should let the call go to voice mail.

"It's all right," Grayson said. "Go ahead and answer."

I did so, but not without a hint of apprehension. My mom was most likely calling because she wasn't pleased with my holiday plans. She'd already let me know that during previous calls.

"Morning, Mom," I said into my phone.

"Sadie, you're awake?"

I couldn't blame her for sounding so shocked. I didn't usually answer my phone before nine in the morning.

"I'm up early today," I said, hoping she wouldn't ask me why.

"Have you changed your mind about coming to Michael's for Christmas?"

"No," I said, wishing she hadn't asked me that either. I repeated the explanation I'd given her at least twice already. "I'm only closing the Inkwell for one day, so it's really not possible."

"I don't see why you can't close the place for a few more days. Christmas is a time to be spent with family, not in some drinking establishment."

"Mom, it's my business, not some rowdy dive bar."

I glanced Grayson's way and caught a hint of a smile on his face as he watched Leo's house.

My mom let out a long-suffering sigh on the other end of the line. Her disapproval of the course I'd recently set for my life wasn't anything new. If she had things her way, I'd be living in Knoxville, working as a lawyer like Michael. The mere thought made me want to cringe. I wasn't lawyer material.

I was steeling myself for another one of my mom's lectures about how foolish I'd been to buy a pub, so I was immensely relieved when she changed the subject.

"Taylor came by for dinner yesterday. Did you know he's off to Costa Rica later this month?"

"Yes, he told me."

There was still a note of disapproval in her voice. She definitely didn't think Christmas was a time to be going on vacation away from family.

"Did you also know that he got another tattoo? Why does he keep doing that to himself?"

I resisted the temptation to roll my eyes heavenward. "He's a tattoo artist, Mom. Of course he has tattoos."

"He's ruining his skin!"

"It's art, Mom. A form of self-expression." I could picture the frown on her face.

"Sadie, please tell me you haven't allowed him to carve up your skin."

"Of course I haven't," I said quickly. "If I let him give me a tattoo, he'd probably do something ridiculous so he could laugh about it for the rest of his life."

This time when I glanced Grayson's way, he was definitely grinning.

A twinge of embarrassment left me eager to get off the phone. "Mom, I should go. I'm kind of in the middle of something right now."

I hoped she wouldn't ask what. If I told her I was on a stakeout, waiting for a chance to snoop around someone's private property, she'd hop into her car, drive to Shady Creek, tie me up, and take me back to Knoxville with her. She'd probably get me one of those electronic ankle bracelets too.

"I hope you'll change your mind about Christmas," she said.

"I'll talk to you soon."

I didn't miss her exasperated sigh, but she allowed me to bring the call to an end.

"Sorry about that," I said as I tucked my phone into the pocket of my jacket. "Did I miss anything?"

I could see nothing had changed at Leo's house. The downstairs light was still on, everything else in darkness, but I'd felt the need to say something. I couldn't help but feel a bit awkward about Grayson hearing my end of the conversation with my mom.

"Did you lie to your mother?" he asked, tearing my attention away from the house.

"What? Of course I didn't."

"So you don't have a tattoo?"

I couldn't see the color of his eyes in the darkness, but I was able to detect a glimmer of amusement in them.

"I never said I didn't have a tattoo," I pointed out. "I said I'd never let my brother give me one."

"So you do have a tattoo?" He sounded mildly surprised, but also interested.

I knew he had tattoos. I'd seen them peeking out from beneath his short sleeves during warmer weather. Not that I'd spent much time checking out his nicely muscled arms.

"Just a little one," I said.

"Where?"

"That's for me to know and you to . . ." I realized what I'd been about to say. "Not," I finished lamely.

I was glad of the darkness. It meant Grayson couldn't see the flaming red of my cheeks. I focused on taking a long drink of my coffee, trying to ignore the weighted silence that had fallen around us. I refused to look his way. I figured he was probably trying not to laugh at me.

Why did I always have to embarrass myself in front of him?

"He's on the move," Grayson said, interrupting my thoughts.

An outdoor light had switched on over the back door of Leo's house. He made his way out onto the steps, pulling the door shut behind him.

I rummaged in my backpack for my own binoculars, but I stopped my search after a quick look through the window.

Leo was heading in our direction.

"Do you think he'll see us?" I asked, hovering on the edge of panic.

Grayson followed Leo's progress with his night-vision binoculars. "No. He's heading for the outbuilding."

I didn't bother to dig out my own binoculars. Leo had left the pool of light near the back of his house, the shadows swallowing him up. I could just make out the dark shape of his figure trekking through the snow toward the ramshackle building near the fence at the back of his property.

When he got close to the building, I could no longer distinguish him from the deep shadows. I was about to ask Grayson for a turn with his binoculars when the outbuilding lit up.

Leo had opened a large door and had switched on an interior light. At first I could see him moving about, but then he disappeared farther into the building, out of sight.

"What's he doing?" Impatience needled at me. "Why isn't he going to work?"

"He must have taken the day off," Grayson said. "He should have left ages ago."

I was about to express my disappointment when Leo burst into view in the rectangle of light created by the open door. As Leo shut off the light, Grayson raised his binoculars to his eyes.

"What the . . ." Grayson said.

"What's going on?" I asked, wishing I could see what he saw. But then I did.

Leo was nothing more than a dark shape to me, but he was tearing across the snow-covered yard. He stumbled and fell to his knees. He scrambled back to his feet and disappeared into the garage. Seconds later, his truck roared off down his driveway toward Hartley Road, away from where Grayson and I were stationed.

"What was that about?" I asked, puzzled by Leo's behavior.

"Something freaked him out." Grayson reached into the backseat for a flashlight before opening his door.

I gulped down the last of my coffee and grabbed my own flashlight from my backpack, hurrying out of the car to follow him.

The cold air stung my face and I immediately missed the relative warmth of the car. Grayson helped me cross a narrow ditch and climb over a half-broken fence to get onto Leo's property. I wasn't thrilled that I needed help, but I was hampered by my puffy, knee-length jacket and I kept sinking into the snow. I winced as some snow slipped down into my left boot, but I did my best to ignore the discomfort.

Once we were over the fence, I switched on my flashlight. Then Grayson switched his on. The powerful beam from his light made mine look pathetic. I kept it on anyway. I didn't want to have brought it for nothing.

It was a good thing there were no neighbors close by. We wouldn't have been able to sneak quietly across Leo's property even if we'd tried. The snow crunched with every footstep, the sound loud in the quiet of the early morning.

The snow was undisturbed on this part of the property and plenty deep. I kept sinking up to my knees as I trudged along. As much as I wanted to keep pace with Grayson, I couldn't, so I gave up trying and followed behind him, stepping into the deep impressions he left as he traversed the yard.

Near the outbuilding, the snow had been trampled down, and we were both able to pick up the pace. Grayson pulled open the door and paused on the threshold, sweeping the bright beam of his flashlight from left to right.

At first all I saw were a few bales of straw, but then I realized there were several bulky objects covered with old blankets.

We moved deeper into the building, leaving the overhead light off so we wouldn't attract attention if Leo returned. Grayson moved off to the left, while I walked straight ahead. Wariness and apprehension had my heart almost tripping over itself. Whatever had freaked Leo out wasn't immediately obvious and I kept expecting something to jump out at us at any second.

I almost yelped with fright when something brushed against my face. I shone my weak light at it and let out a whooshing breath of relief. It was just a cobweb hanging from one of the beams overhead. Fortunately, Grayson hadn't noticed me getting scared by an old spiderweb.

"What do you think frightened Leo?" I whispered.

Instead of answering, Grayson grabbed one of the gray blankets and gave it a yank. As it slid into a heap at his feet, the blanket unveiled a small stack of camping gear. Grayson shone his flashlight at the pile of goods. I noticed that there were some lanterns, camp stoves, and a couple of tents, all still in their boxes.

"A camping fanatic?" I asked, still whispering, even though I didn't know why I was staying so quiet.

"I'm not so sure about that," Grayson said, not speaking much louder than I had.

I approached the bulky object in front of me. I took hold of one corner of the blanket and slowly pulled it free of whatever was beneath it.

We both directed our flashlights at what I'd uncovered. This time instead of camping gear it was a stack of electronics.

Puzzle pieces clicked into place in my head. "Leo's behind the recent burglaries."

"Looks like it," Grayson agreed.

"No wonder he was worried about the police searching his place. I bet the person he was talking to on the phone is his accomplice."

"I'd make that wager too."

We uncovered the third and final stack of goods to find a couple of shiny new bicycles, a golf bag and clubs, and some other assorted sporting equipment.

"Okay," I said, surveying all the goods. "But what freaked him out? Unless someone else stashed all of this here to set him up as the thief?" That explanation didn't feel right.

Grayson didn't buy it either. "If he didn't want the cops searching his property, this is probably why. It must be something else that sent him running."

My apprehension was back full force as we moved farther into the building. We edged around the stack of stolen electronics and Grayson stepped over a bale of straw.

He froze, the beam of his flashlight trained on something on the floor in front of him.

"I think I've found what freaked him out," he said, his voice grim.

I moved over to join him.

He put out an arm to stop my progress. "Don't look."

But it was too late. I'd already seen what was in the beam of his powerful flashlight.

It was Jade Castellano.

And she was dead.

Chapter 21

"We need to stay back," Grayson warned me, taking my arm as I tried to step toward Jade.

"But shouldn't we make sure she's dead?" I asked, even though I knew it was pointless. Her face was such an unnatural shade of gray that there was really no doubt about her state.

"She's been dead for a while," Grayson said.

And likely not from an accident or natural causes. I noticed some bruising around her throat. Had someone strangled her?

I swallowed hard, a sudden wave of queasiness making me regret the coffee I'd had to drink.

Grayson took my hand and led me toward the door. "This is a crime scene. We need to get out of here."

He'd voiced the thoughts that had just run through my head. More thoughts quickly followed as my initial shock slowly wore off.

"I don't understand," I said as we stepped out of the building. "She left town two days ago. I saw her drive away."

"Doesn't look like she got far," Grayson remarked grimly. He let go of my hand and got out his cell phone. "I'll call the police."

I was glad he was taking care of that. My teeth had suddenly started to chatter so hard that I probably wouldn't have been able to speak clearly. I wrapped my arms around me, trying to stay warm, but that was a battle I was quickly losing. The proximity of Jade's body and the freezing early morning temperature had stolen what little warmth I'd carried with me from the car.

"I still don't understand," I said once Grayson had finished speaking with the 911 operator. "Why Jade?"

"A random killing?" he suggested, but I could tell he doubted that theory as much as I did.

"And where's her car?" I asked. "She was driving a white one. A rental, probably."

"She was Freddy's personal assistant, right?"

I nodded. And Mel's ex. My heart constricted. Poor Mel. Even though she was no longer in a relationship with Jade, I knew this wouldn't be easy on her.

"Maybe Leo killed both Freddy and Jade?" I couldn't stop my mind from searching for explanations. "No, that doesn't make sense. If he killed Jade, why would he be shocked to find her body out here?"

I hugged myself more tightly. Nothing was adding up.

"Why don't you wait in the car?" Grayson suggested. "I'll give you the keys so you can turn on the heat."

"That's okay, thanks. I'll stay here."

I was waiting where he was waiting. Finding Jade's body had left my nerves frazzled. I didn't want to wait by myself on the lonely road.

We stayed silent for several minutes, although my thoughts were far from quiet. Even so, by the time the first police car turned into Leo's driveway, I still couldn't explain why Jade was in the shed or who had killed her. Nothing was adding up in my head, much to my frustration.

The cruiser parked next to the garage and two officers climbed out. One flicked on a powerful flashlight and they headed our way.

"Probably best not to mention we were here to snoop," Grayson said quietly.

"Then what do we say we *were* doing here?" I asked.

Grayson didn't answer. The officers were getting too close.

I let Grayson point out where we'd found the body. As he did that, a second police car arrived.

My fingers, toes, and face were numb by then and I longed for another cup of hot coffee, preferably enjoyed indoors next to a crackling fire. As soon as I had that thought, a twinge of guilt made me regret it. I was lucky. I might be cold now, but I could always warm up later. Jade would never be warm again.

After the first two officers on the scene had taken a look at Jade's body, Grayson and I were separated so we could be questioned. Officer Rogers spoke with Grayson while Officer Eldon Howes asked me some questions. I took a morsel of comfort from his familiar face. Although I wasn't a fan of his aunt, Vera Anderson, Eldon was a nice man with kind eyes, though he could be stern when the situation required it.

When prompted, I explained to him how Grayson and I had seen Leo run scared from the outbuilding.

"We decided to see what was wrong. First we found what we assumed were stolen goods. Then Grayson found Jade's body."

"So you knew Ms. Castellano?" Officer Howes asked. He must have recognized her from the investigation into Freddy's death.

"Slightly," I said. "I spoke to her briefly during the ice sculpture competition. I saw her leaving town a couple of days ago, but . . . she obviously never made it back to Boston." I shivered, only partly from the cold.

"And where were you and Mr. Blake when you saw Leo running from the building?"

I pointed toward the gap in the trees by the fence, although it wasn't really visible. One officer had driven a police truck up close to the outbuilding, its headlights illuminating the area. Everything beyond the pool of light was little more than murky darkness.

"Out on that road. We were in Grayson's car."

"Passing?"

"Parked." I tried not to fidget, not wanting to broadcast how nervous I was with the direction the questioning had taken.

"And what were you doing parked on a seldom-used road so early in the morning?"

"Talking." I realized how inadequate that answer was. Flustered, I added, "Getting to know each other."

Oh, sweet Sherlock. That sounded even worse!

Heat rushed to my cheeks and I knew they were a furious shade of red.

"I mean . . . um . . ." I stumbled over my words.

"I understand," Officer Howes said as he jotted something down in his notebook.

I was pretty sure he *didn't* understand, but another officer called his name and he excused himself, leaving me wishing I could disappear into the snow-covered ground.

Grayson was still talking with Rogers. I figured that was a good thing. I didn't think I could face him right at the moment. How long would it be before the entire Shady Creek Police Department thought we'd been parked on the road for a romantic assignation? Probably not long. I just hoped that misinformation wouldn't spread beyond the department.

I watched as Grayson said something to Officer Rogers. When she nodded, he headed my way. I hoped my cheeks weren't still flaming.

"We're allowed to leave now," he said when he reached me.

I followed him through the snow toward his car. I wanted to ask what he'd told the police we'd been doing parked on the road, but I couldn't work up the nerve. I'd already embarrassed myself enough for one morning.

Once we were in the car with the engine running, Grayson cranked up the heat. We didn't speak as he navigated the bumpy, unpaved road. The ride became smoother once we were back on Hartley Road, but I didn't feel any more comfortable. I was embarrassed, sad, cold, confused, and shaken up. My mind was spinning so fast that I couldn't settle on any one thought.

I closed my eyes, trying to calm myself without much success.

"Looks like something else is going on," Grayson said.

I opened my eyes to see the flashing lights of a police car up ahead.

Grayson slowed to a crawl as we passed by the parked cruiser. A police officer was pointing the bright beam of a flashlight down the wooded bank at the side of the road. I caught sight of a white car in a tangle of bushes and branches.

I sat up straight. "Jade's rental car."

"Are you sure?" Grayson asked.

We'd passed the scene now, so he sped up again.

"I can't be positive, but it's the right make and color. And that would make sense, wouldn't it?"

"Somebody ran her off the road, killed her, and moved her to Leo's shed."

I nodded, even though Grayson's eyes were on the road rather than me. My thoughts had taken the same path as his.

But why had someone killed her? And why move her from the car to Leo's place?

When Grayson dropped me off outside the Inkwell minutes later, I was no closer to answering those questions.

I had to take a long, hot shower and drink another cup of steaming coffee before I could declare myself completely thawed out. Once I no longer felt like a close cousin of one of the ice sculptures out on the village green, I headed downstairs to the Inkwell to get ready for the workday.

Booker arrived and got busy with his prep work in the kitchen. This morning he was singing "Last Christmas." I had no need for a radio when he was around.

I joined him in the kitchen as he wrapped up the song.

"When's your next gig?" I asked.

"Tonight." His knife flashed as he expertly chopped up bell peppers. "We're providing the music for the dance at the community center."

"That sounds like fun." The dance was part of the carnival.

"Will you be there?"

"No, but I think my aunt will."

She enjoyed going out dancing with her gentleman friend, Louie. I didn't have anyone to dance with, not that it mattered. I still could have attended the event, but I wanted to stay at the Inkwell. I'd already had enough excitement for one day.

"Did you hear about the incident out on Hartley Road?" I asked as I gathered up some clean glasses to take out to the bar. I was curious to know if the news about the second murder had spread through town yet.

"No. I came straight here from home, so you're the first person I've talked to. I haven't even been online yet today." He grabbed another red pepper. "What kind of incident?"

"There's been another death in town."

"Another one?"

I spun around at the sound of Mel's voice. She stood holding the kitchen door open.

"Was it another murder?" Booker asked.

I nodded, suddenly unable to find my voice. Mel clearly didn't know anything about Jade's fate yet.

"Who was killed?" Mel asked as she pulled her hat off.

I swallowed and put my hand on the edge of the counter to steady myself. I really didn't want to be the one to deliver the news.

"Sadie?" Booker set down his knife and moved to my side. "Was it someone you know?"

"Maybe you should sit down," Mel said with concern.

I shook my head and struggled to make my tongue work. "I'm so sorry, Mel."

Apprehension crept into her blue eyes. "What do you mean?"

"Jade's dead." The nausea I'd briefly experienced at Leo's place made a comeback. Delivering this news to Mel was almost as bad as finding Jade's body.

Mel stared at me, the color draining from her face. "That can't be," she said. "Jade's in Boston. I saw her drive away on Sunday."

"She *left* for Boston," I said. "But she didn't get very far. There's a car in the bushes along Hartley Road. I only caught a glimpse, but it looks like it could be the one she was driving."

"She had an accident?" Mel's usually strong voice had grown faint. "Are you sure she's dead?"

"She might have been run off the road on purpose. Grayson and I found her early this morning. She was in a shed, well away from her car." I put a hand on Mel's arm. "I'm so sorry."

"Is this because of Freddy?" she asked. "Were they killed by the same person?"

"I don't know, but it seems likely."

"But the police arrested Penny," Booker said. "How could she have killed Jade while she was in custody for murdering Freddy?"

"I'm not convinced they've got the right person," I said. "But either way, Penny still could have killed Jade. She's likely been dead for a couple of days."

"Since before Penny was arrested." Booker rubbed the back of his neck. "Geez, Mel. I'm sorry. She was a friend of yours, right?"

Mel nodded but said nothing. I'd never seen her so shaken. I wanted to give her a hug, but I suspected she'd rather I give her some space.

"Why Jade?" she asked, finally speaking. "Why would anyone want to kill her? She was harmless."

"I really don't know," I said, my heart aching.

All three of us jumped when someone knocked loudly on

the pub's front door. I glanced at Booker and Mel before hurrying out of the kitchen to see who was there. I wasn't overly surprised when I found Detective Marquez standing on the other side of the door.

I stepped back to allow her to enter the pub. I quickly closed the door behind her, catching a glimpse of lazy snowflakes drifting down from the gray sky before I shut out the cold air.

"I'm guessing you're here about Jade Castellano," I said.

I figured she probably had more questions for me. I hoped I wouldn't embarrass myself as much as I had with Officer Howes if she asked why I'd been out by Leo's place with Grayson. I also hoped I wouldn't get myself into trouble.

"I am," Marquez said. "But I'm looking for Melanie Costas. Is she here?"

Mel pushed through the swinging kitchen door. "I'm here."

Her voice sounded stronger, back to normal, and grim resignation had replaced some of the shock on her face.

"I just told her about Jade," I said to the detective.

"Do you know why this happened?" Mel asked.

"We're still in the initial stages of our investigation," Detective Marquez replied. "But I was hoping you could help with that. Would you mind accompanying me to the station so we can have a chat?"

Mel addressed me. "Can you manage without me for a while, Sadie?"

"Yes." The word came out more faintly than I'd meant.

Mel zipped up her jacket. "I'll be back as soon as I can."

Chapter 22

My nerves wouldn't stop jittering and a lump of dread sat heavily in my stomach. I tried to make myself believe that Detective Marquez simply wanted to learn more about Jade from Mel, the one person in Shady Creek who'd known the woman. But Mel was already on the detective's radar as far as Freddy's murder was concerned. Even if the police believed one hundred percent that Penny had killed Freddy, did that put Mel in the clear?

I thought it unlikely that the two recent murders were unrelated, but until the police had evidence that they were linked, would Mel be a suspect in Jade's death?

And what if the police came to believe, as I did, that Penny wasn't Freddy's killer? Would Mel then become their prime suspect?

I couldn't keep thinking that way. All it was doing was working me into a near panic.

I opened the Inkwell two minutes before noon, hoping customers would distract me, but no one came through the door. I gazed out one of the windows that overlooked Creekside Road and the village green. The snowflakes no longer drifted lazily to the ground; they were falling thickly and furiously, already leaving a thin layer on the road.

After hurrying upstairs to grab my coat, I spent a few minutes sweeping the front walkway. At the rate the snow was falling, I'd have to repeat the task regularly to keep the footpath clear for customers.

Fortunately, a group of half a dozen tourists arrived as I was dusting the snow off my coat, preparing to head back inside. Others appeared on their heels, looking for a warm sanctuary as the snow continued to fall from the leaden sky.

The influx of customers kept me so busy for the next hour that I didn't have time to worry about anything. While I was in the midst of mixing up three Happily Ever After cocktails and a Milky Way Gargle Blaster, Mel came in out of the snow, pulling off her hat and unzipping her jacket as she made her way behind the bar.

"You're back," I said with immense relief.

"Sorry I left you in the lurch."

"Don't be. It was you I was worried about."

"I'm fine." She shrugged out of her jacket. "I gave the walkway a quick shovel before I came in."

"Thank you," I said as she disappeared into the back.

I delivered the cocktails to a table by one of the windows. When I returned to the bar, Mel was filling pint glasses for two men. I studied her profile, trying to gauge how she was feeling. All of the shock had disappeared from her expression, replaced now with stoicism.

"Mel, you can take the day off if you need to," I said quietly, so no one else would hear.

She delivered the pints to the customers before responding. "Thanks. But I'd rather keep busy." She grabbed a cloth and wiped up a droplet of spilled beer. "Besides, I'm going to need the money to pay my lawyer."

She was about to move away, but I put a hand on her arm to stop her. "Are you really in trouble?" I asked, worried.

"To be completely honest," she said, her face grim, "I think I could be."

I tried not to worry, without much luck. Every moment not spent serving customers or clearing tables turned into an internal anxiety fest. After Freddy's death, I'd vowed to help clear Mel's name, but I'd yet to succeed. With Penny in custody, the pressure on Mel had eased up, until Grayson and I had found Jade's body.

I was certain the two murders were connected. I had a long list of possible culprits for Freddy's death, but what about Jade's? Plenty of people in town harbored ill feelings toward the big-city chef, but aside from Mel, no one here knew Jade.

Did they?

That was the first thing I needed to find out. If I could come up with a list of people who had a connection to Jade, however tenuous, that would give me something to work with. If nobody knew her, maybe she was targeted because she posed a danger to Freddy's killer.

If she'd known something about the murderer, did she share that information with the police? Maybe she didn't realize she knew something important, or perhaps the killer was simply worried she knew too much and didn't want to take any chances by letting her live.

There were so many possibilities, but I needed to start somewhere.

During a relatively quiet moment, I followed Mel into the kitchen, where she deposited a stack of dirty dishes in the dishwasher.

"If it's too painful having me asking questions, tell me," I said to her as she put the last of the dishes in the machine. "But I was wondering if anyone else in Shady Creek knew Jade or had dealings with her while she was in town."

"I don't mind you asking questions," Mel said. "I just don't want you doing anything dangerous on my behalf."

"No danger here," I assured her. "All I'm doing at the moment is trying to sort things out in my head."

Booker spoke up from the prep counter where he was brushing baguette slices with olive oil for a platter of Paradise Lox. "She must have dealt with the organizers of the ice sculpture competition."

"Good point," I said. "Anyone else?" I directed the question at both of them.

Mel wiped her hands on a towel. "The only people I saw her talking with were Freddy, Alma Potts, the competition supervisors, and a couple of reporters."

"Which reporters? Do you remember?"

"Joey and a guy from Boston. I think his name was Miles something. He's the one who tried to get me to trash-talk Freddy."

"He's probably long gone, but I can talk to Joey. Alma organized the competition, so she might know something about Jade."

Alma was the chair of the Inkwell's romance book club and someone I considered a friend. I made a plan to talk with her and Joey as soon as possible. At the moment, however, I had to check on my customers.

When I left the kitchen, I spotted a familiar face and some of my worried tension slipped away. Shontelle hung her coat on one of the pegs by the door and waved at me with a smile. On her way across the room, she stopped to say hello to someone, but then she perched on a stool at the bar.

"It's practically a blizzard out there," she commented, running a hand over her hair.

"I think a lot of people are opting to stay home now," I said, looking around the pub. After an initial rush around twelve-thirty, the crowd had thinned out considerably.

"I'm not getting many people in my store this afternoon, either. My mom's watching over it while I take a late lunch break, but I doubt she'll have many customers to deal with. They might have to reschedule this afternoon's hockey game if the snow doesn't let up."

I'd almost forgotten about the hockey tournament, since the Inkwell was no longer in contention. I wondered when the brewery's next game would be.

Thinking about the brewery led my thoughts to Grayson. Although I'd heard some gossip about the second murder over the past couple of hours, my name hadn't come up, as far as I knew. Maybe Grayson and I would manage to stay under the radar.

I should have known better than to hope for that.

Shontelle picked up a menu, but her brown eyes settled on me. "I'm here for lunch, but I'm also here to see how you're doing."

"You heard?"

"Not long ago. I've known since midmorning that there was some sort of police incident out at Leo Mancini's property, but I didn't know you were involved until Gretchen Dingle came into my shop looking for a Christmas gift for her sister in New Jersey. She said you and Grayson found a body out in a field."

"In an outbuilding on Leo's land."

"Is it really Freddy's personal assistant who's dead?"

"Yes." The image of Jade's dead body flashed in my head, far too vividly.

Some of my distress must have shown because Shontelle reached across the bar to take my hand. "I'm so sorry for bringing it up. Maybe you should sit down."

I gave Shontelle's hand a grateful squeeze. With Mel working and business being slow, I decided I could steal a few minutes away for myself.

"Let me take your order. Then I'll sit with you for a bit."

She requested the Red Cabbage of Courage, a salad made with ramen noodles, grated carrot, sunflower seeds, and—of course—cabbage, all topped with a vinaigrette. She also asked for a cup of coffee to go with it. After I relayed her order to Booker, I poured coffee for both of us and settled onto a bar stool.

"It was a shock finding Jade," I said, "but I don't mind you asking about it. I'm sure everyone will be asking me questions once they know I was there."

"You can always tell them to mind their own business. You can always tell me that too."

I smiled. "That's all right. If I hadn't been involved, I'd be asking plenty of questions. I'm not exactly lacking in curiosity." That was an understatement.

"If you don't mind questions, then I'm going to ask you about Grayson."

"What about him?" I suspected I already knew.

"I heard he was with you when you found the body."

"Technically, *he* found Jade. But, yes, we were both there." I took a sip of coffee. "What else have you heard?" I wondered if I really wanted to hear the answer.

"That the two of you were out that way for a secret rendezvous."

I dropped my head to the bar, resting my forehead against the polished surface. "You heard that from Gretchen Dingle?"

"The news was delivered in gleeful tones."

I groaned. I didn't know Gretchen Dingle, but I knew her reputation. Spreading rumors was her superpower. It didn't matter if they were true or not. As soon as Gretchen got hold of some tasty tidbit of fact or fiction, there was no stopping its spread through town.

Shontelle patted my back. "You're both unattached adults, you know. You don't need to be sneaking around."

I raised my head. "We weren't sneaking around! Well, maybe we were, but not for *that*."

"So your romantic affiliation is no longer a secret?"

"We don't have a romantic affiliation!"

Shontelle was smiling, and her eyes were bright with amusement. "The lady doth protest too much, me thinks."

This time I dropped my head into my hands.

Shontelle nudged my arm. "You know I'm teasing."

I lowered my hands. "I do. I'm just imagining the whole town talking about me and Grayson when there is no me and Grayson."

"Do you want there to be?" Shontelle asked.

She was always interested in the possibility of the two of us getting together.

"Every time I'm with him, I end up embarrassing myself," I said, dodging her question.

"I don't think he minds."

"*I* do."

She took a drink of coffee, but not before I noticed her knowing smile.

"But what do you mean?" I asked, my curiosity nudged wide awake.

She set down her mug. "I'm pretty sure he thinks you're extra cute when you're flustered."

A hint of warmth touched my cheeks. "I'm pretty sure you're wrong."

A *ding* sounded from the kitchen, signaling that Shontelle's lunch was ready.

Saved by the bell, I thought as I slipped off the stool.

Shontelle stayed at the Inkwell for another half hour, but she didn't bring up Grayson or Jade again. I was much happier talking about Kiandra and I told Shontelle I'd take her daughter skating on Sunday morning, as long as the weather allowed it.

By midafternoon, business hadn't picked up at all. That left me with too much time to think and I soon grew antsy. I wanted to take action, to find answers to some of the questions swirling around in my head like snowflakes caught in a swift current of wind.

Mel assured me she could hold down the fort, so I decided to take some time away for sleuthing. I questioned the wisdom of my decision as soon as I stepped out the door. The snow hadn't eased up at all; it was coming down so hard that I could barely see twenty feet in front of me.

I spent several minutes shoveling the walkway and footbridge, but then I tugged my hat down farther over my ears and ventured across the street.

No matter the weather, it was time to seek out some answers.

Chapter 23

My first destination was the thrift shop on Ashcroft Road. When I was halfway there, I realized I probably should have texted Alma to see if she was free to meet with me and where. She worked at the store part-time, but I didn't know her schedule. She easily could have been at home, or anywhere else.

I left my phone in my pocket and kept trudging along. With snowflakes falling thickly and an icy wind whistling through town, I didn't want to remove my gloves to use it. If Alma wasn't at the thrift shop, at least I could take advantage of the shelter to send her a text message.

As it turned out, that wasn't necessary. A woman named Gertrude was behind the counter, but when I asked if Alma was in, she directed me to the shop's back room. I stayed on the welcome mat until I'd brushed snow from my coat and stomped it off my boots. Then I made my way through the maze of shelves and clothing racks to the open door at the back of the store. There I found Alma sorting a big box of clothing that someone had donated.

I perched on a tall, three-legged stool and she kept working while we chatted. I explained that I was on a mission to find out who, if anyone, might have had a connection to Jade.

"Did you speak to her at all before or during the ice sculpture competition?" I asked.

"Oh, sure." Alma flicked her slightly wild, graying hair over her shoulder before picking up a red T-shirt. "I talked to her on the phone a few weeks ago when she was looking to get Freddy registered to compete. I e-mailed her the schedule and rules a few days after that, and I spoke to her briefly a couple of times while she was in town." She folded the T-shirt and set it on top of a tidy pile to her right. "I can't believe she's dead. What a shame. Why would anyone want to kill her? Freddy I can understand, but not her."

"I'm hoping I can find out why. That might lead me to the who."

Alma pulled a yellow and white sundress from the box. "I wish I could help, but we only ever talked about the competition. And I really don't know anything about her."

"That's all right. What about the other people involved in organizing the competition? Did any of them have contact with Jade? The supervisors, maybe?"

"I was the daytime supervisor. Dan and Ruby took the night shift. I don't know if they talked to Jade at all, but I could find out. Let me give them a call."

She set the clothes aside and phoned first Dan, then Ruby. The conversations were short, and from what I heard on Alma's end, I knew what she was going to say before she hung up the phone.

"Neither of them said more than hello to Jade. Sorry we couldn't be more helpful."

"It was a long shot anyway."

As I slipped off the stool, Gertrude poked her head through the door. "Are you two talking about the dead woman?"

"We are," I said. "Do you know anything about her?"

"Only that she was Freddy Mancini's personal assistant."

Gertrude shook her head. "I didn't envy her that job. Do you think the same person killed her and Freddy?" She directed the question at both of us.

"That's Sadie's realm of expertise, not mine," Alma said, sliding a dress onto a clothes hanger. "She's the mystery maven."

"I'm not an expert," I said. "Not by a long shot. But I think there's a good chance one person committed both murders." I pulled my gloves on. "I'd better get a move on. I don't want to be away from the Inkwell too long and I want to see if I can track down someone who spoke to Jade."

"There's always Penny." Gertrude pursed her lips together. "Of course, she's in jail at the moment, so you probably can't talk to her."

I kept my hat in my hand instead of putting it on my head. "Penny? She spoke to Jade?"

"Oh, yes. And it wasn't a pleasant exchange, let me tell you."

Now I was intrigued. "What happened?"

"It was shortly after the ice sculpture competition got underway. I was taking a stroll around the green, having a look at what everyone was up to. It was incredible, don't you think? The way they wielded those chain saws and other tools, turning those blocks into pieces of art. A real marvel."

I forced myself to keep my impatience in check.

Fortunately, Alma prompted Gertrude to get back on track. "What about Jade?"

"Right. She and Penny were over by the bandstand, having words."

"About what?" I asked.

"I haven't a clue, I'm afraid. I couldn't hear what they were saying. But they both looked spitting mad, I can tell you that much."

"Maybe Sybil would know what it was all about," Alma suggested. "She and Penny are close. Maybe Penny confided in her."

I tugged my hat on, making sure it covered my ears. "I'll ask her."

I thanked both women and hurried out onto the street. I was so eager to get to Sybil's yarn store that I barely noticed the snow or the frosty wind stinging my cheeks.

As much as I'd believed in Penny's innocence, I now had to wonder if the police had the right culprit after all. Still, I couldn't be sure, especially since I didn't know what Penny and Jade had argued about.

When I reached Purls of Wisdom, I had to go through the same routine as I had at the thrift shop. I shook the snow from my hat and boots and brushed fluffy flakes from my shoulders. The store was cozy and warm, the colorful yarns giving the place a cheery atmosphere. The upbeat chatter and laughter coming from the table at the back of the store added to the merriness.

A class was wrapping up and Sybil was thanking the half dozen adult students for showing up despite the weather.

To my surprise, I spotted a head of crinkly red hair among the students. I hoped Cordelia was having more luck with her new hobby than she had with hockey, but judging by the tangled mess of yarn she was stuffing into her bag, I suspected she wasn't.

When Cordelia saw me by the door, she waved, a smile lighting up her face. One of the other students started chatting with her, so I focused on Sybil, who was making her way toward the front of the store. I stuffed my gloves into my pocket and met her over by the checkout counter.

"Hello, again," Sybil said with a warm smile. "What can I help you with today?"

"I was hoping for news of Penny," I said. "Is she doing all right?"

Sybil's smile faded. "As well as can be expected, I suppose. She's quite distraught but coping."

"I guess things are even worse for her now that a second body's been found."

Sybil pulled a box out from beneath the counter and set it

down with a thud. "Penny's not responsible for either one. I've known her for years. It's absolutely absurd that she's been arrested."

"I have my doubts about her guilt too."

Sybil removed a handful of packages of knitting needles and slapped them down on the counter. "I don't have doubts. I'm absolutely certain she's innocent."

"Of course," I said quickly, not wanting to annoy her more than I already had.

She reached into the box again and sucked in a sharp breath as she pulled her hand back. She examined her red-painted nails and let out a frustrated sigh. "That's the second nail I've broken in less than a week." After rummaging beneath the counter for a moment, she came up with a nail file. "Penny's hired a lawyer from Burlington. He'll get her out of this mess."

"I hope you're right. Maybe the argument she had with Jade Castellano won't make things worse for her."

Sybil filed her nail with excessive vigor. "Gossiping might, though."

Her voice was chilly enough to rival the winter wind outside and I had the distinct feeling I'd worn out my welcome.

"I really do hope Penny will be okay," I said, taking a step back.

A woman with her arms full of blue and purple yarn approached the counter. Sybil's attention shifted to her and I took the opportunity to slip out of the shop. I had no more information than I'd arrived with and all I'd succeeded in doing was making Sybil think I was a terrible gossip.

"Sadie!" Cordelia called when I was halfway down the street.

I waited as she hurried toward me, her long hair streaming out from beneath her hat.

"How are you feeling today?" she asked when she reached my side.

"I've got a few sore muscles, but otherwise I'm fine, thanks."

She clapped a gloved hand over her eyes. "I'm so sorry. I still can't believe I hurt you and Zoe."

"It's okay, Cordelia. Really." I pulled her hand away from her eyes so she wouldn't end up tripping or walking into a streetlamp. "Are you going to enter the snowshoe race?"

"Gosh, no," she said. "I think I'll stay away from all sports, at least for a while. I don't want to hurt anyone else."

I glanced at her bag. "I see you've taken up knitting."

"I'm trying to, anyway," she said. "It should be safer than hockey, as long as I avoid stabbing anyone with my needles."

"I'm sure you'll do great with it."

She did up the top button of her purple wool coat. "Are you thinking of taking a knitting class? Is that why you came by the store?"

"No. The only things I'm trying to knit together are clues."

Cordelia's blue eyes lit up. "I love a good mystery! Is it the murders you're looking into?"

"Yes."

"But the police arrested Penny Blaine. I heard Freddy's assistant died before that happened, so didn't Penny commit both murders?"

"Possibly, but I think there's a chance she's innocent. I don't want the wrong person going to jail, and if the police figure out that she's innocent, suspicion might fall on Mel."

Cordelia nodded thoughtfully. "I heard she knew Freddy's assistant."

"It seems like she's the only one in town who did. That's not surprising, though, since Jade was from Boston."

"It's strange, though, isn't it? Lots of people in Shady Creek didn't like Freddy, but if no one other than Mel knew his assistant, then why kill her?" Her eyes widened. "Do you think she knew who killed Freddy and that's why she had to be silenced?"

"That thought has crossed my mind," I said.

We were heading north along Hemlock Street, toward Creekside Road. Cordelia lived and worked at her grandmother's beautiful inn up the road from the Inkwell. I could barely make out the shape of the gorgeous Queen Anne that housed the Creekside Inn. We weren't far away, but the falling snow had drastically reduced visibility.

I was, however, able to see far enough to know that we were approaching the town hall. I slowed my steps. I hadn't walked past the building since I'd found Freddy's body. The memory put me on edge, so when Cordelia grabbed my arm, I nearly jumped out of my skin.

"The gingerbread contest!" she exclaimed.

"Sorry?" I said, confused.

"It's part of the Winter Carnival," Cordelia explained. "And the entries are on display at the town hall today. I love gingerbread, don't you? My gran has the best recipe ever. She has to make a double batch each Christmas because I go through it so quickly."

"I love gingerbread," I said when she paused for breath. "My family has a great recipe too, passed down from my Grandma Josephine."

"Do you want to take a look inside?"

We were already at the base of the town hall steps and I was interested to see the creations people had come up with for the contest. I figured I could spare a few more minutes away from the pub.

"Sure," I said.

We hurried up the steps and into the brick building, pausing to brush the snow off ourselves in the vestibule. We wandered into the main room where the chili supper had been held on the weekend. It was quiet in there, no one else about. The tables were still set up, but this time they were covered in white cloths and displayed what I estimated to be at least three dozen gingerbread structures.

"Wow," I said as we approached the nearest table.

There were standard gingerbread houses, but there was also a barn with animals in the farmyard, a gingerbread school bus, and an intricately decorated cruise ship.

"Aren't they incredible?" Cordelia enthused. "I don't know how anyone can do this. The last time I tried making a gingerbread house, the roof collapsed before I could even decorate it."

"I've had that happen once or twice," I said.

"Do you make gingerbread houses each year?"

"No, I haven't for a long time. I did when I was a kid, though."

My mom had helped me with the baking, and my dad had assisted me with the construction. My brother Michael had never shown much interest in gingerbread. He didn't even like eating it, since he wasn't keen on the flavor. Taylor had loved smashing them to pieces and eating them, but I was the only one of the three of us who'd enjoyed making the houses.

Thinking about Christmases past sent a pang of loneliness through me, even though Cordelia was at my side. I was really going to miss my family over the holidays.

I pushed those thoughts aside as we made our way along a table designated for the children's category.

Cordelia moved on ahead of me. When she reached yet another table, she waved me over quickly. "Sadie, check this out."

When I joined her, I nearly gaped in amazement. There was a beautiful gingerbread carousel on the table. It must have taken hours to assemble and decorate. Each piece had been shaped with precision and intricately decorated with icing and candies.

"And this one!" Cordelia had already moved along the table.

I shook my head in wonder. "We have some seriously talented people in this town."

"You can say that again."

This time we were admiring a gingerbread replica of Westminster Abbey, if I wasn't mistaken.

We continued to wander around the room, exclaiming over all the incredible contest entries.

"Penny probably didn't get to enter this year," Cordelia said once we'd seen everything on display.

"Does she usually?" I asked.

"Every year. She always makes the cutest things. But I doubt she had a chance this year, what with getting arrested."

"I wish I knew what happened between Penny and Jade," I said, more to myself than Cordelia.

"You mean why they argued?"

"You know about that?" I said with surprise.

"Sure. I was on the village green when they had their spat."

My hopes spiked. "Do you know why they argued?"

"I heard some of what they were saying," Cordelia said. "Enough to know that Jade thought Penny was a crazy stalker."

Chapter 24

"A stalker?" I had a hard time believing my ears. "Whom did Jade think Penny was stalking? Freddy?"

"That's what I gathered," Cordelia said.

"But why would she think that? My understanding was that Penny hadn't had any contact with Freddy for years. And the one time she tried to talk to him on the green, he pretended he didn't know her. It was only a few hours later that he was killed. How would she have had time for stalking during that narrow time frame?"

"I'm pretty sure it had been going on for years. Maybe Penny hadn't *seen* Freddy for a long time, but it sounded like she'd been sending letters and e-mails."

I took a second to absorb that information. "What exactly did you hear?"

We made our way slowly toward the door, pulling on our gloves and hats again.

"I don't remember word for word, but Freddy's assistant—Jade, right?" When I nodded, she continued. "She told Penny to stay away from Freddy or she'd turn the letters and e-mails over to the police. Penny said she was free to be on the green if she wanted and Freddy wasn't going to stop her from enjoying the Winter Carnival. Then Penny said something else I couldn't hear. I think that's when Jade called her a crazy stalker."

"How did Penny react to that?" I asked, wondering once again if the police really had nabbed the right suspect.

"Her face flushed bright red. I think she was angry, but maybe a bit embarrassed too. I thought she might start to cry, but she took off before I saw any tears."

"Have you told any of this to the police?" I asked as we stepped out into the cold. The snow was still coming down, but not as thickly as when we'd gone inside.

"No, it never crossed my mind to talk to the police. I figured Jade would have told them about the letters and e-mails once Freddy was killed. And then Penny was arrested, so I thought that was that." Cordelia's forehead furrowed with worry. "Should I have talked to them?"

"It might not be a bad idea to have a word with them now," I said, "so they have the full picture of everything that's been going on."

"I've never had to go to the police station before." She sounded both awed and scared.

"It's nothing to worry about," I assured her. "Ask for Detective Marquez. She seems to be in charge of the murder cases."

We'd reached Creekside Road. There weren't many cars out and about, so we crossed without having to wait. We exchanged a few more words outside the Creekside Inn before parting ways, and I returned to the Inkwell, wondering if there was still a murder mystery left for me to solve.

I took advantage of my free time the next morning to get in some training for the upcoming snowshoe race. Before moving to Shady Creek, I'd only been out on snowshoes a couple of times in my life, almost two decades ago when I was living in my dad's home state of Minnesota. I didn't have any real hope of winning the race because I'd be up against people who'd been snowshoeing for years, but I was determined not to come in dead last.

I carried my snowshoes down the road, past the Spirit Hill Brewery, to the start of a trail that led up into the hills. Once I had my feet strapped into my snowshoes, I set off along the track, taking a minute or so to warm up before picking up my pace.

A few puffy, white clouds drifted across the bright blue winter sky, but they didn't blot out the sunlight. I was glad I'd worn a shorter, lighter jacket instead of my knee-length one. Although the cold air stung my bare cheeks, the physical exertion was warming up the rest of me.

I paused for a rest when I reached the crest of a hill, loosening my scarf as I caught my breath. I could hear the occasional call of a bird in the trees on either side of the pathway, but otherwise peace and quiet surrounded me. A bright red cardinal flew over me, bringing a smile to my face. It was nice to be alone with nature. The tranquility was soothing after all the thoughts of murder that had occupied my mind lately.

I was about to continue on my way along the path when I heard a faint noise somewhere behind me. I glanced over my shoulder. The pathway was clear, not another soul in sight. I followed the trail down a slight hill and then quickened my pace, getting as close to a jog as I could with snowshoes attached to my feet.

Snow crunched somewhere in the not-too-far distance. I stopped short, my breaths puffing out of me in misty clouds. I glanced over my shoulder again. I didn't spot anyone behind me, but the small hill I'd come down didn't allow me to see very far. Staying still, I listened for further noises, but heard nothing.

Maybe someone was a long way back, taking the same trail as I was.

It was nothing to worry about, so why did I feel so uneasy?

It was the murders, I decided. Even out here in the peaceful hills, recent events were taking their toll on my nerves. That didn't mean there was any real reason to be scared.

It's fine, I told myself. *Just another person out for a morning trek*.

I set off again but didn't make it far before I stopped once more.

This time there was no mistaking the crunch of snow beneath someone's feet.

I turned around. Seconds later, a figure came into view over the small hill. It was a woman in jeans, a sweater, and snowshoes. As she drew closer, I was able to recognize her.

Lara Hawkes.

I raised a gloved hand in greeting. "Morning, Lara!" I called out.

She didn't return my wave or my greeting, although I knew she'd heard me. Even from a distance, I could tell her gaze was fixed on me.

I waited for her to draw closer. When she was within a few feet, she slowed to a stop.

"All the way out here by yourself?" she asked.

"It's not so far from town." I couldn't help but think it an odd question, especially since she was on her own too. "I'm getting ready for the race on Friday."

"So am I." She eyed me up and down as if assessing her competition. "I hear you were at my mom's store the other day, asking questions about Penny."

I shifted on my snowshoes. Her side of the conversation

lacked any sort of friendliness and there was a sharpness to her eyes that sent a chill creeping over my skin.

"I just wanted to know how Penny was doing. I didn't mean to upset your mom."

"The only thing she's upset about is Penny being in jail."

An awkward silence fell around us. Not even the chirping of a bird interrupted it.

I cast around for something to say. "How's your dad doing?"

"He's fine. Why do you ask?" The question came out like a challenge.

"I know Freddy's death was hard on him, that's all." I wasn't sure why she was acting so cold.

"We're all better off without Freddy."

She was about to say something more, but she snapped her mouth shut when something moved among the trees, grabbing our attention.

A white German shepherd bounded through the snow toward us.

"Bowie!" I crouched down and the dog rushed over to me. I gave his fur a good rub down as his tongue lolled out of his mouth, his eyes bright and happy.

Footsteps crunched through the snow. I straightened up in time to see Grayson coming along a branch of the trail to the right of the main path. He too wore snowshoes.

"I need to get going," Lara muttered.

She stomped past me and turned onto the trail Grayson was on. They paused to exchange a few words and I could have sworn I heard a tinkle of laughter come from Lara. A moment later, she set off again and she soon disappeared from sight.

"Training for the race?" Grayson called out to me as he headed my way.

Bowie trotted over to him as he reached the main trail. I followed more slowly behind the dog.

"I am," I said as we met up and stopped in the middle of the trail. "How about you?"

"I'm mostly out here for Bowie."

"You're not entering the race?"

I found that disappointing. After the disastrous hockey game, it would have been nice to have a chance to beat him at something. Although, knowing my luck with such things, he was probably a snowshoeing champion.

"The brewery's hosting a beer-tasting event on Friday afternoon. I'll be getting ready for that."

"Oh, right." I'd heard about the tasting event. It was part of the Winter Carnival.

"Have your missing books turned up?" he asked as Bowie wandered over to the nearby trees to sniff out interesting scents.

"No." I'd checked after closing the pub the night before. It hadn't surprised me to find that they were still missing.

"I'm sorry to hear that."

Determined not to let my spirits droop, I decided to change the subject. "Have you heard anything more from the *Craft Nation* producer?"

"Actually, there's good news on that front," Grayson said. "Now that the murderer's been caught, the episode's going ahead. They're planning to film it sometime in February."

"That's fantastic! At least something good is coming from Penny's arrest."

"You mean other than getting a murderer off the streets?"

"Yes, I guess there's that too," I said.

"You don't sound convinced."

I tugged my scarf up over my chin. Now that I'd been standing around for a few minutes, all the warmth was seeping out of me.

"I'm becoming more convinced, but I'm disappointed to find out Penny's a killer."

"I get that. She seemed like a nice woman."

"But apparently she had a lot of bitterness beneath the surface, at least where Freddy was concerned." I told him about the letters she'd sent Freddy over the years.

"That's too bad," Grayson said. "I don't think Freddy was worth all the time and energy she must have spent on her grudge against him."

"No. And Jade . . . what a waste." Despite my earlier resolve to keep them high, my spirits were definitely sinking now.

This time it was Grayson who changed the subject. "I've been thinking about Christmas."

"Oh? You're going away after all?"

"No, I'm still staying in Shady Creek. I enjoy cooking, but there's not much point in cooking a big Christmas dinner for one person. I'd love it if you'd join me."

The invitation took me so much by surprise that I stared at him for a second or two before speaking. "Really?"

I wanted to kick myself for my response.

Grayson grinned and my stomach did a somersault. "Really. I'll be making pumpkin pie."

My mouth watered. I'd tasted his prize-winning pumpkin pie back in the fall and I still daydreamed about its incredible taste from time to time.

"Thank you . . . that's . . . I . . ." Why was I stumbling over my words? I pulled myself together. "That would be great. Thank you."

"Good." He held my gaze and my heart nearly tripped over itself. "I'd better get back to the brewery. Enjoy your snowshoeing."

"I will."

"Don't get too close to the trees."

"Tree wells," I said with a nod. "I've been warned."

Several people had given me the same advice.

"See you around." He treated me to another grin before he set off along the trail, heading the opposite way as I was going.

Bowie ran off ahead of him, excited to be on the move again.

I watched until they'd disappeared from sight before resuming my trek. I was thoroughly chilled from standing still for so long, and yet a small glow of warmth in my chest kept me from shivering.

It seemed I wouldn't be alone for Christmas after all.

Chapter 25

Grayson's invitation left me in a good mood that continued into the afternoon. It also didn't hurt that the bright winter sunshine had brought more tourists and locals to the Inkwell. While business had been quiet the day before, now it was steady.

In the early afternoon, Shontelle stopped by for a brief visit. She accepted a cup of coffee but didn't have time to stay and eat.

"I came by to talk about Christmas," she said once she was seated at the bar with a steaming cup of coffee in front of her.

"Can we get together at some point so I can give you and Kiandra your gifts?" I asked.

"That's exactly what I wanted to talk about."

"You tell me when you're free," I said. "You're the one with family coming to visit."

"And you're the one going away."

"No, I'm not. I'm staying in Shady Creek."

"A couple of weeks ago you said Michael had invited you to spend Christmas in Knoxville."

"He invited me." At his wife's prompting, I suspected. "But I decided to stay here."

"And Gilda's going to Savannah?" When I nodded, she said, "Then you'll come to my place for Christmas, right?"

"Actually . . ."

"Sadie, you can't spend Christmas alone."

I hesitated before plowing ahead. "Grayson invited me to his place."

Shontelle's eyebrows shot up. "For Christmas? And you didn't tell me this when we talked yesterday?"

"He only invited me this morning. I ran into him while I was out snowshoeing. He was going to be on his own and apparently he likes cooking Christmas dinner for people."

"Wow. And you keep telling me there's nothing between you."

"There's not," I protested.

"You'll be spending Christmas with him," she reminded me unnecessarily.

"We both thought we'd be on our own. He was just being nice."

"Uh huh." She wasn't buying my explanation for a second.

"He was." I faltered. "Most likely."

This time Shontelle raised one eyebrow.

My nerves jangled. "Maybe I should have said no."

"What on earth for?"

"I don't know!" I grabbed a cloth and ran it over the bar, even though it was spotless.

Shontelle put a hand over mine to still it. "Why are you so nervous?"

"I wasn't until a few seconds ago."

"It's my fault, isn't it?" she said, contrite. "I'm sorry."

"Don't be. I just hadn't thought things through before. It'll probably be a disaster."

"Why would you say that?"

"Because half the time we don't even get along." I thought

about what I'd said. "Well, we get along more than we used to. But still."

"If you're going to worry about it, both of you could come over to my place. If he still wants to cook, he could bring something."

His pumpkin pie, I hoped.

"You've already got your aunt coming to visit," I said.

"The more the merrier."

"But I said yes. I shouldn't back out now. Should I?"

"Only if you're going to stay awake at night worrying about it."

Was I going to do that?

Shontelle finished off her coffee. "I have to get going. Let me know if you want me to invite him. Otherwise, let's get together on Christmas Eve, all right?"

"That would be great."

Shontelle reached across the bar to squeeze my hand before getting up. "Relax, Sadie. Everything will be fine."

I repeated her last words to myself after she left.

I wasn't sure if I believed them.

Later that afternoon, as daylight was fading from the sky, Bobby arrived at the pub and took a seat at the bar. He ordered a pint of beer and a burger but didn't seem quite himself. Although there were people he knew in the pub, he stayed at the bar, sitting alone, focused only on his food and drink. When he finished his burger, he pushed the plate away, his shoulders slumped.

"What's wrong, Bobby?" I asked as he drained the last of his beer. "Has the Penny situation got you down?"

He nodded and nudged his pint glass toward me. When I set his refill in front of him, he shook his head. "If only she hadn't let her bitterness win out."

"Her bitterness toward Freddy?"

"She should have forgotten about him," he said as if he hadn't heard me. "He wasn't worth it."

"So you believe Penny is guilty?" That surprised me, since he'd been willing to lie for her.

"Of course she's not guilty!"

"Sorry," I said quickly. "I thought that's what you were getting at."

He took a long drink of his beer and set the glass down with a thud. "I meant if she'd gone home from the church instead of meeting with that . . ." He seemed to realize what he was about to say and snapped his mouth shut.

"Reporter," I finished for him. When surprise showed on his face, I added, "Penny told me about that."

Bobby lowered his voice. "Nobody else needs to know she's the one who dished the dirt on Freddy."

"Of course not." Except the police, I added in my head, but they already knew. "What were you going to say?"

"If she'd gone home instead of meeting with the reporter, maybe her neighbors would have seen her and could have given her an alibi. A real one. She wasn't sure about talking to the reporter, you see. She almost didn't go to the meeting, but her grudge won out. She wanted to get back at Freddy."

A bell dinged in the kitchen, signaling that an order was ready. Mel set off to retrieve it, so I stayed put.

"You said she was at church? There wasn't a service at that hour, was there?"

"No. She was there by herself, wrestling with her conscience. Too bad it didn't get the upper hand."

I agreed that was unfortunate. If she'd let her conscience guide her, maybe Freddy and Jade would still be alive. I didn't add that last part out loud.

Bobby left a short while later, no less dispirited. He clearly cared for Penny a great deal. I wondered if his feelings were reciprocated.

He still believed in her innocence, but was that because he was blinded by his feelings for her? Or did he know her well enough to be certain she wasn't a killer, despite the bitter grudge she'd harbored for so many years?

I remembered what Shontelle had told me about seeing Penny drive along Hemlock Street right around the time of the murder. There was a church on that street, a couple of blocks away from the village green.

As I mulled things over, I wiped down a table Mel had recently cleared of dirty dishes. When I was done, I surveyed the pub, checking to see if anyone needed anything.

I noticed Emery Leyland at a table with a couple of her friends. She was the daughter of the man who owned the local computer repair store, which was located right across the street from a church on Hemlock Street. But was it *the* church?

A group of four tourists requested two platters of nachos and another round of drinks, so I hurried off to the kitchen. After I'd delivered their food and had mixed their cocktails, I sent a quick text message to Shontelle.

Does Penny go to the same church as you?

While I waited for a response, I kept busy with serving customers. I delivered burgers to a group of tourists from Texas and I mixed up Happily Ever After cocktails for two women seated at the bar. When I managed to sneak another look at my phone, I had a response from Shontelle.

She does. What's up?

Just thinking, I wrote in reply. **I'll tell you more later.**

No one seemed in immediate need of my attention, so I made my way over to the table where Emery Leyland sat with her friends. Emery was in her early twenties and worked as a waitress at Lumière, Shady Creek's nicest restaurant.

"How is everything, ladies?" I asked the three young women. They had several appetizers on their table along with their drinks.

"Delicious," Emery said, and her companions agreed.

"Your dad's store is across from the church on Hemlock Street, right?" I said to Emery.

"That's right."

"Have the police talked to him in connection with Freddy Mancini's murder?"

"Why would they?" she asked with alarm.

"Penny was at the church that evening," I hurried to explain. "If he'd seen her leave, and knew what time he'd seen her, that would be of interest to the police."

"Oh," Emery said with relief. "My dad was out of town for a week, so he hasn't talked to anyone. He got back this afternoon."

"The police seem to have enough evidence against Penny, anyway," one of Emery's friends said.

"Thank goodness," the other woman added. "Who knows how many more people that psychopath would have killed if she was still on the loose."

I wanted to object to the labeling of Penny as a psychopath, but I held my tongue. She had killed two people, after all.

Hadn't she?

A grain of doubt still lingered in my mind, I realized. But surely the police had the right woman. Penny certainly had a motive for killing Freddy, and if she wanted to keep Jade from telling the police about her long-standing grudge against the chef, then she had a motive for the second murder as well.

And yet for some reason I still felt the need to convince myself that the police had nabbed the right person.

I got back to clearing tables and serving customers, and when I glanced Emery's way later on, she and her friends were getting ready to leave the pub. As they wound their way around the tables, heading for the door, I intercepted Emery.

"Does your dad have surveillance cameras outside his shop?"

"Yes. One out the back and one out the front. Why? Are you still thinking about the murder?"

"Yes. It could help to establish a timeline if there was some evidence of when Penny left the church."

"Do you think she's innocent?" Emery asked with skepticism. "I heard she really hated that chef guy."

"I just want to be sure nothing's overlooked," I said.

Emery glanced at her friends, who stood waiting for her by the door. "Let me call my dad, okay?"

She took a moment to say something to her friends and then moved into a quiet corner. She spoke on her phone for a minute or so, and then came back my way.

"He says the police left a message for him while he was away, but he hasn't got back to them yet."

"They're probably wondering about the surveillance footage."

"That's what I told him. So he's going to look through it now. You can go over there if you want. I told him you might."

"Thank you."

She barely acknowledged my words. She was already following her friends out the door.

It wouldn't be long before the dinner rush got underway, but I thought I could manage a short break. I spoke to Mel, and she assured me that she didn't mind me leaving for half an hour or so. As soon as I was bundled up, I hurried across the green and down the street to the computer repair store. A light was on inside, and when I knocked on the door Mr. Leyland answered it within seconds.

"Hi. Sadie, isn't it?" He shook my hand. "Come on in out of the cold."

"Thanks for letting me come over, Mr. Leyland," I said once I was inside.

"No problem at all." He led me over to a desk with a flat-screen computer monitor. "I fast-forwarded through some of the footage from the night of the murder." He shook his head. "What a terrible thing. *Two* murders! I leave town for a week and I come back to find out there's been a crime spree. At first I thought it must have been a deranged tourist in town for the Winter Carnival, but then I heard Penny Blaine was arrested. That's why you're here, though, right? You think she might be innocent?"

"I'd like her to be," I said, "but that might be wishful thinking."

"I understand. I've known Penny since she was a little girl. If she's innocent and I can help prove it, then I'm all for it." He pointed at the computer screen. "As you can see, this security camera doesn't show the church."

The screen displayed a frozen frame of a view of the sidewalk in front of his shop.

"I'm sorry," I said, disappointed. "I guess this was all for nothing then."

"Not so fast." He clicked the mouse. "First, watch this."

The time code on the screen counted away the seconds, but nothing else changed for a moment. Then I noticed movement in the upper left corner.

A red car had pulled up to the curb, not much more than its wheels showing.

"Now we have to fast-forward again," Mr. Leyland said.

With another click of the mouse, the recording zoomed forward, although it was hard to tell from the static image. Nobody walked past the office and the car remained parked by the curb. After the time code had moved forward about an hour, Mr. Leyland switched the video back to normal speed.

A few seconds later, the car drove away.

My hope of finding important evidence evaporated.

"Thanks for going to the trouble of showing this to me," I said. "Unfortunately, we don't know whose car that was. Even if we could prove that it was Penny's, which is doubtful, this footage doesn't show where she went between parking her car and driving away again. For all we know, she could have run over to the town hall, killed Freddy, and run back."

"That's true. Let's try the other camera."

"The one out the back?" I asked, confused. I didn't see how that could help us.

"No, out front."

"Emery told me you only had one camera out front."

"That used to be the case, but then those break-ins started a few weeks ago. My buddy Pete Mintzer owns the dollar store across the street, right next to the church. We were talking about ways to beef up our security and we decided to add extra cameras. Now I've got one trained on his business, and he's got one aimed at mine."

"And yours shows the church?" I asked with a hint of renewed hope.

"It does. Not the entire front of the building, mind you, but it shows the front door."

He maneuvered the mouse and called up the footage from the second camera. With a few more clicks, he accessed the files from the day of Freddy's murder.

I tried not to fidget with impatience as he got the recording to the point where the red car drove up in front of his office. This time, all we could see was the roof of the car, until someone climbed out of the driver's side. That same person crossed the street and walked into the church.

"That's Penny, right?" I said.

It was a woman, but she never faced the camera, so it was hard to be sure of her identity.

"I think so."

I was disappointed that Mr. Leyland didn't sound any more certain than I did.

He fast forwarded through the footage until the front door of the church opened again. The same woman emerged from the church and walked across the street, getting closer to the camera.

"It *is* her!" I said with excitement.

There was no doubt about it now. The light of a nearby streetlamp lit up her face, making it clear enough to identify.

As we continued to watch, Penny climbed into the parked car and drove off.

"What do you think?" Mr. Leyland asked as he stopped the recording.

"I think you should share this with the police as soon as possible," I said.

"This could help Penny?"

"Very much so," I said.

If the time code was accurate, Penny had driven away from the church right before Shontelle had seen her. And that meant she didn't have time to stop and kill Freddy before heading off to meet the reporter.

Chapter 26

Before I'd left Mr. Leyland's shop, I'd experienced a sudden rush of uncertainty. I was worried that when presented with the video footage, the police would say that Penny could have gone out the back door of the church, killed Freddy, and then gone back through the church in the hope of establishing an alibi.

However, when I'd voiced that concern to Mr. Leyland, he'd quickly put it to rest. He attended the church regularly. Apparently, the back door was for emergency use only. If anyone opened it, an alarm would sound, so the only way Penny could have entered or exited the church was through the front door.

That meant she was innocent. I was sure of it now.

But *somebody* was guilty of killing Freddy and Jade. Somebody who was still on the loose.

And what was good news for Penny could be bad news for Mel. She'd probably be Detective Marquez's prime suspect now.

I tossed and turned that night, troubled by those thoughts. When morning arrived, I was no less uneasy. I felt like I was letting Mel down. I wanted so badly to prove her innocence, but the only way I could do that was to find out who the real killer was, and I hadn't made much progress.

I spent some time in my cubbyhole of an office, paying bills and placing some orders with the Inkwell's suppliers. That helped to keep my mind from going in circles, at least for a little while. I was getting tired of sitting at my desk when I received a text message from Shontelle.

Guess who's playing hockey this morning.

The brewery? I wrote back.

Will I see you there?

I'll watch for a while, I replied. **I could use some fresh air.**

It took only seconds for Shontelle to write back. **Fresh air. Right. Wouldn't want to miss out on that.**

She followed that up with a winking emoji.

I responded with one with its tongue sticking out.

When I reached the outdoor rink, Shontelle was already there. She waved and I joined her on one of the wooden benches.

"I brought you some hot chocolate," she said, handing me a cup.

"Mmm. Thank you." I took a sip of the rich, delicious drink. It was nice and warm, but not too hot.

The hockey players were out on the ice, warming up. The Spirit Hill Brewery was set to play the grocery store's team. I picked out Grayson among the players. He was chatting with Jason while he stretched at the far side of the rink.

"Is your mom watching the store?" I asked Shontelle.

"She is. She wanted me to have a chance to get out and enjoy some of the Winter Carnival."

"That's nice of her."

"I don't know what I'd do without her," Shontelle admitted.

As a single mother and a business owner, Shontelle had a lot on her plate. I didn't know how she managed to juggle everything so well. Some days I felt overwhelmed by the responsibilities that came with running a business and I didn't have a child to look after on top of that. Luckily, her mom seemed to enjoy helping out, both with the shop and with Kiandra.

The half dozen picnic tables and benches had filled up with spectators, and the game was about to get underway. The players took up their positions at center ice, Grayson included. The puck dropped and the game began.

Shontelle nudged me with her elbow. "So, what have you decided to do about Christmas?"

"I haven't decided anything," I said as I watched Jason pass the puck to one of his teammates.

"Then your plans with Grayson still stand?"

"For the moment."

I was relieved when two women came over to say hi to Shontelle, putting an end to our conversation. Shontelle introduced me to the women, who both had daughters in Kiandra's class at school, but when they started chatting about upcoming school events, I focused my attention on the game.

Grayson had a good scoring chance, but the opposing team's goalie snatched up the puck, preventing it from crossing the line.

I cheered on the brewery's team as they got ready for another face-off.

As I watched the game, I thought about all the reasons why it would be best to renege on my acceptance of Grayson's invitation and suggest we both go to Shontelle's place instead.

For starters, we had a tendency to rile each other up. At least, he had a tendency to rile *me* up. And I seemed to have a habit of embarrassing myself whenever I ended up alone with him.

What if the dinner turned out to be painfully awkward?

I recalled the conversation we'd had in his car before we found Jade's body. I'd managed to say—or almost say—something embarrassing, as usual, but I wouldn't have described the time spent with him as awkward. In fact, it had been nice to get to know him a little better.

Maybe I was overthinking things.

That was most likely the case.

I let out a groan as the grocery store's team scored the first goal of the game. My disappointment vanished minutes later when Grayson got a breakaway and scored a beautiful goal.

I jumped up from the bench and cheered along with some of the other spectators in the small crowd.

Grayson zoomed past. His eyes locked on mine and he grinned at me before hopping off the ice to take a seat on his team's bench. My heart did a funny flip-flop as I sat back down next to Shontelle. Her friends had moved on to find seats elsewhere and she was smiling at me.

"You can't deny he's got a great smile," she said.

Great smile, great eyes, great—

I stopped my thoughts in their tracks.

Despite the cold air, my cheeks heated up.

"Sure, he's attractive," I said, trying not to sound too interested.

"Attractive, charming, successful. Do I need to go on?"

"Nope. Not necessary." I kept my eyes focused on the game.

"I'm sure Lara Hawkes could add to the list."

My gaze snapped her way. "Lara?"

"I saw them at the bank yesterday."

My stomach gave an unpleasant quiver. "Together?"

"They didn't arrive together, but Lara was clearly hoping they'd *leave* together."

"Did they?"

Shontelle clapped, reminding me that I was supposed to be watching the hockey game.

She let out a sound of disappointment. "Too bad."

I had no idea what had just happened on the ice because all my attention was fixed on Shontelle.

"Did they?" I asked again.

Her eyes were wide with feigned innocence. "Did who what?"

"Shontelle!"

She laughed, but then put an arm around me and gave me a squeeze. "You have nothing to worry about, Sadie. He wasn't the least bit interested."

I didn't like how relieved I felt. I had enough on my mind without falling for Grayson Blake.

I forced myself to refocus on the game, but my attention was diverted only moments later.

"Did you hear about Penny Blaine?" a woman seated on the bench next to ours said to the man beside her.

"I heard she was arrested. That's old news now."

"Not *that*. She's going to be released. Probably tomorrow, if not today. Apparently there's evidence that she didn't kill Freddy Mancini after all."

"Is that true?" Shontelle whispered to me.

"The part about the evidence is," I said. "I hadn't heard that she was going to be released, but I figured that would probably happen."

"Let me guess," Shontelle said. "You're the one who found the evidence."

"I might have helped," I admitted. "But the police probably would have discovered it eventually."

I explained to her how Mr. Leyland had been out of town and hadn't checked his security footage or spoken to the police until the day before.

"I hear that woman who works at the pub had it in for Freddy and his assistant," the man on the next bench said.

I stiffened, my cheeks burning with indignation.

"He means Mel, doesn't he?" Shontelle said quietly.

I nodded, too upset to speak. I hated the fact that rumors were flying about Mel. Even worse was the fact that the police were probably thinking along the same lines.

A whistle blew, bringing the first period of the hockey game to an end. I noted that the scoreboard had the game tied at one.

I stood up. "I'd better get back to the Inkwell. It's almost time to open for the day."

"Will I see you at the light parade tonight?" Shontelle asked.

The parade was one of the highlights of the Winter Carnival, so I'd been told. Each year people spent weeks, even months, planning and constructing their floats.

"I'm not sure," I replied. "I'd like to, but I'll have to see if I can get away from the pub."

I said good-bye to Shontelle and set off for the Inkwell, feeling even more unsettled than I had during the night.

When I arrived back at the pub, Mel was already there for her shift and Booker was at work in the kitchen.

"How's the brewery team doing?" Mel asked when I told her I'd been at the outdoor rink.

"The game was tied when I left," I said.

"Are you rooting for their competition?"

"Because the brewery's team beat ours?"

Mel shrugged. "You do seem to have a rivalry with Grayson."

I thought I detected a hint of amusement in her eyes, but I couldn't be sure.

"I wouldn't call it a rivalry," I said. "More like a friendly, competitive spirit."

Shontelle would have laughed at that.

"And, actually," I continued, "I was cheering for the brewery."

"That's probably a good thing, since we do business with them," Mel said before changing the subject. "I'm guessing you'll have a lull tonight during the parade, but be prepared for a rush after it's over. That's what happens every year. People like to come in for a drink and something to eat after standing out in the cold."

"In that case, I'll make sure the overflow rooms are ready."

I flipped the CLOSED sign on the front door to OPEN and then checked out the Stewart Room. I'd given it a good clean recently, so everything was still shipshape. I checked the Christie Room next.

As I ran my gaze over the room, I zeroed in on the shelf to my left. There was no longer a gap between the books. I hurried over to the shelf. My eyes hadn't played a trick on me. The missing books were back in place. I removed them from the shelf and carefully opened the covers, one at a time. There was no doubt about it. They were definitely my books. The inscriptions from my dad proved it.

I flipped through the pages and found with relief that both books seemed unharmed. Maybe someone had simply wanted to borrow them and didn't want to ask, for whatever reason. Or maybe they'd stolen the books and then their conscience got the better of them.

I sank down into the nearest chair, the books still in my grasp, as I blinked away tears. I'd thought the books were gone forever, and having them back in my hands brought me such a rush of relief and happiness that it was almost overwhelming.

My tears under control, I set the books back on the shelf and left the room.

Mel was in the midst of lining up clean pint glasses on a shelf under the bar.

"Mel, has anyone else been in here this morning?"

She seemed surprised by the question. "Booker's here, of course. His girlfriend was with him when he arrived, but she only stayed a few minutes. And Gilda stopped by briefly. She was wondering if you were going to the parade tonight. Oh, and Rick from the brewery brought today's delivery." She placed the last glass on the shelf. "Why? Is something wrong?"

"No. It's the opposite, really." I told her about the reappearance of my missing books.

"That's strange. I didn't see anyone go into the Christie Room, but I was in the back at times."

The front door opened and the first customers of the day hurried in from the cold.

"It doesn't matter," I said to Mel.

I put a smile on my face and greeted the customers. I got them settled at a table and returned to the bar while they looked over the menus.

Mel had her phone out, but as I approached, she tucked it into the back pocket of her jeans, her face grim.

"Have you heard that Penny Blaine's going to be released from custody?" she asked me.

"I found out a little while ago," I said, my unease returning.

I could tell she knew as well as I did that Penny's good fortune didn't bode well for her.

"I think you should start looking for a replacement," Mel said in a low voice so the customers wouldn't overhear.

"A replacement for what?" I asked.

"For me."

I gaped at her. "Mel! Don't be ridiculous."

"It would be the smart thing to do, Sadie."

"But you're innocent."

"I might end up having to prove that in court."

I shook my head, not wanting to believe it.

"I can recommend someone," Mel said.

"Let's not jump off that bridge until we get to it, all right?"

"I'm pretty sure it's right in front of us."

Fear settled heavily in my stomach.

No matter how much I wanted to deny it, I knew what Mel said could be true.

Chapter 27

When Mel's shift ended, she told me she was going home to call her lawyer. While I figured that was a good move, I wished she didn't have a need for legal representation.

"I feel so useless," I confided to Damien after I'd brought him up to speed. "There must be something I can do to help her."

"She's got a lawyer. That's what she needs most." Damien shot a glance my way as he filled a pint glass with Hopposites Attract, one of the beers supplied by Grayson's brewery. "She definitely doesn't need you getting in trouble trying to hunt down the real killer."

"The only thing I plan to hunt for is more clues."

"Same thing, isn't it?"

He didn't give me a chance to respond. He set the pint glass on a tray with two others and carried it over to a table where three men were eating nachos and burgers.

With a blast of icy air, the front door opened and seven new customers came into the pub. As they shed their outerwear I realized that Grayson was one of the new arrivals, accompanied by members of his hockey team.

They claimed two adjacent tables, talking and laughing as they got settled. Damien was closer to the group, so he took their drink orders while I stayed behind the bar. Grayson detached himself from the group and headed my way. I tried to ignore the flutter of butterflies in my chest as he approached.

"Is this a celebration?" I asked when he reached the bar.

"More like commiseration."

"You lost?" That surprised me, considering how jovial his teammates were. "No one seems too upset."

"It was a good game and we had fun." Grayson glanced over at his team. "Plus, the drinks are on me."

"Ah," I said with a smile. "Is Damien getting you something?"

"He is, but I wanted to run an idea by you."

"Oh?" I wondered if he was about to change our Christmas plans.

"How about next year the brewery and the pub have a combined hockey team?"

The suggestion was so unexpected that it threw me for a second.

"You'd want to do that?" I asked once I'd collected myself.

"I think we'd be a force to be reckoned with."

I pictured us playing together rather than against each other, Jason, Mel, and Damien also on our team. It made me look forward to next year.

"You know what?" I said, smiling again. "I think you're right."

As the hour of the parade drew closer, business slowed, as Mel had predicted.

"Why don't you go check out the parade for a while?" Damien suggested.

"Don't you want to go?" I asked.

"I've been more times than I can count. I'd rather stay here where it's warmer, to tell the truth. My girls will be there, though."

"Aunt Gilda and Shontelle will be too."

"Go on then," Damien said.

"All right. But I'll do my best to beat the crowd back here."

I filled a travel mug with hot chocolate from the kitchen and bundled up before heading outdoors. A sizable crowd milled about on the green and people lined the streets around the square. On my way across Creekside Road, I waved to Bobby. He was working crowd control, wearing a bright orange reflective vest and keeping people off the streets, which had been blocked to keep vehicle traffic away.

I set off in the direction of Aunt Gilda's salon, hoping I could find her. With the streetlamps providing the only light, it wasn't easy to pick familiar faces out of the crowd.

As I edged my way toward Sycamore Street, I nearly bumped into a short, plump woman.

"Sorry," I apologized as I sidestepped to avoid her.

Before I got any farther, I realized I recognized a man up ahead.

"Hello, Mr. Hawkes," I greeted as I stopped next to him.

"Hello," Eli said as he regarded me with confusion.

I could tell he didn't know who I was.

"I'm Sadie Coleman. I own the Inkwell Pub."

"Oh, right. Here to see the parade?"

"Yes, if I can find a good spot."

I thought I caught a glimpse of Aunt Gilda across the street, and for a second I was torn between heading her way and staying put. My desire to help Mel won out.

"You were at the town hall the night Freddy was killed," I said to Eli.

He seemed surprised to find that I was still next to him. "Yes," he said after a moment. "I was." He looked more closely at me. "Are you the one who found him after . . . ?"

"That's right."

"A terrible business," he said with a shake of his head. "A real shame. Freddy should've had decades ahead of him."

"Did you notice anything suspicious that night?" I asked.

"I couldn't have. I left before Freddy did."

"Nobody was loitering outside when you left?"

"Not that I noticed."

Lara elbowed her way through the crowd to get to us. "You leave my dad alone!" she practically hissed at me.

I took a step back, startled by the vehemence behind her words.

"Now, Lara. There's no need to be rude," her father admonished.

"She's the one being rude by pestering you with questions!"

"I didn't mean any harm," I said.

Lara continued as if she hadn't heard me. "Leave me and my family alone." She took her father's arm. "Come on, Dad. Mom's waiting for us down the road."

I stared after them as they made their way around the spectators milling about on the green.

Music blared in the distance and an excited murmur ran through the crowd. The parade had started, and I still hadn't found Aunt Gilda. I stood on tiptoes to peer over the shoulders of the people in front of me, but I couldn't spot my aunt. Giving up, I moved along the green until I found a spot where I could get closer to the road. I'd just have to watch the parade without Aunt Gilda's company.

As I claimed my spot by the curb, I noticed a shimmer of colored lights down the road. The music grew louder. The song was an enthusiastic rendition of "Walking in a Winter Wonderland." The first float came into view, garnering cheers from the crowd. Towed by a pickup truck adorned with lights, reindeer antlers, and a red nose, the float had been decorated to look like a magical winter forest. Snowmen danced among trees decked out with bright lights, accompanied by bouncing and prancing children dressed up like cute woodland critters.

The next float was a compact version of Santa's workshop. Several elves were busy making toys while shimmying to the music, but Saint Nick was nowhere to be seen.

The first song came to an end and another one started up. This time it was "Jingle Bells." People in the crowd began singing along and several kids bounced up and down in time to the music.

The next float was decorated to look like a gingerbread house. A gingerbread man stood in the open doorway, waving to the crowd.

All of the floats that followed were bedazzling with their lights and decorations. Bringing up the rear was one of the trucks from the local fire department, its siren off but its lights flashing.

The children in the crowd jumped and cheered with excitement when they realized Santa Claus was on board. The kids got even more hyped up when Santa waved to them and tossed handfuls of lollipops to the people lining the street.

One lollipop beaned me right between the eyes. Luckily, it didn't hurt much. I handed it to a little boy holding his mother's hand, the flashing lights of the fire engine reflected in his wide eyes. His face lit up when I handed him the candy.

As the fire engine turned the corner, the crowd around me began to slowly disperse. I figured I'd better head back to the Inkwell, but that wasn't as easy as I expected. Children were running across the green in the hope of getting another look at Santa—or another lollipop—as the parade meandered along Hemlock Street on the far side of the square. Parents followed behind them, some chasing and some unconcerned, while other people wandered off in all different directions.

I had to keep darting around slow-moving clusters of people and I almost got my feet stepped on by a large man who towered above me. I quickly ducked out of his way, saving my toes in the nick of time.

I let out a sigh of relief as I managed to break free of the thinning crowd. Something niggled at the back of my mind and I paused. My subconscious was trying to tell me something, but what? I glanced around, searching for whatever might have triggered the feeling.

Emery and her friends were in the crowd behind me, along with a couple of other people I recognized as Inkwell customers. Nothing clicked together in my mind. The feeling faded, but the memory of it left me on edge.

A hand closed around my arm. I gasped and spun around.

"Aunt Gilda," I said with relief. The smile spreading across my face faltered when I saw her expression.

"Oh, honey," she said sadly. "I just heard the news."

"What news?" I asked, apprehension settling in my stomach like a lump of lead. I didn't think she was talking about Penny's release.

"About Mel. You haven't heard? The police showed up at her apartment and arrested her."

Chapter 28

I didn't sleep well that night, but probably better than Mel did. I couldn't stop thinking about her locked away in a cell. It wasn't fair or right and I worried that she wouldn't be free anytime soon. I really had let her down, even though I knew she'd never see it that way.

In the morning I didn't bother getting dressed right away. I should have been getting ready for the snowshoe race, but Mel's situation had left me far too dispirited to compete in the event. When I checked my phone, I found a good-luck text message from Shontelle. I sent her a quick reply, telling her about my change of plans.

I curled up on the couch with a book and a cup of coffee. The book ended up on the side table a few minutes later. I'd read the same paragraph several times and couldn't get my mind to focus.

Wimsey was lounging on the back of the couch. I ran my hand over his silky white fur.

"What should I do, Wims? I feel so useless."

Wimsey closed his eyes with contentment. Human troubles didn't concern him. Lucky cat.

I let out a deep sigh and then nearly jumped out of my skin when my door buzzer sounded. My phone chimed at the same time.

It's me at the door, the new text from Shontelle read.

I hurried downstairs, still in my pajamas. I unlocked the pub's front door and shivered as Shontelle breezed in with a blast of bone-chilling air. I shut the door quickly and rubbed my arms.

Shontelle took in the sight of my pajamas. "You aren't even dressed!"

"What's the point?" I asked. "The pub doesn't open until noon."

She put a hand to my back and steered me to the stairway that led to my apartment. "You've got a snowshoe race starting in one hour."

"I told you I decided not to enter."

"You have to."

"I can't. Not with Mel locked away in jail." I opened the door at the top of the stairs and led the way into my apartment.

"And what can you do about her being in jail?" Shontelle asked.

"Nothing."

"Exactly. You've been looking forward to this race for weeks, Sadie. Do you think Mel would want you to drop out because of her?"

"No, she wouldn't," I said without any doubt.

Shontelle shooed me toward my bedroom. "Then go get dressed."

My spirits were still drooping, but I did as I was told. After all, racing would be more fun than moping.

Thanks to Shontelle hurrying me along, I arrived at the race's starting point with enough time to get some stretching in before the event began. The size of the crowd gathered at the edge of the snowy field surprised me. Aside from my fellow racers, who were strapping on their snowshoes, there had to be at least fifty people milling about, waiting to cheer on their friends and family members when the race got underway.

I spotted Sybil and Eli Hawkes in the crowd and remembered that Lara was one of my competitors. A moment later, I spotted her. She was up closer to the starting line, chatting with a few other racers, her snowshoes already on. She wore the same sweater she'd worn to the book club meeting—the sweater with burnt-orange yarn knitted into the pattern.

The suspicions I harbored about Lara resurfaced, stronger than ever, but I smiled, distracted from those thoughts, when I saw Aunt Gilda among the spectators.

"I was starting to worry," she said as she made her way over to me.

"I wasn't going to come," I said. "Shontelle convinced me that I should."

"I'm glad she did. You've been looking forward to this." Aunt Gilda patted my back. "Try not to worry too much about Mel, honey. Things will work out for her."

"I hope you're right."

She melted back into the crowd as I set my snowshoes on the ground.

"Smile, Sadie."

I glanced up in time to see Joey snap my picture.

"You took me by surprise," I said. "I hope that photo won't end up in the paper. I probably look like a deer caught in headlights."

"Nah. You look great."

I doubted that but thanked him anyway as I strapped my left foot into its snowshoe. "How much do you know about Jade Castellano?"

"I know you were there when her body was found. Which means I should be asking *you* questions."

I saw Grayson approaching us and I momentarily forgot

what Joey had just said. I fastened the strap of my right snowshoe and straightened up.

"Nice day for a race," Grayson said.

"It is," I agreed, smiling as I glanced up at the clear blue sky.

"I'll catch you later, Sadie." Joey headed off to chat with some of the other racers.

I thought he sounded a bit disappointed and I realized it might have something to do with the way I was smiling at Grayson.

I reined in my expression. "Here to watch?"

"Not for long. I need to get back to the brewery soon, but I wanted to make sure I stopped by to wish you luck."

"Really?" That surprised and pleased me. Maybe we really could get along well enough to survive Christmas dinner together. "Thank you."

A whistle blew before either of us could say anything more. A man wearing a red vest over his jacket stood by the starting line, waving his hand in the air.

"Racers, to the line, please," he called out before saying something into a two-way radio.

I got jostled by a few people as I made my way to the starting line, everyone jockeying for a spot. I glanced over at the crowd to my left and saw Grayson chatting with Aunt Gilda. They seemed deep in conversation. I wondered what they were talking about.

I didn't have much of a chance to think about it. My fellow racers and I were told to get set and then the whistle blew again.

The whole pack of racers charged away from the starting line. I nearly got tripped up by Lara when she pushed past me and trod on my snowshoes. I glared at her back as she dashed off ahead of me. If she thought she could intimidate me, she was dead wrong. All she'd done was spark my competitive spirit, which had so far been absent that morning.

I picked up my pace but didn't let myself go too fast. The

race was fairly long, so I needed to conserve some energy for later.

The race route traversed a local farmer's property. It started in an open field, near the road. After crossing the field, we would enter a track through the woods. I hadn't followed the route before, but I'd heard that it would wind in and out of the forest, going up and down a few small hills.

By the time I reached the edge of the woods, the racers had spread out from our initial big group. Lara and half a dozen others had pulled ahead to form a small cluster in the lead. About twice that many racers were lagging behind, bringing up the rear as a group. The rest of the competitors, myself included, were spread out between the two packs. I figured I wasn't in a bad position. There was still a chance I could catch up to the leaders if they started to lose some steam.

That didn't hold true for long, however. As the race progressed, I dropped farther behind the leading group. Clearly the training I'd done hadn't been enough to make me competitive with the fastest snowshoe racers in town. I wasn't the only one falling farther behind, though. Those in my wake had also slowed, widening the gap between me and the next racer.

As I rounded a bend on the track that led through the forest, I found myself racing on my own. I couldn't even hear the sound of my competitors ahead of me or behind me. I tried to keep my pace up, but it was harder to stay motivated without other racers in sight.

I rounded another bend and descended a gentle hill. At the bottom of the slope, the trees ended and the trail led out into another field. Across the open expanse of snow, I spotted a table and a man wearing a bright red vest over his jacket, indicating that he was an event volunteer.

I was approaching the halfway point of the race.

As I neared the table, I noticed that it had paper cups of water set out on it. I was already hot from the effort of snowshoeing and I kicked up my pace, the promise of water drawing me onward like an oasis in a desert.

Before I reached the table, the man in the red vest moved off toward the tree line. When I drew closer I realized he was tacking a bright orange trail marker to a tree. It must have fallen from its place on the trunk.

A quick glance over my shoulder told me that I still didn't have any racers on my tail, so I stopped by the table and downed a cup of water.

"You're doing well, Sadie."

I realized then that the man in the red vest was Bobby.

"You're not too far behind the leading pack," he said as he approached the table.

I drank down another cup of water. "I doubt I can catch them, but I'm going to try."

"That's the spirit."

If not for the trail marker, I would have followed the path straight ahead of me instead of the one that entered the woods off to my right. It was a good thing Bobby was there to replace the fallen flag.

"Thanks for the water," I said as I set off again, entering the forest seconds later.

The path was windy and wove its way up a steep hill. By the time I reached the top of the incline, my lungs were burning and I was gasping for breath.

I didn't want to stop, but I had no choice. I leaned forward, my hands on my knees as I struggled to catch my breath.

The forest was silent around me. Not even the chirping of a bird could be heard. I looked back down the hill I'd just climbed, but the twists and turns prevented me from seeing if anyone else had begun the ascent behind me.

More slowly than I would have liked, I resumed my progress, following the trail down into a small dip before climbing upward again.

Something didn't feel quite right, but I wasn't sure what.

Then it hit me. There weren't many snowshoe tracks ahead of me. It looked as though two or three people had followed this trail since the last snowfall, but not the six or seven people I knew were ahead of me in the race.

I paused, wondering if I should turn back. But surely Bobby wouldn't have steered me along the wrong route.

Still feeling unsure, I kept going forward, until I reached the top of the next hill. The tracks in the snow ahead of me turned around, heading back the way I'd come. And I soon saw why. The path followed a gentle slope down to a cliff that overlooked a small valley.

Bobby *had* sent me the wrong way.

How he'd made such a mistake, I didn't know. Maybe he'd taken over for another volunteer and when he'd realized that the trail marker was lying in the snow he'd tacked it back up in the wrong spot. Maybe when it had fallen, the wind had blown it a ways.

Except there wasn't any wind.

However it had happened, I definitely wasn't on the right trail.

I let out a sound of disappointment. There was nothing to do but turn around. I'd most likely finish the race in last place now, but there was nothing I could do about it.

I retraced my steps, going as fast as I could, not wanting to show up at the finish line ages behind everyone else.

As I was about to descend the largest hill, I spotted movement through the trees.

I paused, breathing hard. Something red moved along the pathway, around one of the trail's many twists and turns.

Bobby, I realized, in his red vest.

Was he coming to tell me about his mistake?

He disappeared from sight for a second and then I caught another brief glimpse of him. But this time I saw more than his red vest. I also noticed his knitted hat.

My heart stuttered and fear formed a heavy lump in my stomach.

The hat was the same one he'd been wearing when I saw him at the parade, but only my subconscious had grasped its significance that night. Now it was glaringly obvious. The hat was gray, with a decorative pattern in burnt orange. The same shade of yarn as I'd seen on the ice pick driven through Freddy's heart.

Bobby wasn't coming to tell me he made a mistake about the race route.

He was coming to kill me.

Chapter 29

I turned faster than I thought possible on snowshoes and galloped along the trail.

What do I do? I screamed in my head.

There was a killer twice my size, and likely with twice my strength, charging up the trail behind me. And I was heading straight for a cliff.

What I needed was my cell phone.

I reached for my jacket pocket.

Oh, for the love of Dame Agatha! I wasn't wearing a jacket. I knew I'd get hot during the race, so I'd only worn a long-sleeved shirt and a sweater, and in my rush to make it to the starting line on time, I'd forgotten my phone at home.

I desperately hoped that wouldn't turn out to be a deadly decision.

My pace frantic, I glanced over my shoulder. Bobby wasn't in sight at the moment, but I knew it wouldn't be long before he made it through the dip in the trail and could see all the way down to the cliff's edge.

I didn't have a plan, other than to try my best not to panic—

something I was barely succeeding at—but when I reached the cliff, I had to make a decision.

I couldn't go forward and I couldn't go back.

My only option was to veer off the path and into the forest. But no matter what I did, Bobby would see my tracks.

I grabbed a broken evergreen branch and swept snow over my tracks as I sidestepped into the forest. As soon as I was within the tree line, I dropped the branch and dashed deeper into the woods, tree limbs snagging at my hair and sweater. I made it no more than fifteen feet before I had to stop. The undergrowth and fallen branches made it impossible for me to get any farther on snowshoes.

Crouching down, I hurriedly unstrapped my snowshoes and kicked them free of my boots. I grabbed one snowshoe in each hand and climbed over a fallen tree. On the other side of it, I sank knee-deep into the snow. I struggled onward.

It didn't take long for my legs to start to burn. My heart was ready to beat right out of my chest from a mixture of fear and exertion.

"Sadie!" Bobby's voice rang out like a gunshot.

I dropped into a crouch again, terrified that he could see me through the trees.

"I know you're out here!"

So he couldn't see me?

I realized I was holding my breath and forced myself to let it out. Peering through the trees, I spotted Bobby's red vest. He was out on the trail, near the edge of the cliff. He turned my way and I ducked down again.

Think, I ordered myself. *You need to get out of here.*

But how?

Bobby was so close that he'd hear me if I moved. The snow would crunch under my feet and twigs would snap. I couldn't avoid that.

I needed to wait for the right opportunity.

Cautiously, I raised my head. I had to peer around the trunk of a bare-limbed sugar maple to catch sight of Bobby this time.

Maybe *this* was my opportunity.

He had his back to me and was moving slowly toward the trees on the other side of the path.

I knew I might not get another chance to make a run for it. I almost ditched my snowshoes, but I'd need them if I managed to break free of the forest.

Gripping one in each hand, I crept through the trees, trying to move as quietly as possible. I needed every second I could get for a head start.

"You can't get away, Sadie."

Bobby's voice sent my heart into my throat. A branch hidden beneath the snow snapped when I stepped on it. I winced and froze. Hardly daring to breathe, I turned my head until I caught a glimpse of Bobby. He still had his back to me. I crept onward.

"This is my cousin's land," Bobby called out. "I grew up roaming through these woods. Wherever you hide, I'll find you."

His calm confidence spiked my fear. I moved faster, desperate to put more distance between us.

A branch caught on my sweater and then snapped free, rustling against other branches as it whipped back.

"There you are."

The words chilled me right through to my bones.

"Come out, come out!"

Bobby was following the path now, watching me as we moved parallel to each other, about forty feet between us. I pushed aside some evergreen branches and clambered over a tangle of undergrowth and fallen, spindly trees.

"Why did you do it, Bobby?" I asked, unable to take the silence that had fallen between us. "Why did you kill Freddy and Jade?"

Bobby kept his pace casual while I struggled to make my

way through the woods, sometimes sinking down to my knees in the snow.

"With all the questions you've been asking, I'd have thought you'd know," he said.

"How do you know I've been asking questions?"

"I saw you grilling Eli at the parade. Plus, Lara was complaining about what a snoop you are. I knew you'd cause me problems if I let you keep on nosing about."

I was finding it harder and harder to keep myself from panicking. I was hoping to break out of the woods, onto the pathway where it curved around. But even if I did that, Bobby wouldn't be far behind me, and without my snowshoes on, I'd be at a disadvantage.

"You still haven't told me why you killed them," I said.

"Both for the same reason."

Suddenly that reason was as clear to me as the cloudless winter sky.

"Penny," I said. "You're in love with her."

"How could I not be?"

I could see the trail ahead of me now.

"So you killed Freddy because of the way he treated Penny?" I knew I was right.

"He broke her heart all those years ago, and then he showed up here in town and treated her like dirt. He didn't deserve to live. You should have been mad at him too. He stole your friend's tools. He dumped them by the town hall but then decided to do a better job of it. I caught him in the act of moving them to the alley."

My foot slipped and I nearly twisted my ankle. "What about Jade?" I asked as I recovered, using one snowshoe as a crutch to leverage me up out of the deep snow.

"I went to the police station to tell them I was with Penny when Freddy was killed. That woman was there, telling an officer about all the letters and e-mails Penny had sent Freddy over the years. She told the cop that Penny was bitter and crazy." He let out a growl of anger that nearly froze my heart with fear. "Nobody talks about my Penny that way."

Bobby was the crazy one, and I was next on his hit list.

"Why did you leave Jade's body at Leo's place?" I asked, hoping to distract him until I could make my move.

"It was a coincidence that I managed to run her off the road near his property. Then I figured, what better way to make him look even guiltier than he did already?"

I was only half listening to him. The trail was just twenty feet ahead of me now.

Still gripping my snowshoes, I charged forward, stumbling and flailing. Out of the corner of my eye, I saw Bobby break into a loping run on his snowshoes.

I burst out of the forest. I tried to run along the trail, but I kept sinking deep into the snow. I needed my snowshoes on.

I glanced over my shoulder as I dropped them to the ground. I could hear Bobby coming, but he was still around the bend.

My breaths shallow and fast, I strapped my snowshoes on as quickly as I could, my fingers feeling clumsy and uncooperative. I had the straps fastened within seconds, but it felt more like hours.

As I straightened up, Bobby came charging around the curve in the trail. He was only thirty feet away from me and closing in fast.

With a gasp, I broke into a run, moving faster than I ever had before on snowshoes.

But it wasn't fast enough.

With every step I could hear Bobby gaining on me.

I felt rather than saw him loom behind me. I swerved off toward the tree line, hoping to dart out of his grasp.

He tackled me from behind, the force of the impact knocking the air out of my lungs. I fell forward and hit the snow.

I kept falling.

My foot caught on something and my face hit a wall of snow.

For a second I didn't move, too stunned to react. Then I became aware of the snow filling my mouth and the fact that I was upside down.

I flailed, trying to right myself.

Something fell on top of me, making it hard to move.

Snow, I realized.

Don't panic!

I stopped flailing. My mind finally caught up, sifting through the last few seconds to make sense of my situation.

When Bobby had tackled me, we'd fallen into a tree well, headfirst. I could feel one of Bobby's legs tangled with mine.

It took every ounce of my self-restraint to keep myself from flailing again. I was headfirst down a hole, half buried with snow, trapped with a murderer.

I carefully moved my arms, trying to prevent more snow from falling off the tree's lower branches. I scooped snow away from my face so it was easier to breathe. Then I felt around for something to grab on to. My gloved fingers found the rough bark of the tree trunk. I snaked my arm through the snow to wrap it around the trunk, anchoring myself so I wouldn't fall any deeper.

I tried to remember what I knew about tree wells. It wasn't much, other than the fact that they were dangerous and extremely difficult to get out of on your own. My feet, with my snowshoes still attached, were caught on something. I could barely move them.

At least I had an air pocket around my face. That would buy me some time. But would it be enough?

I tried to tunnel my right arm through the snow, thinking that if I could hug the tree trunk, maybe I could slowly haul myself upward. Instead of the trunk, my right hand touched something else. I brushed the snow away as best I could in the confined space.

A scream tried to work its way out of my throat, but I bit it back.

I'd uncovered Bobby's face, less than a foot away from mine. His eyes were closed and he didn't stir.

Had he suffocated under the snow?

The urge to flee, to get away from him, was so strong that I had to focus on nothing but breathing for several seconds to keep myself from panicking.

He can't hurt you, I told myself.

Not until he wakes up.

That unwelcome thought popped into my mind.

Was he dead or unconscious? I didn't want to stay in the tree well long enough to find out.

I needed help.

I tried yelling, but the sound was muffled by the snow. No one would hear it. Someone might discover that Bobby and I were missing, but it could be ages before they searched this trail. And they might not find us even if they walked right past this tree.

Trying to keep my fear under control, I stared at Bobby's snow-dusted face. I'd thought he was a nice, affable man. Now the sight of him filled me with terror.

I noticed his red vest peeking out from beneath the snow. The volunteer at the starting line had a two-way radio. Maybe Bobby did too.

My heart soaring with newfound hope, I carefully tunneled my right hand through the snow. The thought of Bobby regaining consciousness and opening his eyes horrified me, but if I wanted to survive, I had to keep searching for the radio.

My gloved fingers blindly followed the fabric of Bobby's jacket. My movements dislodged more snow and it cascaded down onto my face.

I couldn't breathe.

I spat the snow out of my mouth and shook my head. I drew in a breath and opened my eyes. The new snow hadn't filled my airhole. That brought me a sputtering of relief.

A second later, that relief bloomed.

My hand closed around Bobby's radio.

Chapter 30

I hummed the tune of "Sleigh Ride" as I parked my car in Grayson's driveway. Colored lights outlined the front door and the floor-to-ceiling windows of his blue-and-gray house. I grabbed the bottle of wine and the box of maple sugar candies I'd brought and climbed the two steps to the door.

I was about to press a finger to the doorbell when the door opened, startling me.

"Merry Christmas," Grayson said with a smile.

Was it just me or were his blue eyes brighter than usual?

My heart fluttered. "Merry Christmas."

Once inside, I presented him with the wine and candies and shed all my outerwear. It was only a two-minute drive from my doorstep to his, but the wind felt like it was swooping down from the Arctic, so I'd bundled up before leaving.

"The tree is beautiful," I said as he led me into his living room.

The Douglas fir took up one corner of the room and was decorated with lights, garlands, and colorful baubles. Flames danced and crackled in the fireplace, giving the room a cozy, cheery feel.

"Thank you." Grayson stopped to admire the tree as well. "Decorating the Christmas tree is one of my favorite holiday traditions."

"Mine too."

I smiled at him and I could have sworn that a spark of electricity shot through my body when our gazes locked. We stood there, staring at each other, my heart thudding away, until Grayson cleared his throat.

"Would you like some hot apple cider?"

"Please."

On the way to the kitchen, I stopped in front of a large bookcase that rose all the way up to the ceiling. Every shelf was filled. I spotted some familiar titles, including ones by Michael Crichton, Tom Clancy, and Louise Penny.

So Grayson was a reader, after all. I smiled.

His comment about me not snooping far enough made sense now. When I'd peered through his window back in the fall, I hadn't seen the bookshelf. If I had, I never would have mistaken him for a nonreader.

Tearing myself away from Grayson's book collection, I followed him into his modern kitchen. I'd peeked into the room before—through the window while I was snooping—but it was even more impressive now that I was inside and breathing in the delicious aromas emanating from the stove and the wall ovens.

"Oh, my Lucy Maud." My gaze settled on a pumpkin pie sitting on the granite countertop. "Is that *the* pumpkin pie?"

"It is."

My mouth watered.

Grayson ladled cider into a mug from a pot on the stove. Of course he'd made the cider himself. Was there anything the man couldn't do?

"How are you?" he asked, his face serious.

"Great, thanks."

He handed me the mug. "For real?"

I breathed in the delicious scent of apples and spices. "Yes. Bobby's locked away, Mel's free, and it's Christmas. All is well."

Aside from the fact that I missed my family.

I was relieved that I'd so far had only two nightmares about my frightening encounter with Bobby and the tree well. I knew it could have been the end of me. It would have been, if not for Bobby's radio, which I'd used to summon help.

Bobby was still unconscious when rescuers pulled him out, but he woke up in the hospital later, with police officers by his side, so I'd been told. I'd heard through the town grapevine that the remnants of the gloves Penny had knitted for him were found in the fire pit behind his house. The gray-and-orange gloves had matched his hat. He'd pretended he'd lost them, because they got covered in blood when he stabbed Freddy.

I tried to banish my unpleasant memories and took a sip of apple cider to soothe me. It worked wonders.

"I'm glad nothing worse happened to you," Grayson said.

His gaze met mine and again I felt a jolt of electricity surge through my bloodstream.

He stepped closer. "Sadie . . ."

The doorbell rang. Startled, I nearly spilled my apple cider.

Grayson touched a hand to my arm. "Excuse me a moment."

I followed him out of the kitchen, my heart beating faster than normal. I lingered by the Christmas tree as he crossed the living room to the front door.

"Merry Christmas!" I heard a familiar voice say.

I didn't think I could have heard correctly. I set my mug of apple cider down on a side table and hurried to the foyer.

I wasn't mistaken.

"Aunt Gilda?"

"Merry Christmas, honey." She wrapped me in a hug as Grayson shut the door behind her.

I returned the hug, surprised and confused, but ready to burst with happiness.

"I don't understand," I said when I pulled back. "You're supposed to be in Savannah."

"Not this year." Aunt Gilda gave me another squeeze before unbuttoning her coat. "I'm going for New Year's instead. I wanted to spend Christmas with you and we decided to surprise you."

I glanced at Grayson. He was grinning.

"Is that what you two were whispering about at the snowshoe race?" I asked them.

Grayson laughed. "We weren't whispering, but yes."

"I wanted to be here for your first Christmas in Shady Creek," Aunt Gilda said.

"I'm so glad you are," I told her.

She handed me a gift bag.

"But you already gave me a gift," I protested.

"And now I'm giving you another one."

I peeked into the bag and saw a thin, square book.

While Gilda unwound her scarf and Grayson hung her coat in the closet, I pulled the book out of the bag. Tears welled in my eyes. It was a photo book, the kind you could design and order online. On the front was an old photo of my dad lifting me up so I could put a star on the top of our family's Christmas tree.

I opened the book and turned the pages. Aunt Gilda had filled it with pictures from Christmases past, mostly photos featuring me and my dad. Here and there, among the pictures, were copies of the inscriptions he'd written in the books he'd given me over the years.

Suddenly everything made sense. "I thought someone had stolen the books," I said, struggling not to cry. "But then they reappeared."

Aunt Gilda squeezed my arm. "Oh, honey. I'm so sorry. I was hoping you wouldn't notice they were gone. I only took two at a time so it wouldn't be so obvious. I'm sorry for making you worry."

I shook my head. "It's okay. Better than okay." I closed the book and hugged it to my chest. "This is perfect. Thank you."

"I know you miss him, but you've got beautiful memories."

I nodded, fresh tears welling in my eyes. "I do."

I slipped the book back into the gift bag for safekeeping. Grayson offered Aunt Gilda some apple cider and she followed him toward the kitchen. I was about to trail after them when the doorbell rang again.

"Sadie, would you mind getting that?" Grayson called as he disappeared from sight.

I set the gift bag on the foyer table and wiped away the stray tear that had managed to escape one of my eyes.

I opened the door, wondering who else Grayson had invited to dinner.

My jaw dropped.

I let out a scream of excitement and threw myself at my younger brother, wrapping him in a bear hug.

"Taylor!" I squeezed him hard before stepping back. "I can't believe it."

Taylor grinned, the cold wind ruffling his blond hair.

"Merry Christmas, Sis."

I pulled him inside and shut the door.

Grayson and Aunt Gilda returned to the foyer, Gilda with a steaming mug in hand. They both had smiles on their faces.

"You were in on this too," I said to both of them.

"We thought it would be a good surprise," Aunt Gilda said.

"You're not kidding."

I hugged Taylor again. I hadn't seen him in months and I'd missed him terribly.

"I don't understand. You were going to Costa Rica."

"Still am," he said as he pulled off his gloves. "Just not for another four days."

I shook my head in disbelief.

Aunt Gilda put an arm around my shoulders. "You've had a lot of changes in your life over the past year. We wanted to make sure you had a memorable Christmas."

I beamed at all three of them.

"It's a perfect Christmas," I said. "Absolutely perfect."

Cocktails & Recipes

Count Dracula Cocktail

4 oz blood-orange juice
2 oz cranberry juice
½ oz simple cinnamon syrup
¼ oz coconut rum
cinnamon stick

Fill a cocktail shaker ¾ full with ice. Add all ingredients. Shake vigorously and strain into a glass. Garnish with cinnamon stick. Makes one cocktail.

Evil Stepmother Cocktail

1 oz vodka
½ oz sour mix
3 oz white grape juice
3 oz ginger ale

Fill a cocktail shaker ¾ full with ice. Add vodka, sour mix, and grape juice. Shake vigorously and strain into a glass. Add ginger ale and stir. Makes one cocktail.

Evil Stepmother Mocktail

½ oz sour mix
4 oz white grape juice
4 oz ginger ale

Fill a cocktail shaker ¾ full with ice. Add sour mix and grape juice. Shake vigorously and strain into a glass. Add ginger ale and stir. Makes one mocktail.

Paradise Lox

12 baguette slices, ¼ inch thick
2 tablespoons olive oil
6 tablespoons salmon cream cheese
1¼ teaspoons lemon juice
1¼ teaspoons dried dill
3 oz lox

Preheat oven to 350° F.

Brush both sides of each baguette slice with olive oil. Place slices on baking sheet and bake in oven for 3 to 4 minutes. Turn slices over and bake for another 3 to 4 minutes. Remove from oven and let cool.

Mix together the cream cheese, lemon juice, and dill. Spread some of the mixture on each baguette slice. Top with a piece of lox. Serve.

Acknowledgments

I'd like to extend my sincere thanks to several people whose hard work and input made this book what it is today. I'm truly grateful to my agent, Jessica Faust, for helping me bring this series to life, and to my editor, Martin Biro, for taking a chance on this series and for his enthusiasm and guidance. The entire Kensington team has been fabulous and I love the beautiful covers the art department has created. I'm also grateful to Samantha McVeigh and the rest of the publicity department for all their hard work. Thank you to Sarah Blair and Jody Holford for reading my early drafts and cheering me on, and to the Cozy Mystery Crew, my review crew, and all my wonderful friends in the writing community.

In USA Today *Bestselling Author Sarah Fox's delicious Pancake House Mystery, it's up to Marley McKinney to sort through a tall stack of suspects . . .*

CRÊPE EXPECTATIONS

Although it's a soggy start to spring in Wildwood Cove, the weather clears up just in time for the town to host an amateur chef competition. Marley McKinney, owner of the Flip Side pancake house, already signed up to volunteer, and chef Ivan Kaminski is one of the judges. But when Marley visits her landscaper boyfriend Brett at the site of the Victorian mansion that's being restored as the Wildwood Inn, she discovers something else pushing up daisies: human remains.

The skeleton on the riverbank washed out by the early-spring floodwaters belonged to eighteen-year-old Demetra Kozani, who vanished a decade earlier. While the cold case is reopened, Marley must step in when some of the cook-off contestants fall suspiciously ill. Stuck in a syrupy mess of sabotage and blackmail, it falls to Marley to stop a killer from crêping up on another victim . . .

Read on for a special excerpt of* Crêpe Expectations*,
on sale now.

Chapter 1

A banner with bold lettering rippled in the breeze. It gave a snap now and again when a stronger gust tried to wrest it free of the table it was fastened to, but it remained in place, the thick paper refusing to tear. So far the banner had done its job, grabbing people's attention and directing them to the table where I sat with a stack of papers in front of me.

"Looks like we've got the makings of a great competition this year," Patricia Murray commented from the chair next to mine.

"I had no idea it would be this popular," I admitted, running my eyes down the list of names written on one of the papers.

I leaned back in my folding chair and stretched my legs under the table set up in the parking lot of Wildwood Cove's grocery store. It was early on a Saturday afternoon, and normally at that time of day I'd be at my pancake house, the Flip Side, closing up and tidying the restaurant. Today, however, I'd agreed to volunteer my time to help with registration for the Olympic Peninsula's annual amateur chef competition.

Each year, one of the peninsula's communities hosted the

competition, and this time it was Wildwood Cove's turn. The event would take place over the following three weekends, and already several residents of Wildwood Cove and other towns had signed up. I'd been sitting at the registration table for two hours, and people were still arriving to put their names down for either the teen division or the adult category.

"I was worried with all the rain this year that most people wouldn't want to come out and participate," Patricia said. She owned a bed-and-breakfast three properties away from my beachfront Victorian, and she was also on the organizing committee for the amateur chef contest.

"We're definitely lucky the weather decided to change," I said before Patricia greeted the latest person to approach the registration table.

I'd spent many of my summer vacations in Wildwood Cove while growing up in Seattle, but I'd only moved to the seaside town permanently the previous spring and had never been present for the cooking competition. It sounded like fun, though, and I was eager to be involved with the community, so I hadn't hesitated to volunteer when Patricia had asked me to help out. My participation would be limited to assisting with registration, but I'd been assured that I was providing some much-needed help.

As Patricia registered a teenage girl with dark hair even curlier than mine, I breathed deeply, enjoying the fresh air and the lack of rain. The peninsula had seen very little sunshine over the past two months, and the rainfall had been so heavy and persistent that the nearby river had flooded its banks, damaging some homes and causing a slew of problems. Now that we'd had a few days without any rain, the floodwaters were finally receding, allowing everyone to breathe easier, even though many people had a long road of cleanup and restoration ahead of them.

I sat up straighter when I noticed a fifty-something woman

approaching the registration table. She had her light brown hair tied back in a bun, and she walked with careful steps. A man about her age followed along behind her and hung back when she reached the table. I greeted her and provided her with the registration form. Her name was Dorothy Kerwin, I noted as she filled in the form with her name, address, and the division she was entering. When she'd completed the form, I provided her with the booklet that every entrant received. It contained the rules and the event schedule.

"Hi, Dorothy," Patricia said with a smile when she'd finished registering the teenage girl. "How are you doing these days?"

"Better, thank you," Dorothy replied with a hint of a smile.

"Are you ready to go, Dot?" the man hovering behind her asked as he glanced at his watch.

"Sorry," she said to me and Patricia. "I'd better be on my way."

Despite the man's impatience, he didn't hurry Dorothy once they set off, one of her arms tucked into his.

"Had you met Dorothy and Willard Kerwin before today?" Patricia asked me once we were alone.

"No."

"The poor woman has been through a lot over the past year or two. She fell off a stepladder and broke her back, and then her twin sister passed away while Dorothy was still in the hospital."

"That's terrible," I said, with a surge of compassion for the woman.

"I think this is the first time she's participated in any community event since all that happened, so it's nice to see her getting involved."

I was about to agree with her when I caught sight of my boyfriend, Brett Collins, out of the corner of my eye. I smiled and waved as he approached, carrying two take-out cups from the local coffee shop, the Beach and Bean. The light breeze ruffled his blond hair as he reached the table.

"A coffee for you, Patricia," he said, setting one of the cups in front of her. "And a matcha latte for you, Marley." He handed the second cup to me.

We both thanked him. Since no one was waiting to be registered at that moment, I got up to give him a hug and a quick kiss.

"Did you get something for yourself?" I asked.

"Yep. A sandwich and a coffee. I put them in the truck."

"I'm guessing you have to head back to work now?"

"I do, but I should be done for the day in about three hours."

He was on his lunch break from his landscaping work at an old Victorian mansion that would soon be opening to guests as the Wildwood Inn. Brett ran his own lawn and garden business, and the new owners of the mansion had hired him to landscape and prepare the gardens before the inn's grand opening, which would be marked by a garden party later in the month. The mansion's owners, Lonny and Hope Barron, had spent the past several months restoring the Victorian and getting it ready for its new life as an inn.

"I'll see you at home, then," I said, leaning into him for another hug before reluctantly releasing him.

"Hello, everyone!" Brett's sister, Chloe, breezed over to us, her blue eyes bright.

She caught sight of the cups Patricia and I held. "Drinks from the Beach and Bean? That's where I'm headed."

"That makes more sense," Brett said.

"More sense than what?" Chloe asked.

"For a second there I thought you were here to register for the cooking competition."

"Why wouldn't that make sense?" Patricia asked as Chloe's smile morphed into a frown.

Brett slung an arm across Chloe's shoulders. "Because my kid sister couldn't cook to save her life."

"I can so cook," Chloe retorted, giving him a shove. She looked to me for support.

"You make good cookies," I said. "I know that much."

"You mean the ones *Jourdan* made for the Fourth of July barbecue?" Brett asked, referring to their cousin.

"Hey, I helped," Chloe protested.

"Right. I seem to recall that you spooned the dough onto the cookie sheets and Jourdan did the rest."

"I'm sure you can cook," I said to Chloe, wanting to placate her before things escalated.

"Of course," Brett said, trying to keep a straight face. "She can make toast, rubbery scrambled eggs, and pasta—as long as the pasta comes from a store and the sauce comes out of a jar." He addressed his sister. "And what about that time you tried to cook a family dinner and nearly burned down the house?"

Chloe's gaze hardened. "It was a tiny little fire, and I put it out right away."

I couldn't help but laugh, and beside me Patricia was struggling to contain a smile.

"You're no help, Marley," Chloe said, turning her frown on me.

"I'm sorry." I quickly took a sip of my latte to keep myself from laughing again.

Chloe grabbed a pen off the table. "Registration form, please," she said to me.

I glanced at Brett and then back at her before handing over a form.

"What are you doing?" Brett asked.

"Exactly what it looks like." Chloe wrote her name on the form. "I'm signing up for the competition."

"Hasn't the town seen enough disaster lately with all the flooding?"

Chloe pressed the pen so hard against the paper that I was

surprised when it didn't tear. "Just you wait. I'm going to make you eat your words."

"They'll probably taste better than your scrambled eggs."

Chloe threw the pen at him. He caught it right before it smacked him in the face.

Chloe passed me the completed form, and I gave her a booklet.

"You'll see," she said, swatting her brother's arm with the booklet before storming off, heading in the direction of the coffee shop.

"Brett," I said, "you shouldn't tease her like that."

"But it's so fun," he said with a smile.

I shook my head, and he wrapped his arms around me.

"I've got to run," he said into my ear. "See you later."

After giving me a quick kiss, he left for his truck, parked on the street. A group of three teenagers arrived to register for the youth division, so Patricia and I kept busy for the next several minutes. Two adults registered after that, but then we had another lull. Patricia's cell phone rang, and she got up from the table, walking a few steps away before answering the call. While she was still occupied, Logan Teeves arrived and asked to register. Logan was seventeen and lived next door to me with his dad, Gerald. He'd dated Patricia's daughter, Sienna, for a while, and although they'd broken up, they were still friends.

"I didn't realize you liked cooking," I said as Logan filled out the registration form.

He shrugged and brushed his fair hair off his forehead. "My dad doesn't cook, so we'd always be eating takeout and frozen dinners if I didn't learn." He shrugged again. "It's kind of fun."

"Well, I think it's great that you're entering." I handed him a booklet. "Good luck."

Logan wandered off, and Patricia returned to the table, dropping into her seat with a worried frown on her face.

"What's wrong?" I asked.

"That was Sid Michaels on the phone."

"The owner of Scoops Ice Cream?"

Patricia nodded. "He was supposed to be one of the judges for the competition, but now he has to make an unexpected trip to San Francisco. He's not sure when he'll be back, but he thinks he'll be gone at least two weeks."

"So now you need another judge," I surmised.

"As soon as possible. Would you be able to step in, Marley?" she asked.

"I could," I said slowly, "but I don't eat meat."

"Right. And that would be a problem, especially for the first challenge."

On the opening day of the competition the contestants would be cooking main course dishes, with the dessert challenge the following week.

Patricia swiped away a strand of dark hair that the breeze had blown across her face. "How about Ivan? Do you think he'd be willing to step in?"

"To be honest, I'm not sure." Ivan Kaminski was the Flip Side's talented chef. He was a wizard in the kitchen and more than qualified to take on the role as judge for the competition, but he wasn't the most social man, and I wasn't sure how he'd feel about taking part in the event. "I could ask him, though."

"Would you?" Patricia said with obvious relief. "That would be fantastic."

"When do you need a definitive answer?"

"As soon as you can get one?"

I pulled my phone from my pocket. "I'll send him a text now, and if I don't hear back from him today, I'll talk to him about it in the morning."

"Thanks, Marley. That's a huge help."

I really wasn't sure how Ivan would respond to the request, but I decided to do my best to convince him to help with the judging, even if it did put me in direct line of one of his intimidating scowls.

A few minutes later I received a curt text message in response:

We'll talk tomorrow.

I didn't share the reply with Patricia, not quite knowing what to make of it. At least he hadn't said no outright, but I wasn't entirely sure what to expect in the morning.